The
Hungry
Earth

For Kate

The Hungry Earth

SEÁN KENNY

WOLFHOUND PRESS

First published 1995 by
WOLFHOUND PRESS Ltd
68 Mountjoy Square
Dublin 1

and Wolfhound Press (UK)
18 Coleswood Rd
Harpenden
Herts AL5 1EQ

Wolfhound Press receives financial assistance from the Arts Council/An Chomhairle Ealaíon, Dublin.

British Library Cataloguing in Publication Data
A catalogue record for this book is available from the British Library.

ISBN 0 86327 479 X

Typesetting: Wolfhound Press
Cover design: Daire Ní Bhréartúin
Cover illustration: 'Harvest Moon' by Jack B. Yeats. Private collection. Courtesy of Dr Michael W.J. Smurfit.
Printed in Ireland by the Guernsey Press Co Ltd, Guernsey, Channel Isles.

ACKNOWLEDGEMENTS

This story grew out of a workshop I attended in Los Angeles in 1992 entitled 'Return to Innocence: A Healing Journey for Irish Catholics'. Many thanks to Doctor Garrett O'Connor and Fionnula Flanagan for creating that experience, which convinced me of the connectedness between past and present.

Thanks to Bill Corr, John Harney, Mary Kenny, Anne Kenny and Colman Ledwith for comments on the early drafts. To Steve Goldsmith for the same, and above all for opening the door at Wolfhound. Likewise to Dan McLoughlin, and for unlimited access to his computers in Fermoy, and to Michael and Tricia Flynn for making that last trip to Ireland possible.

Infinite thanks to Doreen Kenny and Finbarr Kenny for help with the mortgage, and to Justin and Helen for putting up with one topping on their pizzas all this time.

Finally high praise to Seamus Cashman for taking the risk and to Adrienne Murphy for turning a manuscript into this book.

... to forge in the smithy of my
soul the uncreated conscience of my race. *James Joyce*

CHAPTER ONE

Turlough Walsh dug his hands deeper into the pockets of his pleated trousers. Through the window of his third floor office, made to look as if it possessed twelve panes of glass, he looked down on the Friday evening traffic. The rain had stopped again and the office workers at the bus stop on the far side of the street were inspired to fold their umbrellas, stern faces still eyeing the oncoming traffic though, lest a truck sweep in close and spray them with muddy water.

It was after six. He could tell that just by the sight before him. If it was any earlier people would still be joining that despondent queue, but these were the last, and they would probably all fit on the next bus. Had MacCarthy left yet? As at the end of so many similar weeks, Turlough reminded himself that the man was a workaholic, that he showed no signs of succumbing to any stress-related illness any time soon, and, with little remaining justification for it, still saw himself as the driving force behind this whole practice.

Yet everyone could see that it was the younger partners who made it all happen. And far more would get done if they weren't all so preoccupied with staying on the right side of that misbegotten old bollocks. With these unsatisfying thoughts

Turlough Walsh decided that he had given enough of himself, for yet another week, to the accountancy practice that employed him, turned from the window, flicked the power switch on his PC, stalked across the carpet to where the jacket that matched his trousers was hung, twirled the sheer fabric expertly from the hanger and onto his arms in a single movement, checked for the presence of his car keys and stepped out of his office.

His secretary's work station was devoid now of the paper tasks that filled her day, and she too had fled to wherever it was she went when she wasn't doing his bidding here. One small square yellow note stood out on the veneer surface, causing Turlough to frown at her carelessness in not bringing it to his attention before she left, but then picking it up and reading it he saw it was from his wife, who had probably said not to interrupt him.

'Important looking letter for you from west.'

What kind of a message was that? Should he call? MacCarthy's light was off. No. Nuala would extract a commitment to be home at some specific time, and he felt like kicking back for a while here in town. Turlough sauntered through the open area, pleased that most of the other partners' offices were also dark. There was one that was not, however, and on passing its open doorway he felt compelled to look in. Finucane's head swung back and forth between a ledger and a computer terminal that was reflected in his large spectacles.

'Burning the midnight oil, Ed?' he asked without crossing the threshold. The other looked up.

'What?'

Finucane seemed startled by the unexpected interruption, but then everyone had that effect on him.

'If you can't get it all done in eight hours, might as well give up.' Turlough smiled as this jibe clearly wrenched Finucane's attention away from whatever arcane numerical task he had been grappling with.

'Ah, I've mountains of work here yet,' said Finucane, 'be

here all day tomorrow too.'

'The client won't pay for that, you know,' Turlough replied, shaking his head.

Finucane acknowledged this with a raised-eyebrow nod, then lost eye-contact as if believing the interlude was at an end.

'Come on, and I'll buy you a drink?' Just for a moment the dire thought occurred to Turlough that he might have overdone the heartiness, and that Finucane might actually take him up on this offer, but he didn't, just shook his head and mumbled something, the columns of white figures dancing around in his glass lenses as he did so.

Turlough breezed on toward the lift. Not that his movements bespoke his actual mood. Anything but carefree inside this building, he had long since learned the usefulness, and at times the necessity of such dissimulation. As the doors closed and he descended alone to street level he lapsed into a pensive stare, more appropriate to the inner machinations of his complicated existence.

Had he already told Nuala what time he would be home? They weren't having company tonight, he was sure of that, but still, she might be irked. A letter from the west. America? The doors of the lift slid open and he passed quickly through the lobby, out and down the new granite steps onto the old granite slabs of the footpath. The cold air, the roar of a bus taking off, and the steady clicking of a woman's shoes as he overtook her all lifted his spirits. But it was momentary, and thoughts of work soon caught up on him again.

Yes, it had been another disastrous week. Not that he was to blame, clients came and went all the time, but he was still one of the most junior partners, and he would not be immune to the repercussions if the others all got hungry at the same time. That was why he absolutely could not afford the slightest squint of disapproval from MacCarthy. It might be taken as the signal for a feeding frenzy.

Fine then, let Nuala get into one of her moods. The days when she could pussywhip him were long gone. And they both knew it. Seeing a break in the traffic he dashed across the street and continued hurrying all the way to the door of the bar. Perfect timing as it was starting to rain again. Even the entranceway was thronged and he had to shoulder his way through just to find a point where he could look out across the ocean of faces that were seated everywhere.

'Turlough!'

You could always count on one of the juniors to be on the lookout for you. What was the fellow's name? He knew it would come to him as he slid past the well-heeled and well-spoken, well-met and well-oiled by now, the elite of white-collar Dublin, amongst whom he was always at home. Desmond! That was it, but was it his first or his last name?

'Here, take my seat.' This came from one of the other suits at the same table.

'Thanks lads, but I tell you what, I see O'Brien at the bar and I need to have a quick chat with him. Give me about twenty minutes and I'll be back.'

'We got the tickets for Paris!' he heard from one of them as he shuffled away, catching O'Brien's eye and giving him the nod for a pint. That was good news anyway. He needed a weekend away from Nuala and the kids. Whoever thought of having rugby matches in Paris in the spring was a genius. An Irish male genius.

'Here long, Jim?'

'About twenty minutes, what kept you?' replied Jim O'Brien, flicking back the long lock of grey hair that was intended to camouflage his receding hairline.

His scalp shone with condensation, caused by the masses of damp clothing worn into the bar. His hairstyle was sure to fail him under those circumstances, and with increasing frequency as the evening passed. Turlough was thankful he didn't have that problem. Granted, he was a bit grey around the ears, but there was no loss of growth, and he would never have to cultivate a combover. No, there was nothing that would cause a woman to hesitate at the sight of him.

'Oh, we've so much going on I'm swamped. Thought I'd never get away tonight,' he replied.

'Well, by God, you're the only one that has that problem,' said O'Brien.

Turlough took the brim-full pint glass of black stout proffered to him, mind churning for something else to say that would keep the conversation on business for another while. O'Brien was all gossip, about anything, so much so that you often had to think back over it all later and filter out the plausible from the purely speculative.

'You've been around a lot longer than me, Jim, what do you think MacCarthy will do about it?'

O'Brien swished his own half-empty glass of red beer about, generating a new frothy head on it.

'It's not all up to him these days,' he replied, 'I mean it was once, but now he has his masters, in London, and New York, and God knows where. Oh, I'd say heads will have to roll, there's just no way round it, but sure you have little to worry about. Your star's still in the ascendant.'

Turlough nodded, gulping back his first drink of the week, and scanning the bar for familiar faces while he had his head raised, first to his right, then to his left.

'Ah, Jim, you're the only one that's got any security,' he said, lowering his arm. 'You can always count on our glorious political leaders to create new tax problems from now till eternity. Sure, people must be begging you to tell them some new loophole every year.'

They both grinned and nodded at this.

'What you say is right enough,' O'Brien continued, becoming serious again, 'but that doesn't mean they'll always want yours truly around to dispense these pearls of wisdom. Every mucksavage that ever passed the civil service exams wants to get into the Department of Finance, and every one that does wants to get out and become a tax consultant.'

'Yes, but they're not all cute hoors like you.'

'Now that's rare praise, coming from Turlough the

bloodsucker.'

They both laughed. If Jim O'Brien was stroking him, so what? It was a pleasant way to put the week behind them.

'There's Terence Mulholland and Jack O'Toole holding court over in the corner.' Turlough looked away quickly as he said this so that these other two partners would not catch his eye.

'The Cork mafia,' said O'Brien.

'O'Toole's not from down there.'

'No, but he'd have himself castrated if he thought it would give him the accent. And isn't he from some part of the bog?'

'See, there's where the rest of us lost out, Jim. Wrong accent, wrong sport.'

'Ah well, we're all different. Nothing wrong with that.'

'Ah get serious, man.' Turlough was enjoying this conversation now. 'Look around the bar at all the young crowd from the office. I'm sure the first time any of them get the chance to pay homage to the holy ground of MacCarthy's corner office they think those are pictures of a rugby team on the wall.'

'You could be right.'

O'Brien seemed to be hearing this one for the first time, though Turlough himself had heard it from someone else and the notion of this generation seeing Gaelic games as no more than distant folklore had surprised him too.

'It's just as well they're not allowed to address the old fucker directly. That would be an instant end to their promising careers.'

'I'm sure they're all too busy wetting themselves,' said O'Brien. They both nodded agreement at this, smiling at the images they had conjured up. Turlough cast his eyes about the noisy lounge again and caught an unexpected glance of what looked like Caitríona's hair amongst a crowd around the corner of the L-shaped bar. Surely not. Needing an excuse to keep looking there, he beckoned to a barman.

'Yessir?' enquired one of the many serving staff, with the

industriousness of a paper-hatted server in one of the now familiar fast food restaurants sprouting ever faster in new variations around the city.

'Same again.'

He went about the task without comment, leaving Turlough free to observe the long dark hair, partially hidden by a neck scarf, though what he could see had a sheen that would make any man want to know more. Was it her?

'Have yourself and Nuala any plans for the holidays this year yet?'

O'Brien's question tore him away before she moved her head.

'What? Oh, no, no, unless she's booked something and hasn't told me yet.'

Jim O'Brien shook his head at this, a delegation of arrangements that would be unthinkable in his own family life. The hair glistened behind its owner.

'Sure how would she know when you'd have the time off?' he asked.

For a moment Turlough wondered was this a come-on. But it wasn't. He did such a good job covering up, even from the people who knew him well, his less than blissful home life, that O'Brien had taken his previous remark, which he should never have made, and wouldn't have if his mind hadn't been on Caitríona, as a jest, or at least an exaggeration.

'Eh, well, we've more or less settled on doing something late in the summer....'

The two drinks arrived and Turlough fished out his wallet and handed over a twenty. The hoodlike mass of dark hair swung slowly around, as though knowing it was being watched, and he saw that it was Caitríona's pale face, but before her blue eyes locked onto him, he switched his gaze back to the barman who was handing him coins and crumpled notes by way of change.

'Bringing the kids?' asked O'Brien.

'What? Well, eh, that depends. I mean, they might not want

to go. It might interfere with their own busy social schedules.'

'Ah, they'll hardly say no to a chance to fly off to the sun!'

'I don't know about that. Gearóid might go if he thought there was some good water sport in it, if we went to Club Med again. But Emily would just whine the whole time.'

'Difficult age, young teenagers.'

'Bloody right. Didn't I tell you they just about refused to go to my granduncle's funeral back in December?'

'You mentioned that alright. He was the old fellow that lived over in the west somewhere, wasn't he?'

Was that the west Nuala had been referring to? Mayo? 'Yes. Mad old codger. Never married, the one thing he got right, spent half his time in and out of the loony bin, but still you have to show your respects to the dead!'

'And did they go?'

'Who?'

'Your kids, to the funeral?'

Turlough nodded, frowning at the memory of that trip. He should have gone alone. Nuala had been even worse than the two children, lighting into him with a vengeance when they got lost outside Killala, then fuming away quietly while he bought drinks for all the local mourners. And they'd had a real headbutting all the way back.

Unbidden, the memory returned of pulling the car over and screeching at her: 'What was I supposed to do? Run up there with the keys to the BMW in one hand and the wreath in the other, fling the fucking flowers into the grave after the old bollocks, bless myself and take off again?'

But even that hadn't put an end to it. She had retaliated by pointing out that it was all just deception anyway, in case there might be anything in it for him, that he hadn't seen his granduncle in years, wouldn't know him in the street, and had made right fools of the lot of them by trying to play the big shot in front of all those locals who had their own slant on everything.

He had felt obliged to do that because they had been so late.

Why hadn't he asked someone the way? Ask who? There wasn't so much as an animal in a field to be seen, just walls and rocks and wet ruins everywhere. Horrible. He should be canonized, or whatever, for his patience with Nuala.

'There's a young lady eyeing you from down the back.'

O'Brien's comment pulled Turlough back from his unpleasant reminiscence. He looked up, and this time Caitríona caught his eye and waved, flashing a quick smile.

'I take it you know her?' asked O'Brien.

'Eh, yes, her father's on the committee in the yacht club....' What was she trying to do to him?

'She has that look of money about her alright.'

'I'd better go and say hello. I'll be right back.'

Turlough slid out into the empty space between the crowds standing at the bar and the crowds sitting at the tables, already beginning to thin as the bar entered that lull between the after-work drinkers going home and the out-for-the-night crowd coming in.

He shuffled deliberately around to where Caitríona stood, as though he were headed for the toilet, feigning surprise and halting when she detached herself from those she was with at his approach.

'Fancy meeting you here!' she exclaimed, this time beaming.

'I was going to call you later on,' said Turlough, a half-truth, since he had not intended to contact her until early the following week.

'Then I've saved you a phone call, haven't I?'

Turlough demurred, digging his left hand into his trouser pocket while rubbing the back of his neck with his right. Desmond and one of his cohorts passed by, on their way for a piss, nodding deferentially.

'I'll be right over,' said Turlough as they passed, taking in Caitríona with guileless vertical sweeps of their eyes. She ignored them completely, fixing her gaze on an antique mirror on the far wall, advertising some long forgotten brand of whiskey.

'Some of your foot soldiers?' she asked when they had gone.

'Yes.' Indeed, they had just done him a service, solving the problem of what to do next here. 'What brings you to this neck of the woods?' he asked.

'I should ask you the same thing.'

'Look, you know this is the company watering hole. That's why we never meet here.'

'Well, I'm out with friends for the evening.'

Turlough cast a glance at the others she was with. Theodora he knew, and the others, another woman and two men, were vaguely familiar. He had no desire whatsoever to meet any of them, and hoped they would continue to ignore him.

'Would you like to have dinner with me instead?' The words were out before he knew it. He was irritated with himself, and with her for catching him off balance like this. He liked to plan his meetings with her very carefully in sadvance. He just had too much on his mind.

'You mean tonight?' She cocked her head to one side in surprise. 'Like, walk out of here right now? Together?'

'No, no, no! Later.'

He saw she was enjoying this, knowing she had him running, and learning far too much about him. He had to turn it around. What was she doing here anyway? She must have known she was very likely to run into him. He assumed he was one of a list of men she went out with, and that unless he contacted her he would never hear from her again; as far as he was concerned, these were the rules of enagagement. Was she now changing that?

'How much later?' she asked.

'An hour.'

'Okay.'

'Downstairs. Verdi's. Will you book it?'

'Sure.'

They smiled at one another as if ending a casual chance encounter and Turlough continued on his way to rid himself of his first pint.

'Say hello to your father for me!' he shouted back by way of an afterthought, for the benefit of the now returning Desmond and friend, and anyone else from the office who might have been watching.

'Be right with you lads,' he told the two younger men as they passed, 'I want to settle up with you for that ticket.'

He entered the brightly lit, tiled, deodorized, sanitized, colour coordinated lavatory, stood at an empty spot in front of the long white porcelain urinal, and relieved himself. Then he walked to the bank of sinks and looked at his face in the fully-mirrored wall.

For some strange reason he remembered being here before they had spent a fortune renovating the whole place. He had been a student, on a pub crawl, and there had been someone playing a guitar in the dimly lit bar outside, and someone else had passed around a joint and when he had come in here there had been a stench, piss on the wall so old it was crystallized, and the freezing night air had come in through broken, barred windows, and there were no mirrors, and if there had been a sink it probably didn't work, and he certainly hadn't used it.

Now he carefully washed and dried his hands, and took a comb out of his jacket pocket and made his hair look exactly the way it had when he had blow-dried it that morning, a look he knew made his face appear narrower and younger. He was slightly in need of a shave, but she would have to put up with that. Now he would be really late home. A sheep, not a lamb, to yet another slaughter of words....

'Let's join the lads,' said Turlough returning to Jim O'Brien.

'Fair enough. While you were gone, Mulholland just tipped me off that MacCarthy's going to call a management meeting for next Wednesday.'

'Fucking marvellous! He probably won't start the meeting till six, not wanting to lose any partners' billing time, though if we'd any sense we'd just bill them all anyway, and then we'll all be there till the small hours.'

Turlough knew his comment was superfluous, but he wanted to vent his anger at the fact that Mulholland had been in the know, even though he, Turlough Walsh, had been the last to leave. Where was the fairness in that? By God, the sooner that cantankerous wizened old Cork bastard, with his stupid pictures of himself and those other Munster shitheads who had played Gaelic games in the year dot, the sooner he croaked, and the more painfully, the better.

It was enough just to have been born in the wrong parish as far as that lot were concerned, let alone to best it over them by being a native of the capital city. It was all their fault, them and their pulpit-pounding priest friends, and their civil war politics, with their sanctity of marriage and their special place of the church superstitious nonsense, all their fault that he couldn't just openly walk out of here with Caitríona, buy her dinner, fuck her, and shout from the rooftops that he was having an affair, or that she was his mistress, or anything he liked, as he could surely do in any other civilized European country.

'So how do you rate our chances at the triple crown this year boys?' asked Turlough, as he and O'Brien pulled up two stools, and the younger accounting staff shuffled theirs into a tighter arc to make room for the senior dignitaries, whose presence in their midst, with the infallible career advice it might bring, was the high point of this Friday evening ritual.

CHAPTER TWO

Turlough's leathersoled feet tapped their way briskly down the stone steps. Verdi's held a unique position in the spectrum of the city's restaurants. More elegant, and expensive, than any of the other basement establishments on the same street, it could be counted on not to fill up with a younger and noisier crowd.

He swung through both doors and began walking toward the back without looking around. All of the tables he passed were small, lit by oil lamps, each decorated with a pink stem rose. This overstated romanticism was one of two deterrents to its use for business entertainment.

Caitríona was there, twirling a glass of white wine. She was not, as she had told him on their first meeting, a champagne person.

'Not here too long I hope?' he asked, sitting down.

'About half an hour.'

She did not appear too put out by her wait, content to mention it and let it pass.

'Have you looked at the menu?'

She nodded as he picked up the padded document. This was the other reason you could not bring clients here, and were unlikely to bump into any of the other partners. The menu consisted of only three choices, two of them fish, and even these varied unpredictably with the chef's opinion of the sea's bounty.

They ordered and the waitress picked up the wine from the ice bucket.

'They didn't have the same year we had last time,' said Caitríona.

Turlough took in the label, an unusual Chablis, tasted the wine, pursed his lips and murmured approval. She smiled at this. She must have been sitting there long enough to weigh up the risks of her little decision before he arrived and was pleased now at her success.

'You know you could make life very difficult for me coming to that place when it's packed full of people I work with,' he said, anxious to deal with this matter first.

'You said you liked to take risks,' Caitríona replied.

He knew she was needling him, but with a clever cutting charm rare in a woman. It was her most appealing quality, this way of hers of always being out in front of herself, sparring with you, challenging your ideas, never letting her guard down, or demanding to be listened to, or sympathized with, or to have all her own mundane little problems heard or understood. He could easily, though he didn't, relate to her.

'Being here is a risk,' he declared, 'being there is folly.'

'Turlough's folly!' She laughed, musically, at this. 'This isn't the nineteenth century, you know,' she continued, shaking her head at him.

She was wearing an open-necked white shirt, the sleeves carefully rolled up almost to the elbows, the little gold cross she always wore around her neck flashing as her head tilted back with this gaiety.

'Yes, yes, not all that long now till it'll be the twenty-first century,' said Turlough, 'and by then we'll all have deluded ourselves into thinking we can do anything we like, but it just isn't true.'

'Oh, come on!' She leaned forward and put her hand on his.

'None of those idiots give a damn what you do with your personal life. You told me yourself one of the other partners is gay.'

'Well, that's different.'

'All the people I work with know I'm seeing a married man and it doesn't seem to bother them.'

'Oh, I'm not saying it would bother them in any real sense, but they could use it against me.'

'Aaah!' Her mouth lingered open as she pondered this idea.

'Yes,' he reaffirmed, 'and they would!'

Was she really so naive? Apparently so, but then she spent her days designing advertisements, and perhaps in that world it was an advantage to be somewhat changeable and flaky, but not in his, most certainly not.

'Well how would they?' she asked.

'Questions get asked,' he replied, 'by clients, by banks, even to get nominated onto the boards of paper-holding companies....'

'Mmmm...it's all really Machiavellian, isn't it?'

He nodded at that. Whatever turns you on, he thought. He had often heard that power was an aphrodisiac, but this was the first time it had actually worked for him. There had been other excursions beyond the conjugal bedchamber, but they'd either been in the we-were-both-drunk-let's-forget-it or sex-for-gifts, favours, or promotion categories. He knew Nuala liked to look on him as powerful and successful, but that was different, was marital territoriality, because then whenever she succeeded in getting him to do anything it made her feel all the more potent herself.

Food began arriving and Turlough's mind continued to wander back and forth between the two women as he ate. Nuala had never, ever, been like Caitríona, but if Caitríona got married would she become like Nuala? Most people's wives seemed to have a common agenda, to which they might intermittently contribute some of their own earned income. Buy a house, have kids, buy a bigger house, go to Spain this summer, go to Greece next summer, go to Florida....

When did they change? Wrong question. Why did they change? Yes, what was the answer to that? He was sure that like everything else on the planet it could be explained by the unalterable laws of economics. Supply and demand, that was it. Caitríona supplied him with all the female affection she could because she had as yet unfulfilled, if skilfully hidden, demands for the same stuff. Let her get married though, and she, like all the others, would believe she was now in possession of an inexhaustible supply of this emotional nectar, and would promptly cease putting out the effort that secured it in the first place. Pleased with his own answer to both of his own questions, Turlough reached for the wine.

'Were you really going to call me?' asked Caitríona.

'Yes.'

He poured, emptying the bottle. Good, she'd had two glasses before he got there, enough to loosen her up for later on. He felt a tingling in his groin at the prospect. Why was it that sex was the one thing that, no matter how well you visualized it from the last time, you had to keep doing it again and again to produce the same effect?

'And what were you going to say?' she asked.

The coyly put question was all he could have hoped for, a perfect lead-in, a sure sign they were still on the same wavelength.

'I was going to ask you to go to Paris with me for a weekend.'

'When?' Her eyes widened and she beamed back at him.

'Weekend after next.'

There was a momentary pause, her gaze shifting to one side, then back again.

'Okay,' she said brightly, shrugging as if to show that she had settled some secret little conflict in her head.

Outside, the damp clung to everything, lending a sheen to the brick walls of the Georgian buildings, making haloes in the air round the street lights and leaving the road surface slick everywhere. They passed through an arched passageway which led to the rear of these same facades, all alike, all with the same twelve-paned windows that diminished in size with each ascending floor.

The big gleaming car was parked where once there had been a mews to house the horses of the gentry who had built and lived in these splendid brick abodes. It always pleased Turlough to make that comparison. Didn't it add to the aura of power about him? The headlights of his car flashed at them as he disabled its alarm, then unlocked and held open the passenger door for Caitríona.

'Your place?' he asked as all the lights and symbols of the instrument panel and the car's elaborate stereo came alive.

'Okay.'

He detected a flatness about her reply that bothered him and they were over the Grand Canal and headed for the flatland area where she lived before either of them spoke again.

'You know,' she said softly, 'I don't just let you fuck me because you take me out and spend money on me....'

Good God, what was he supposed to say to that?

'Well, okay then, I won't take you out any more. I'll just call round every now and then and hop into bed with you!'

She swung round and stared at him.

'You would, wouldn't you?' she asked.

Where was she going with these questions? If he did show up out of the blue would there be someone else in the bed with her? He would rather not know. The less he knew the better. The whole point of indulging in this illicit entertainment was to make things be the way he wanted them to be. Did she not realize that? Still, he had better back off.

'Of course I wouldn't. I mean it was only a joke. What was I supposed to say to a comment like that?'

'Well, you could have done better than that anyway.'

'Than what, Caitríona? What do you want me to say? That

I'm glad you feel that way? Okay then: I am!'

She was looking out the window. Time to appeal to female emotion.

'No, really, I mean it,' he said. 'You're a really special person.' He stroked the side of her face, but she only pouted. 'Why else would I take you to Paris with me?'

She brightened up at this reminder. Why wouldn't she? She was a twenty-three year old girl putting up with having a good time in order to have a better time. They cruised past the two storey red-brick house that contained her flat without finding a parking space.

'Oh God, I just thought of something!' she cried, looking out the window at where she lived. 'My sister's there for the weekend.'

Turlough groaned loudly. 'Can't you just give her some money and send her out to the pub?' he asked.

'It's almost closing time, and she probably has her friends around too.'

'Well this is a fine time to be thinking of this.'

'Sorry. What do you want to do?'

'Let's find a dark lane!'

He noticed her stiffening a little. Then the sister story was a lie. He smirked involuntarily at her predicament. She didn't want to make love tonight but she didn't want to blow her Paris trip either. He reached over and turned up the car's heater, then in silence they prowled the web of dark streets until he found his way into the unlit yard behind a butcher shop.

She was all hands right away, feeling for the zip of his trousers as soon as they started kissing.

'Let's see here, how do we want to do this?' he mumbled, reclining the back of his own seat and pulling her over onto him.

'Don't want any embarrassing stains, do we?' she chided, sitting back up to partially undress. He reached over and began undoing the front buttons of her shirt. The first time they had done it in this car, which was the first time they had done it, he had recklessly pounded away into her on the passenger seat, and she had lain there while it all leaked back out again, and the upholstery had never fully recovered, nor could it be replaced since the original had been custom-ordered.

He began to feel one of her breasts through the lacy bra, but she seemed unimpressed and busily hitched her already short skirt up to her waist, freeing herself to climb astride him, clamping him between her knees. He wondered if she could feel the bulges in the sides of his hips that would be absent in a younger lover, though they were by no means out of control yet.

She bent down and they kissed, her silky black mane flowing down both sides of his face, shampoo fragrant, her gold cross tickling his chin. He reached between her legs and slid his fingers up and down the outside of her panties, feeling the flattened springy little hairs through the thin fabric, but before he could work his way round the elastic rim he felt her grab him by the wrist.

'Let's just make this your night, Turlough,' she whispered, releasing his wrist and reaching for the other cylindrical piece of flesh near at hand, which, however, was anything but bone-like.

How much had he had to drink? Not too much. No, all that was lacking here was stimulation, and she was pumping away vigorously to remedy that. Then what was holding him back? There was some mental block, some logjam in the stream, preventing him from sending the necessary hormones to the necessary blood vessels.

Caitríona changed hands a few times, then tired of that approach and got back onto the passenger seat to kneel back on her haunches, get her face down there and try with her mouth for a while.

What was it he asked himself? He stroked the back of her head, smoothing down the dark mane, and frantically tried to free himself of every stressful thought he had had that day, but that just brought them all flooding back. MacCarthy, Mulholland, O'Brien, the long phone calls to his juniors in other parts of the country.

No, it wasn't any of that anyway. Was he afraid of doing it with Caitríona again? Was it because he wasn't wearing a condom? That had been her choice. Surely that should help, make her tongue feel all the more exquisite. Why? Did she already know she was HIV positive, or did she have syphilis or something? Was she some kind of crusading sexual serial killer out to infect all men who were unfaithful to their wives?

No, no! Was there anything undesirable about her then? Was there any mannerism, or smell, or anything about her body that was physically undesirable? Certainly not, although her breasts were not in the same category as Nuala's at all. Nuala's mysterious message about a letter from the west! Was that it? Then the thought of his wife brought the germ of an idea into Turlough's head, and it grew and grew until he was sure he knew what was wrong with him.

Guilt! He was inexplicably experiencing a feeling of guilt. But why now? His marital infidelity had never troubled him in the past, and now that Nuala had as good as told him that she was not above the occasional fling herself, Turlough believed she had given him a licence to pursue whatever potential sexual conquests came his way.

And yet here he was, in the middle of such an opportunity, and he could not get a hard-on because he was feeling guilty about what he was doing. He was sure that's what it was. He became intensely aware of Caitríona then, heard her sucking on him, felt her fingers kneading the organ lower down, and began to sense its every tiny movement. Instantly he felt a surge of pleasure, and his member grew so fast she gagged, but she knew now success was at hand, and swung back onto him, pulling the crotch of her panties to one side to let him slide deep into her.

He gasped as she rocked back and forth over him, the only

motion possible within the confined space, but it was more than enough, and in sudden, quick, hot spurts it was over, though she seemed not to notice for another few moments, and then stopped and slumped down onto him, both of them breathless from the task of satisfying, once more, the most primal urge of Turlough Walsh.

Preoccupied with this guilt notion all the way back to her flat, he was pleased that she chose not to interrupt the silence until they got there, and when they did she asked a parting question that would now put all his thoughts in order.

'I suppose you think I'm a cheap slut?'

'No,' he replied. Technically he was telling the truth. He thought she was a slut, but not a cheap one, since she had the good taste to go out with him.

But there was the confirmation of the whole thing. The very fact that she asked meant that what he thought of her mattered, whereas he neither knew nor cared what she thought of him. She kissed his cheek and left.

He was almost tempted to take her to a nightclub and dance with her, sensing that she would enjoy that, but while he was weighing it up she was gone, slamming the door hard, and in response he drove away before she had even passed through the gate.

It began to rain again but he was indifferent, musing on what he had now labelled his guilt-trip all the way, so happy with this new insight into himself that he began to whistle and strum the steering wheel with his fingers.

It was really very simple. Because Caitríona was confused by her feelings for him, in fact because she was unable to reconcile her greedy desire to go to Paris with her temporary lack of sexual desire, brought on by who knows what female maladjustment, she had experienced some sort of guilt back there in the car.

And, because he was an intelligent, sensitive man, he had allowed that guilt to be transferred to him, almost wanting not to have sex with her, because she was indifferent to having it with him! He shook his head slowly. It was all very well to be a carrier of these emotional diseases and inflict them on other people, that's how you got them to do things for you, but he was always careful not to get infected himself, not even by someone as beautiful and accommodating as Caitríona. So tempting. Yes, take her east, to Paris, but let her mystery endure. Turlough's folly? No, a lesser man would surely have succumbed, but he had overcome. And come.

He rolled down both front windows as he swung onto the tree-lined lane on which he lived, listening to the hiss of the powerful car's wheels as it glided over the rain-soaked asphalt, the night air flapping through his jacket, purging the car of any lingering female odours.

He turned into the driveway of his latest home, acquired two years previously, concurrent with the knowledge that he was about to be promoted to partner, and noticed as he pulled up beside his wife's car that there were many lights on. Nuala was still up.

'I'm home!' announced Turlough, slamming the heavy oak hall door behind him.

'What kept you till now?' asked Nuala's voice from the landing above.

'Oh, there's more trouble brewing and I had to be sure I knew where Mulholland was on it all...feed him some truth serum...just politics, nothing constructive. Jim O'Brien wanted to have a chat with me too.'

'You're always chatting with him. I wish you'd let me know when you're going to be so late. If you're looking for food there isn't a bite to eat.'

She began to descend the stairs.

'Well it's Friday night. I'm never home before eight.'

'It's midnight Turlough.'

He looked at his watch and blinked in surprise.

'Oh, gosh! Well, I'm not hungry, I had a sandwich with the

crowd of them. Why are you still up?'

Nuala reached the bottom of the stairs, and sat down, drawing her legs up inside her long silk nightdress.

'Didn't you get my message? A letter came for you today,' she said, pointing to the hall table, 'and it has the address of a solicitor in Killala on it.'

'Killala? Christ, could you not have been more specific! "West" you said!'

'And isn't it west of us?'

'Ah for God's sake! I thought it might have been a job offer from Hawaii or somewhere like that! Well why didn't you open it?' he asked, reaching for the long white envelope and turning it over a few times before tearing away the end of it.

'It looks very official and it's addressed to you.'

He shook his head at this illogical answer, which suggested that she would certainly have opened it if it had been personal. There was a single sheet of the same solicitor's notepaper inside that said:

Dear Mr Walsh,

I represent a party interested in acquiring the property of your late uncle Bernard Patrick Walsh, God have mercy on him.

As with many such premises handed on by way of inheritance there are complications of which you should be apprised. Not the least of these is that the deed search has revealed no title deed and also the fact that all members of the Walsh family residing on the estate in question seem to have died intestate, or insane, or both.

Please contact my office and make an appointment to come here for a meeting with me. It would greatly facilitate the conveyancing of this property if I could appoint you custodian of your uncle's estate and have you sign various documents pursuant to my client's purchase.

Yours faithfully,

Thadeus O'Gorman.

Turlough handed his wife the letter to read.

'Jesus, woman, why didn't you open the damn thing and call me?' He paced around as he spoke, irritated. 'I mean, what does this culchy shyster think he's playing at? If I've inherited something, and if I have I wish someone had told me before now, then how does he know I'd want to sell it again at all? How much is it worth?'

'What are you so upset about?' asked Nuala, folding the letter and handing it back. 'It seems we've just come into a farm in Mayo that we knew nothing about!' She clapped her hands in delight at the thought.

'Ah, get a grip on yourself woman! First of all, Uncle Bernie was my granduncle, not my uncle, and there are lots of other grandnephews and grandnieces dotted around the world, so I doubt I have any legal right to the place. Secondly, there's something crooked about this. It looks like we'd never have heard about the place at all if some greedy local yokel hadn't put his eye on it. And thirdly, as I said, why the fuck didn't you call me so we don't have to wait till Monday to find out more about it all?'

'If you'd come home from work you'd have known about it sooner.' Nuala stood up and began ascending the stairs again.

Turlough raised his hand above his head and waved the letter up at her. 'Don't be so bloody stupid! This is a small fucking country with only one fucking time zone,' he yelled, 'so if I was finished work in Dublin then so would Thadeus gobshite O'Gorman be finished in Killala!'

He gulped at his own half-assed remark, but she was good at bringing out the worst in him, and besides, this attack was a good defence for his tardiness.

'Be quiet!' she hissed back down, 'You'll wake up the kids.' He ignored this remark, switched off the lights and followed her up the stairs. When he reached the bedroom, Nuala was just sliding into sleeping position in the king-size bed, bare shoulder and one silk strap exposed to view. He reminded himself that the price of this nocturnal elegance was that their central heating went on burning what was left of the world's fossil fuel day and night, all year round, and that he was paying for it, every month.

'I left a list on the kitchen table of things I want you to get at the garden centre in the morning,' she told him, dozing, 'I have to go into town and get a few bits and pieces for tomorrow night. Oh, and Gearóid has a match tomorrow, so you'll have to bring him to that if I'm not back.'

With that she fell into a contented sleep, leaving him to mull over where they were going that required the purchase of 'bits and pieces', her euphemism for a shopping spree on Grafton Street, but he was too addled to recall. Surely there would be no need for him to actually go back to the wilds of Killala? After all, he thought, pulling off his shoes, Uncle Bernie had died intestate because he was insane, had been a lifelong alcoholic when he wasn't on shock treatment, had never had a job of any kind, never attempted any kind of farming other than the wretched and unnecessary pursuit of growing his own potatoes, and, therefore, had surely gone to that great pub in the sky with the arse out of his trousers, penniless, yes, destitute, and so, beyond any doubt whatsoever, landless . . . .

CHAPTER THREE

Emily was lying on the couch, reading a magazine, watching TV and listening to a CD when Turlough came down next morning.

'Has your mother gone yet?' he asked from the doorway.

'What?' The thirteen year old viewed him upside down, head leaning backward over the couch, hair hanging down in a wavy mess.

'I thought you would have gone with her. She might have bought you something.'

'If you give me money I'll take the bus in now.'

Turlough shook his head at this outspoken greed and wandered on to the kitchen. She would milk some unfortunate man for everything he was worth one of these years. Just like her mother.

He examined the squares on the calendar behind the door to see if they gave any clue as to where they were going that night but found nothing. These social events that Nuala sprang on him were annoying. He flipped up the page to assure himself that she had made no plans for the weekend he was going away with Caitríona, saw that it was empty, picked up a marker from the counter and wrote in thick letters: 'Rugby–Paris'.

He found the list of items to be bought at the garden centre and decided to do that first and get it out of the way.

'Do you want to come shopping with me?' he asked Emily as he passed by again.

'No!' she responded, predictably enough.

The place was crowded with people and he had to get in line to pay for the bulbs and fertilizer and sweet pea seed Nuala wanted.

'That time of year again, Turlough!'

Turlough swung around at the sound of his name to see Dara Mooney and his wife, whose name he couldn't remember, standing behind him, both of them with potted plants in their arms.

'Oh, yes, yes indeed. The next spell of good weather and the grass will shoot up.' He detested this kind of small talk, but you had to say something by way of greeting.

'Is your boat in the water yet?' asked Mooney, pursuing the one thing they had in common and the reason they knew each other — they were members of the same yacht club.

'Oh, God, no, I haven't had time to think about it at all yet. Been very busy, you know.'

They both nodded. It was well known that he had made partner and it was expected that this would cut inroads on his leisure time.

'We did pretty well in the frostbite races this year,' said the wife, reminding him that they were dinghy sailors, much lower in the pecking order, onshore as well as off, than those who raced keel boats, like himself.

'We'd have won the series easily if we'd been able to make every race,' added Dara Mooney.

Now what kind of a stupid comment was that to make? Was he supposed to commiserate with them or congratulate them on their prowess?

'Nuala gave up on the house plants years ago. We had one that looked like that,' he said, nodding at the dracanea

Mooney's wife was holding, 'but she insisted on pulling all the leaves off it that had anything wrong with them, until there were so few of them left the thing just gave up.'

Mooney's wife shook her head slowly at this wanton cruelty, but Dara was willing to dispense advice on the problem. 'You really have to situate these plants carefully, keep the leaves well sprayed in the winter, and talk to them.'

'They need to know you're non-violent,' added the wife.

'Oh!' said Turlough, nodding as if absorbing this information with great interest.

'And since we're vegetarians,' Mooney went on, 'well, maybe that explains why our house plants do so well.'

It was all Turlough could do not to splutter at this nonsense, but he was saved by reaching the cash desk.

'Well, nice talking to you both,' he said before leaving, barely resisting the temptation to point out to them that all these orchids and bromeliads and such like did perfectly well in tropical rain forests filled with carnivorous headhunters.

'Sure, we'll see you tonight, won't we?' said Mooney.

'Oh? Eh, right!'

'Now don't tell me you're not going to go, after paying for the tickets?' added the wife.

'Oh no, no, we'll be there.'

'Cheerio!'

'Bye. See you later!'

He turned his back on them and hefted the fertilizer out to the car.

'For Christ's sake why didn't you tell me we had something on in the yacht club tonight? Do you get some sadistic pleasure out of the thought of me making a fool of myself in front of people we know?'

Turlough yelled these words at his wife that afternoon as soon as she walked into the living room, still clutching the various bags, decorated with the logos of the city's most expensive stores, which contained the 'bits and pieces' she had spent her day buying.

'You forget everything, Turlough,' she replied, 'you have a head like a sieve.'

'Well, you should have written it up on the calendar.'

'If you'd come home....'

'Don't start that again,' he warned.

'Anyway,' she went on, putting her bags on the armchair, 'it's nothing to do with the club, it's a fund raiser for the Olympics. There'll be a couple of thousand people there.'

'Who are we going with?' he asked, looking at his watch.

'The Kents. We're meeting the Flahertys there.'

He grunted approval at this. Larry Kent was thinking of taking a share in the boat; Mark and Veronica Flaherty, who co-owned the vessel, were two of their oldest friends.

'I suppose it's monkey-suit?' he asked, getting a couple of nods from Nuala as she unpacked a new glittery purse from one bag and pulled a shoebox from another.

There could easily have been two thousand people there, no problem at all, Turlough mused, surveying the huge hotel ballroom.

'But if they revalued the D-mark, wouldn't that help?' asked Larry Kent.

'Not at all,' said Mark Flaherty, 'it would only make a worse mess of everything. We'd be crippled by our own interest rates.'

'What do you think, Turlough?' asked Larry.

'About what?'

'Ah, he's too busy looking at all the skirt going by,' said Mark.

'I was not!' Turlough replied, shooting a wary glance at Nuala, but she was engrossed in some chitchat with Veronica. Philomena Kent, chain smoking as usual, was the only one of the three women tuned into the men's conversation.

'They're talking about the economy,' she told Turlough helpfully.

'Oh, right, well you know how I see it. Governments should stay away from economic meddling. They have nothing to contribute, and they only get in the way. At best. More often they bungle things, which creates more debt, which causes them to hike up taxes, which makes the economy worse, and so it goes on, just throwing good money after bad.'

'But you have to have some government services,' said Larry.

'Ah, you do in your arse!' said Turlough. 'You just think that because you make a living selling equipment to hospitals.'

'Right,' said Philomena, 'and he'd make more money if all the hospitals were private, like in America.'

'No he wouldn't,' said Mark, 'because he wouldn't be able to rip them off so easily.'

'That's true,' added Turlough, 'They wouldn't buy all that overpriced antiquated junk you sell them if they had to compete for patients.'

'You have to wait years for some operations in the UK now,' said Mark, rowing in with Turlough on the side of private enterprise.

'You could be dead before they got around to you,' said Philomena.

'Yes,' said Turlough, 'but you're only outraged at that thought because you think it's immoral. What we're saying is that it's sheer incompetence, caused by this huge government meddling.'

'Roll it all back then, is that it?' asked Larry.

'Absolutely!' said Turlough. 'It's the only hope if we're to compete with Asia. Let supply and demand, market forces, take over. We'd all be way better off.'

Shushing sounds rippled through the dining room, cutting off any response to Turlough's comment as the wail of a microphone being adjusted came across the loudspeakers.

'Oh God, are we going to have speeches?' asked Mark.

'There's Irish logic for you,' said Turlough. 'What's the point preaching to us about all this? We've already coughed up.'

A man with a gold anchor on the breast pocket of his jacket was at the microphone.

'...great pleasure...to you...the Minister...,' was all Turlough heard him say. Then another man with a sheaf of paper in his left hand trotted up the steps and there was applause as both of them shook hands.

'Minister for what?' asked Turlough.

'Ssshh!' said Nuala.

'For Sport,' said Mark.

'Never knew we had one,' muttered Turlough.

'...thank everyone here tonight for their tremendous support...,' said the Minister for Sport.

'I think he's only a Junior Minister,' said Larry softly.

'...together with the proceeds allocated to this from the national lottery...,' the Minister continued.

'The bloody lottery paying for Dara Mooney to go sailing,' said Mark, shaking his head.

'You're joking,' said Turlough. 'That half-witted vegetarian is on the Irish Olympic team?'

'Ssshhh!' said both Nuala and Veronica.

'...minimize the burden on the taxpayer....'

'I mean there you have it!' said Turlough, throwing up his hands and ignoring the renewed shushing of the women at the table. 'If self-serving cretins like the Mooneys want to go to the Olympics they should bloody well save up their own money. This is the kind of malarkey that brought down the Soviet Union.'

'...another example of outstanding talent from a small nation....'

'Talent?' quizzed Turlough, 'Talent is when you can sing or act, instead of having to fuck all the judges....'

'For God's sake!' said Nuala.

'Or juggle,' said Mark.

'Talent is the opposite,' said Turlough, 'of whatever stuff politicians are made of.'

Even the three women tittered at that one. The Junior Minister for Sport folded up his papers and put them in his pocket, indicating that he was more or less finished.

'And I just want to conclude by saying,' he said, 'that the present government is committed, like no government before it in the history of the state, to excellence in the field of sport.' He paused, compelling those at the tables nearest him to applaud weakly. 'And that we, as a maritime nation, will always look to you sailors amongst us, to show us where we can all go together, if we put our minds to it.'

Turlough watched, clapping and shaking his head at the same time, as this woolly-minded exhortation was followed by pumping the hand of the man with the anchor on his blazer and then a sprightly descent from the stage to offer the same influential right limb to all those seated at the front tables.

The rest of the night passed in a combination of lighthearted argument, dancing, buying rounds of drinks and mingling with the others who were there from their yacht club. He noticed that Philomena did not dance with Larry, who did however dance with Nuala. Surely the two of them weren't going to crank up that old merry-go-round again? He watched as they returned, laughing, to the table. Philomena just smoked on, heedless, as Larry adjusted Nuala's chair. A woman never opens her heart to the same man twice, he reminded himself. But then that wasn't what Nuala had opened for Larry Kent.

The function reached its boisterous conclusion, everyone doing the hokeypokey, and as they parted with the Kents in the foyer he saw Larry's hand slide down over Nuala's buttock, in jest, maybe, but not unwelcomed. Veronica, who seldom drank anyway, drove the four of them home and the Flahertys came in for a pot of tea, giving the women one last chance for a disparaging review of the outfits worn by everyone else, while Turlough and Mark mulled over the calendar in the kitchen, making tentative arrangements to launch their boat.

*

'Is Mark going to Paris with you?' asked Nuala later as she began removing her jewellery, chains and beads clattering on the marbled top of her dressing table.

'He doesn't know yet. Probably.'

'Well, Veronica says he's not. They have too many debts at the moment.'

Turlough brooded on this. Was it a test question? Was she trying to catch him out in a lie? He looked across at her and she smiled back at him, raising her eyebrows as she wriggled out of her evening dress, an expectant look that reassured him the question was without malice. He was glad he had not struck out with a comment on Larry.

He was not at all averse to making love to his wife; they did so about twice a week, usually on weekends, usually after socializing with their friends, the one pastime that significantly increased their tolerance of their own company. He watched as Nuala went on undressing until she was completely naked, then whipped down the bedcovers and lay back sideways across the sheet, feet on the floor, hands behind her head, smoothing out her permed, tinted hair.

Was it the idea of him kneeling at her altar of pleasure that she liked most? No, the corollary with prayer, if it occurred to her, would not sit well, and certainly not on a Saturday night when she would be mulling over which Mass they would be going to in the morning and what they should all wear. But not now. He knew this pose, this bliss-expectant, inhibitionless interlude. Do this for me and you can do anything you like to me.

Supply and demand, thought Turlough as he finished pulling off his own clothes and went over to her — it was as simple as that. And theirs was a market that had long since reached equilibrium. He knelt down. The stable bottom of the curve, that's where they were, at rest, motionless. Wasn't that what drove him in his pursuit of Caitríona, he asked himself, hands caressing his wife's smooth thighs?

And it was. He wanted to set the pendulum swinging again; to upset this balanced give and take; to energize his life so that he would not just grow old without feeling it, numbed, calcified in some irreversible process, until he could no longer tell the difference between life and death, and faded away, like everyone else, like Uncle Bernie.

'What? Yes, I'll hold. And tell him this is the third time I've called.'

Turlough swivelled back and forth at his desk, as far as he could with the phone to his ear. It was Monday afternoon and he held the still perplexing letter in his other hand, no nearer to speaking with its author. And he had a meeting in five minutes that was sure to go on late.

'Mr Walsh?'

A distant tinny voice came over the phone.

'Yes!'

Turlough straightened up and stopped swivelling.

'Good afternoon, Mr Walsh, this is Thadeus O'Gorman.'

'Hello, Mr O'Gorman.'

There was a pause at the other end.

'And what can I do for you?' asked the voice at the far end, breaking the silence.

'It's about this letter you sent me.'

'Oh, yes?'

'You say my granduncle, Bernard Walsh, left some sort of estate.'

'Oh, that's right. Yes, I recall now. But of course you understand I'm not acting on his behalf, I never met the man, but on behalf of my own client.'

'Eh, yes.' Turlough was glad that had been clarified. 'But you seem to think that I can be of some help.'

'I do, yes,' O'Gorman continued. 'Apparently you gave out a business card in Moran's Public House after the funeral, and since you're the only direct descendant of these same Walshs known to us we were hoping you might be able to sign off on a few things....'

'Have I inherited some land?'

'There's a house and land involved.'

'Where Uncle Bernie used to live?'

'I believe so.'

'Will I need my own solicitor?'

'You'd have to ask him that question.'

Turlough shook his head at this obtuse response.

'I mean,' he continued, 'would it be a conflict of interest if you were to handle both sides of this transaction?'

'Oh, I see! I don't think so. It might be less expensive too.' There was another pause. 'And more rewarding.'

Turlough nodded and smiled, grasping the situation at last.

'Who has the title deed?' he asked.

'Well now, that's a mystery that might never be resolved, but you can leave all the details of the conveyancing to me. Are you familiar with the Land Reform Acts?'

'No.'

'Well, you see, I am. So when could you come over here and see me?'

'When would be convenient?'

'I'm here all the time.'

Turlough clenched his free fist. These country people were insufferable. It had taken all day to get O'Gorman to answer his phone and now he says he's there all the time!

'Let me get back to you. It'll be some time in the next few weeks.'

'Fair enough. God bless.'

Turlough put the phone down and stroked his chin with his left hand. He had been wrong to think of not going to Killala, but right to disabuse Nuala of the idea that there would be any money involved. Now he could go down there, sell off the place, have the money paid to him in trust as executor of the will, and take it out of the country with him when he went to Paris.

He stood up and clapped his hands. Uncle Bernie had lived,

intermittently, in a hovel on an acre or so of land. But whoever bought that site would automatically get planning permission to build themselves a new house, and so would be prepared to pay a pretty penny for it.

Turlough looked at his watch: three minutes to four. He picked up a scratch pad and his gold pen, walked out the door of his office, was handed the file relevant to his four o'clock meeting by his secretary as he passed, swung right, and made for the practice's main conference room, where MacCarthy was about to hold one of his dreaded revenue meetings.

CHAPTER FOUR

Turlough looked at his watch yet again as he passed the road sign on its two striped legs that announced he was in the town of Killala. It was just after six, dark, and much later than he had originally planned.

The shops in the town centre were all lit up, all open for business, so he took that as a hopeful sign. He should have called O'Gorman's office to say he would be late, but that would just have caused more delay. Then, stopped at one of the town's few traffic lights, he once again felt lucky, spotting the gold lettering that advertised O'Gorman's business on three upstairs windows on the opposite corner.

Parking, he walked back to the panelled door, lined down both sides with the brass plates of each individual practitioner of the legal arts housed within, but the door was locked.

'Suffering Jesus!' he exclaimed, standing back to look at the glass fanlight above the door. The hallway was in darkness. Turlough shook his head in disgust and walked round the corner in search of a phone. Thadeus habeus corpus O'Gorman must surely live nearby.

He found two new-looking phone booths, but neither contained a phone book, and the operator was no help. He asked in the various shops from which you could see the gold lettering, but all he got was blank stares and 'sorry'.

Eventually he gave up and, slowed down now by the lack of any clear purpose, wandered back to the car. Should he just find a hotel for the night? What a waste of time! And he had to be back in Dublin no later than lunch time tomorrow.

Then, tapping his fingers on the steering wheel, an idea came to him. Maybe the night would not be a complete waste of time after all. He gunned the engine, swung out of the parking space and took the main, and only, road west out of Killala.

Soon he passed through the main, and only, street of Ballycastle and then he had to start thinking hard, looking for features he recognized. He doubted he could find Uncle Bernie's house, even in daylight. He had only been there once, as a young child. The family had been in Sligo on one of those childhood holidays that were now all merged together in his memory when his father had decided to take them on an excursion to Mayo to visit his mad uncle.

That was the first and last time he had met Bernard Patrick Walsh alive and it came back to him that he had gotten into trouble that day for knocking down a part of the stone wall across the road, and no one seemed to care that, wearing short pants, he had stung both legs badly with nettles at the same time.

He had been eight years old: thirty-one years ago! There had been one other trip to this part of the country, and at the time he had not understood its significance. He had waited on a bench within view of the porters in an institution he'd assumed was a hospital, somewhere near Ballina, while his father had 'just signed a few papers to help poor Uncle Bernie.'

A crossroads loomed up, with its black and white pole on which were bolted the cast iron signs, with their raised lettering in both Irish and English picked out in black paint, pointing to various towns, none of which he knew. But the junction itself was familiar from the day of the funeral back in December.

Turlough turned right and after another few miles, snaking around dark hills, black pools and boggy fields of reeds, he came on the destination he was looking for. 'Yes!' he shouted as he drew level with a two storey building on his right.

Above the door, in a panel that ran the full length of the nineteenth-century facade were large raised Gaelic-style letters that read 'Moran's'. To the left in smaller letters was the word 'lounge' and to the right the word 'bar', and in much smaller hand painted letters beneath all of this was inscribed, 'licensed to sell wine, spirits and tobacco'. Beer was not mentioned.

He reversed his BMW into a space between an old Cortina hitched to a small trailer, containing two bales of hay, or straw, or silage, or whatever was sold in bales at this time of the year, and a huge green tractor, its rear wheels spattered with what smelled like cowshit.

Pushing in one of the two stiff doors, which swung noisily shut behind him, Turlough found himself in the bar area and walked across well-worn black and red tiles to one of the empty stools at the counter, feeling overdressed as the ruddy-faced man on the far side eyed his silk tie.

'Good evening,' said Turlough, settling onto a stool.

'What'll it be?' asked the other.

'I think I'll try a pint of stout,' said Turlough, watching as the proprietor's giant hand gripped a pint glass, and held it, vice-like, beneath the appropriate tap.

'Have I seen you before somewhere?'

The question was put to Turlough without eye contact. There were three other customers in the bar, all old men. One sat beneath the front window, intent on the evening paper, and the other two occupied opposite ends of the bar.

Unless all four of them had Alzheimer's they would surely remember him from his largesse at the funeral, though he had no idea whether any or all of them had been present that night. He had spent most of his time commiserating with mourners in the lounge, where they had been served by a woman who must have been this fellow's wife. But he had bought drink for the whole bloody place.

'Ah, some of my people were from these parts, on my father's side. Just like to drop by when I get the chance.'

He clasped his hands around one knee. He would remain noncommittal and see how they reacted.

They did not react at all, leaving Turlough to fumble for his wallet as the questioner topped off his drink and slid it across to him, leaving a trail of creamy froth on the wooden surface.

'Are you Mr Moran?' he asked, handing over a twenty, the biggest note in his wallet.

'No.'

'Oh, eh, is he around then?'

The man to the right found this very amusing. His body shook with the effort of laughing with his mouth closed. Turlough turned to the man on the left, a diminutive specimen in an ancient suit and cloth cap, who stuck his finger in his ear, twisted it around, turned to look at the stranger and shook his head.

'There isn't one,' said the proprietor, pressing his palms on the countertop. 'My wife is the last of the Morans.'

'Oh, oh I see,' Turlough replied. 'Well, I'm sorry to hear that.' That didn't go over well. 'I mean it's sad, all the emigration and all that. Less people around. Can't be good for business....'

The right palm in front of him left the countertop, swung through ninety degrees and came forward.

'Donal Cohan,' he said, waiting immobile until Turlough understood the gesture and reached out his own hand, to be squeezed painfully and not shaken.

'Turlough Walsh. Pleased to meet you.'

'Would you be anything to Bernard Walsh then, God have mercy on his unfortunate soul?'

'Well, yes, eh, in fact that's why I'm here, I mean in this part of the country at all.'

'Is it the land you're after?' This question came from the chuckler on the right.

'Whisht!' said Cohan, glaring at him. 'Take no notice of him.'

Aha! The game was in play.

'As a matter of fact it is that piece of land that brought me here.'

'You're less than a mile from it,' said soft-cap on the left.

'But poor Bernard left no heirs,' said Cohan, adding: 'He was also the last of his line.'

'Ah well now, that's not quite accurate,' said Turlough, 'and in fact I just had that very conversation with a solicitor in Killala, who seemed to be similarly misinformed.' He lapsed into a deliberate silence, and took a long swig of his black pint, knowing he was watched now from all four points of the compass. Their move.

'Will you have another one of those?' asked Cohan, pointing to the now half-empty glass as Turlough lowered it to the counter again.

'Well....' Turlough looked at his watch.

'This one's on me,' said Cohan.

'Oh, gosh, well, alright then.'

It was an hour or more before the conversation returned to the issue, with Turlough buying the three patrons a round, and the chuckler buying one in return in the meantime. For the most part they asked him highly speculative questions, about politics and the economy, and he gave them long-winded, and equally speculative replies.

'You know,' said Cohan, 'I don't think we'll ever see prosperity in these parts again.'

'What do you mean "again" Donal?' asked the chuckler.

'You see, isn't this the problem with us,' said Turlough.

'With who?' asked Cohan.

'The Irish. All of us.' He gestured with both hands, taking in the whole of the bar by swinging around on his stool.

'What do you mean?' asked the newspaper reader, sternest of the four, face frowning over at the thought that he was about to hear something disparaging about his race.

'What I mean,' said Turlough, 'is that we're so caught up in the past, and even in the problems we all have today, that we can't see what a fantastic future this country has!'

He had them. Time to land this puppy, as the Americans would say, and get what he came for.

'You look around, Mr Cohan, and say to yourself that you'll never fill this bar again, but that's not true. There's a tremendous demand for property out here again, what with all these people who are working from their homes with computers and faxes and all. Now, the reason I say that is because, well, take this place up the road that I inherited....'

He saw Cohan glance to the chuckler, then fix soft-cap with a glare.

'I have offers on that,' Turlough declared, 'sight unseen, from prospective buyers in Dublin, that are well over twice the kind of offers we were talking about in Killala this afternoon.'

'Arra, Christ!' said soft-cap, 'Bernie Pat was hardly sitting on thirty thousand all those years!' He looked imploringly at the roof. 'Oh, if only the poor divil had known!'

'Quiet!' yelled Cohan, storming down the bar and grabbing soft-cap's elbow. 'You've had enough for tonight, Morris, get on out of here home!'

Cohan dislodged Morris of the soft cap from his stool and sent him tottering against the side wall.

'God, what have I done?' he asked, readjusting his archaic headwear as he stumbled toward the door. 'Isn't my money as good as the next person's?'

'Go on, get on home!'

Cohan was flushed and angry, disappearing out of sight into the back of the pub as the door slammed behind soft-cap, the informer.

'I hope that wasn't my fault!' said Turlough, shaking his head at the remaining pair, but neither of them replied, perhaps fearful of being barred from their watering hole too.

It was all Turlough could do not to smile. Now he knew both the offer price and the buyer: fifteen thousand from Cohan! That would be a tidy enough sum, would pay for any number of little getaways with Caitríona, or any other Caitríonas that came along. And maybe Cohan would go higher for a quick deal!

'You know, I haven't seen this place of Bernard's, God rest him, in thirty years,' said Turlough, turning to the newspaper reader. 'What condition is it in?'

That thawed them a little.

'I'd say fair.'

'Ah, hardly even that,' said the chuckler, 'There's probably dry rot in the roof, and no insulation whatever.'

'And where exactly is it?' asked Turlough, to emphasize how little he knew about this property, and thus, hopefully, for Cohan's benefit when he returned, his willingness to bargain reasonably over it.

'Just go straight on,' said the reader, 'and you can't miss it. It's the first old cottage on your right –'

'It is not!' protested the other man.

'Ah, let me finish! It's the first one that's right up against the road. And you'll know you've passed it if the road starts going downhill. About, oh, two miles from here.'

Cohan returned, looking in no better form than when he had left.

'We were just talking about the property while you were gone,' said Turlough, 'and of course I have no idea what it might really be worth. I suppose, like everything else, it's all a question of supply and demand.'

'Is that so?' said Cohan with a coolness that was offputting.

'You know,' said Turlough, lowering his voice conspiratorially, 'I wouldn't be averse to a, perhaps, lower offer from someone here in the area who was in a position to move on it right away....'

'There's only going to be the one offer,' Cohan replied,

folding his great brawny arms in a gesture of finality.

Turlough attempted to feign a look of disbelief, but as he did so a wooziness, brought on by drinking on an empty stomach, overtook him, and he had to adjust his position on the stool suddenly, reaching with both hands for the edge of the counter.

'I wouldn't be so sure about that,' he replied.

'Ah, well you see I am.'

Turlough blinked at Cohan who looked warily at his other two customers then back again, and leaned forward.

'I just got off the phone,' he said slowly, 'with Thadeus O'Gorman....'

'What?'

'Yes, Mr Walsh, and he says you never met this afternoon....'

'Well, we spoke several times on the phone, so he knows the score,' Turlough shouted, 'and I must say Mr O'Gorman's professional conduct leaves a lot to be desired in this matter.'

Cohan snorted, the reader coughed repeatedly and the chuckler lost control of himself, laughing uproariously at the glass in front of him.

'You're not the undisputed inheritor of that cottage,' said Cohan, pushing his face menacingly close.

'That has yet to be established,' Turlough replied. 'I'll have you know it was my father had Uncle Bernie committed, and he died of cancer ten years ago himself, so as his heir I'm the one that'll end up executor of that estate!'

Before he'd even finished the sentence he'd forgotten what exactly he had said, but these three were not about to have any more entertainment at his expense. Turlough stood up, deciding his best course now was to retreat, let Cohan and O'Gorman talk again in the morning and present him with their offer.

'You're a liar and a blaggard, Walsh!' said Cohan, 'Go on then, get out of here, and maybe we'll be in touch, and then again maybe not!'

Cohan waved a hand toward the door as Turlough moved

none too directly across the room.

'Bloody ignorant culchies!' he shouted as he reached it, 'Sucking the country dry with farm subsidies and dole!'

'Go on! Get out! And don't darken my door again!' bellowed Cohan.

'Oh, don't bloody worry, you serve a lousy pint anyway!'

Cohan's face turned purple at this last insult and he lunged around the counter, but his two regular customers came to Turlough's defence, rising to their feet as if to block the publican's path.

'Let him go, Donal!' said one.

'He's gone, forget about him!' said the other, 'You've done all you could.'

Outside, Turlough paused for a moment, so that the closing door slammed into his shoulder. He grunted, allowing the blow to set him staggering toward the parked Cortina. Then the cold air seemed to sweep away whatever sluggishness had overcome him in the bar and he walked round and unlocked his own car.

The horn blared to life, shattering the absolute calm. Frantically he removed the keys and fumbled for the control of his alarm, but in doing so dropped the whole bunch, in the shadow created by the one streetlight, and had to crouch down and feel around for them.

By the time he found them, deadened the horn, and slumped into the driver's seat, Cohan, the other two from the bar and some other customers who must have been in the lounge were all gathered in the doorway, while still more faces peered out the lounge window.

Turlough ignored them all, started the engine, and roared away into the night. He had no idea where he was going, remembering that he had intended to ask was there a bed and breakfast nearby, but he could hardly do that now, and besides, he wouldn't put it past the whole godforsaken lot of them to poison him over this worthless postage stamp of dirt.

He knew he was going the in wrong direction, and decided

to make a U-turn, head for Killala and if he couldn't find a hotel there go on to Ballina. But the car was hemmed in by stone walls on both sides of the road, and before any suitable turning place presented itself a yellow warning sign flashed past with the symbol for a steep descent.

Then he realized where he was and sure enough, as they had told him, Uncle Bernie's cottage appeared on the right hand side of the road, its gable end lit up against the black sky beyond by the headlights. Ivy had made its way up the stonework, losing some of its more recent plaster, and only one of two clay chimney pots remained atop the brick chimney.

Turlough slowed down as he drew level with the house, then, on some impulse, pulled over and stopped outside the front door. Somehow, in this darkness, it didn't look as run down as he had expected. A suspicion crept up on him that perhaps there was more to this little scheme than the natives would ever admit to....

In the glove compartment was one of those small, expensive metal flashlights that was invaluable when he had to fold up sails and stow gear late at night. He took this out, twisted it to the on position and stood up out of the car.

Both of the cottage's front windows had net curtains that reflected back the light. Going to the letter box in the solid front door he could only open it wide enough to shine the light at a small patch of bare wooden floor. He examined the lock, all of whose chrome plating had long since turned to black oxide scales, tried a few of his keys in it without success and decided to turn his attention to the back of the building.

Turlough scrambled over what might once have been a functioning gate, now choked with brambles, and swished through an overgrown patch of grass to find that the back of the house gave onto a sloping field whose shape and boundaries were lost below in darkness.

He turned his attention once again to the dark, silent building. If anyone was in there they had left no signs of their presence outside. He had to lean over an overgrown privet bush to see in the first window, shining his light through a missing corner and waving it around to reveal a fireplace in an otherwise empty room, and he was obstructed by a rusting steel barrel full of rainwater from seeing in the other window.

You couldn't be up to these locals. If there were squatters involved in all this they had no doubt been warned that he might come prowling around during his visit. But he would have to get in somehow and find proof. Then he heard a sudden rustling in the grass nearby and caught the red eyes of some small animal in his beam, but it vanished immediately.

Turlough shook his head, heart pounding, took a few deep breaths to settle himself back down, and felt an instant need to rid himself of the liquid he had consumed in Moran's Bar. He turned off the flashlight, put it away, walked a few paces back from the cottage and urinated with prolonged satisfaction on what might once have been a flowerbed.

The cottage, seen from back here, was a perfect picture of the desolation of rural Ireland. No improvement had taken place for at least a generation, and anyone mad enough to set up home in this place deserved the fate that awaited them: to end their days as alcoholic freaks in Moran's Bar.

Turlough grimaced, disgusted at such a prospect, zipped himself up, and eyed the building with renewed determination. Surely the back door would give way to a good push? He took a run at it, swinging his shoulder round at the last moment and felt it give a little.

One more try. He backed up again, smoothed down his suit and attacked with more momentum. There was a loud crack as the lock broke, then an amazing thing happened, so fast that Turlough had no time to react: the top half of the door flew back out of sight.

The bottom half remained where it was, providing a waist-high fulcrum over which Turlough somersaulted into the room, thinking, as he flailed hopelessly for a handhold, that someone must have set a trap for him, and, as his skull banged heavily off the first floorboard it met, that he would see to it that half-doors were made illegal because of this, and then, as the rest of his body crashed to the ground ahead of him, in absolute darkness, he lost consciousness.

CHAPTER FIVE

It was light outside as he came to and somewhere in the distance a donkey brayed. At first Turlough was afraid to move, wondering had he broken any bones but slowly, as his head cleared, he recalled where he was and what he had done, and the urgency of getting back to Dublin overcame all else.

His first clue that something strange had occurred was when he pressed his palms against the floor to raise himself. It was not made of wood; it was just hard cold earth. He looked around and saw that he could no longer be in the same place.

He was in what appeared to be an outhouse of sorts, with stone walls, roughly quarried and fitted together without mortar of any kind. Had he wandered in here after his fall? Was he concussed from the blow? The doorway of this place had no door at all, just a canvas sack that swung in and out in the breeze.

And then in one of its movements, the light from outside played along the far gable wall and Turlough saw that he was not alone. A man lay on a low wooden bed beside a blackened alcove that must have served as a fireplace.

'Who are you?' asked Turlough brusquely, deciding as he stood up that this fellow was surely a vagrant and might be capable of any mischief. There was no reply. Rising to his full height, Turlough discovered that this cottage was of miniature proportions, his head now among the roof beams, where he had to swat away a sticky cobweb that clung to his face.

'Wake up!' he shouted, stooping down again to shuffle over to the prone figure. It was an old man, with a wispish beard and unruly matted hair, and a face black, filthy to the point of being unrecognizable. Turlough gave the bed a tap with his foot, but the occupant did not stir even as the wooden frame itself creaked back and forth, as though it bore no weight.

Only then did it occur to him that he was looking at a corpse, and as if the wind were listening to his thoughts, a fresh gust came flapping into the room and whisked away the dead man's ragged cover.

'Oh, Jesus!' Turlough looked away as fast as he could, ducked and made for the doorway clasping his hand over his mouth, both to keep out whatever foulness must be about and to stop himself from vomiting. He pushed through the canvas, ripping it away, then frantically shook it free of his hand, lest it too was diseased.

The feeling of nausea passed, but the image of what he had just seen kept returning. A skeletal frame with black skin stretched over it, hands clawed across the stomach as though it were a source of pain right to the end, and parts of all the man's fingers missing....

'Christ almighty, where am I?' he asked, looking around, hoping to see his car.

Instead, the sight that Turlough Walsh beheld was unlike any he had ever seen or imagined before. In front of him, the land sloped gently away, levelling out after about a mile and giving way again to wild looking hills in the distance. But in between, and in every direction he could see, was a patchwork of walls and hedges, defining fields the size of Dublin gardens, and within each there were one or more small stone cottages. All of the land had been tilled and the soil arranged into neat brown ridges, dark in the troughs, dried and lightened by this fresh wind across their wide flat crests.

The homes were so close to one another, and the fields so small, that it was indeed as densely populated as most suburbs. And there were people around, ragged looking children playing, old people sitting here and there in ones and twos, and men, making their way in dark groups along the narrow unpaved roads, as if heading for some single destination, a common place of work somewhere.

Yet nowhere did he see any vehicles, let alone his own, and as he let his eye wander he saw that they would be of no use here: all the roads impossibly narrow, with abrupt corners, deep ruts, and massive boulders protruding out from the sides.

If it were not for the masses of people everywhere, and the extent of the cultivation, and the lack of any modern houses whatever, he could perhaps have convinced himself that he had somehow, mysteriously, ended up on the Aran Islands, or some other remote tourist spot. But they were all near the sea, which was nowhere to be seen.

And all these people! His accountant's mind began calculating, multiplying, but in the end he gave up. The population of this wide valley was more than most Irish towns, and yet there was no town anywhere in sight, no tight cluster of buildings, no church set amid trees, no trees at all. He gave up surveying the larger view and turned his attention to his immediate vicinity.

The stone hut from which he had emerged was sited very similarly to Uncle Bernie's house, but the land it gave onto stopped at a much nearer wall, and beyond that was another squarish field. The one he was standing in showed no signs of having been tilled lately, was in fact overgrown with weeds, but the one beyond was as well tended as any of the others.

He heard voices.

'I found one!'

'Show me! Show me!'

They were children's voices, from in front of him. He walked down toward the wall, stepping gingerly amongst the weeds, but picking up an inch of heavy muck on his soles nonetheless.

'Is it fresh?' said one child.

Turlough looked over the wall. Below him were two youngsters, on their hunkers, intent on this find. As he leaned over his hand moved a rock, startling them. Big blue eyes looked up at him from thin faces.

'Excuse me, I wonder could you tell me where exactly I am?' he asked.

One was a girl, perhaps a little older, the other a boy. They looked up at him, then at each other, then at the object of their attention in the long grass at the base of the wall. Turlough saw that they were torn between flight and the loss of whatever was there.

'What have you found?' he asked, smiling and raising his eyebrows.

'An egg,' said the girl.

'Oohhh! Let's see it!'

The child reached into the grass and removed a brown egg.

'Now, how did that get there?' asked Turlough.

The girl laughed at this, and the boy laughed because she did.

'One of the hens laid it, of course!' she told him, standing up to give him a closer look.

'Is this your brother?' asked Turlough.

'He's one of them. I have two brothers.'

'And what are your names?'

'I'm Nan, and he's Séamus.'

The boy straightened up beside her. Both were ragged looking young children, hair chopped short but still unkempt, barefoot, with muddy knees, but they both had bright alert eyes, and when they smiled they showed healthy white teeth. He thought at first they might be scavenging itinerants, but something about their manner, the fact that they held their ground made him doubt that.

'Where do you live?' he asked, and they turned and pointed to the house that occupied the far end of their field.

'Well, do you think someone in your family might be able to give me directions? You see I'm lost.'

The girl took off at a run toward the house, followed by her brother, shouting: 'Mam! Mam! There's a man here and he's lost!' While they jumped from ridge to ridge across the field, Turlough swung himself over the precarious wall, feeling the stitching give in his right sleeve as he reached out to balance himself.

His shoes were now so muddy he lost interest in preserving them, and plodded resolutely across the field to this other stone cabin, a longer version of the one he had just left.

As he did so, its occupants gathered outside: a woman, a teenage girl holding an infant, Nan and Séamus. All of them were barefoot, though the older girl and woman wore long dark dresses and had shawls wrapped round their shoulders.

Was he dreaming? Was that it?

'Good morning,' he said, addressing the woman.

'God bless you sir,' she replied, curtseying slightly.

'Emmm, I wonder if you could help me?'

'We have very little to spare,' the woman replied hastily, 'what with five children in the house.'

'Oh, no, I'm not looking for food or anything like that,' said Turlough. The last thing he wanted was to be invited into another of these filthy huts. 'No, it's just that I'm not from here, and I'm lost.'

'Well, where is it you're looking for?' she asked.

'Killala.'

'Well, you're a day's walk from there.'

'I have a car.'

'Ah, well then you need only take any road east and ask along the way.'

'Yes, but I've lost my car too.'

The woman looked at her oldest daughter.

'What colour was the horse?' asked the girl, rocking the infant gently back and forth as she spoke.

This must be a dream.

'Not a cart!' he shouted, 'A car, a motor car, a BMW in fact!'

The two children gathered themselves more closely about the others at this outburst.

'I've come here on business from Dublin, and I have to get back again!'

'Oh Mam, he's from the Board of Works,' said the older girl excitedly. 'Sir, I'll take you out to where they're putting in the new road.'

'Are you the new Inspecting Officer, sir?' asked the mother.

'Emmm, well let me talk to someone there,' said Turlough, perking up at the mention of a new road.

'That'd be the best thing,' said the mother. 'Let you take him, Bríd. If you hurry you might catch up on Mick-Óg and your father.'

The girl handed the infant to her mother, rubbed her hands on the sides of her dress and said: 'Come on, so!'

'Can we go too?' asked Nan, still holding her egg.

'No Nan, it's too far, but ye can run on down as far as the corner with them.'

The two younger children put their own interpretation on this instruction, skipping along beside Turlough and Bríd for a mile or more, joined here and there by other skinny barefoot friends, who appeared out of the doorways of more of these same stone cottages.

Every one of these buildings, none of which had a plumbed wall or squared corner, was in need of repairs. Some had pieces of roof missing, most were missing doors or windows, and all had weeds growing out of the thatch, itself long since in need of replacement.

'Why doesn't anyone do something with these houses?' he asked, but Bríd did not appear to understand the question.

'How old are you?' he asked, changing the subject.

'Fourteen,' she replied.

He looked at her as they tramped on together. Yes, she was about that age, the gangly look of childhood gone, a woman's hips on her, and a beautiful oval face, cheeks rouged by the weather, the same clear blue eyes as her siblings, and fine dark eyebrows that he wanted to tell her never to pluck. Beneath these two beacons of innocence and across her straight nose ran a light speckling of freckles, and if her long wavy brown hair never saw shampoo, still it shone with frequent brushing.

'Fourteen,' he repeated, 'and is that your little baby?'

'Maura? Mine?' Bríd stopped dead at this thought. 'Oh, sir, that's an awful thing to say!' She blushed, violently, more than Turlough had ever seen anyone do so before.

'Oh, well, gosh, I'm sorry, really. Yes, you're right, that was a terrible thing to say. You were just so good with the child.'

Bríd folded her arms and walked hesitantly on.

'I have a daughter a year younger than you myself,' he said, watching as she brightened up at this turn in the conversation. He had misread her, and what was the point dreaming about a girl a year older than your own daughter? Alright, if she had already had a child with someone else...but no, it was just too perverse!

'And you live in Dublin?'

'Yes.'

'What does your daughter wear?'

This simple question at last brought home to Turlough the impossible, incredible truth. He stopped and looked all around him once more.

'Where are we?' he asked. 'We're in Mayo, aren't we?'

'We are, in Erris. Over that hill is Glenamoy.'

He shook his head, knowing that was not what he had really meant to ask.

'I mean, when is it? What date is it?'

'Well...,' Bríd began, counting off on her fingers.

'Just tell me the year!'

'1846.'

Turlough felt dizzy. He screwed his eyes shut and blinked several times, but Bríd was still there, and all the little farms, and the stony laneway they were following was the best there was, and there was no way to get from here back to Dublin, not by lunch time, not ever!

'Do you believe in magic?' he asked Brid.

'Oh, sir, it isn't right to be talking about such things and the faeries listening the whole time.'

She gasped and backed away from him, then made the sign of the cross.

'Ah, so you are superstitious?'

'Oh no sir, no I'm not. Not at all.'

'Do you know where I've come from?' It was no use. She could see he was somehow bewildered and there was no way he could explain it to her.

'You're halfway there now sir,' said Bríd, 'Just follow this road on straight and you'll come across them all. I have to get back.'

'But Bríd....s'

She turned her back on him, gathered her shawl outside her long hair and hurried away.

'What's your father's name?' he asked, but she just shook her head and began running, then just as he turned away he heard her shouting back at him:

'Kernen! Tomás Kernen! K-E-R-N-E-N! And be sure and give my brother a job too!'

He shook his head and smiled at her saucy demand. Employ them as what? Did she not know that you couldn't move these days without a degree? He might spare a few words of advice for the brother, but that was it. As soon as he found out what was happening he would have to get back to Dublin by whatever means possible.

Continuing alone down the pathway, everything seemed all the more dreamlike. Yet this could not be a dream. The wind blew clouds slowly across the sky, made his suit flap about him, and whistled in his ears. And he was beginning to feel hungry. The world was following all of its natural laws, so it must be real. Turlough shivered and dug his hands deep into his pockets. Whatever had happened, he needed to find people a lot more educated than those kids to explain it to him.

Why was it 1846? That wasn't a year that stood out for any reason. Let's see, 1803 was the Act of Union, or was that the year they hanged Robert Emmet? Let no man write my epitaph. What about Wolfe Tone? No, he was further back. 1789? No, that was the French Revolution. A tale of two cities. Something to do with O'Connell maybe? Catholic emancipation. Yes. He had done that. About then. Maybe.

He passed a small church on his right, set in a field bigger than most others, bounded by a higher stone wall, one that surely predated all the other ones, and yet they were higgledy-piggledy affairs while this was a straight perpendicular work of cut stone. Still, it too was falling down, and through the gaps he saw that, like most country churches, this one was surrounded by graves, some with upright inscribed stones, others with slabs that lay on the ground.

He stopped, thinking of going in, but there was no one there and he needed to find people who could help him, live people, not dead ones, so he hurried on, ignoring the women and children who stared at him as he passed their hovels. What's wrong with this picture, he asked himself, to pass the time?

Aside from the fact that it really did look like a scene from the nineteenth century, there were other things amiss. There were people everywhere, not doing very much, but they were there. And then it came to him: there were no farm animals. He had heard one donkey, come across a few chickens, and that was it.

Obviously they didn't keep grazing animals in any quantity since they had tilled all the land, but still you would expect them to have horses, pigs, and to see an occasional cow. Then, as if his very thoughts had triggered it, he heard the distant sound of hooves, and looking back saw a horse-drawn buggy approaching, driven by a single man in a red military uniform.

Turlough waved his arms and the fellow slowed from a canter to a trot as he drew abreast.

'Good morning!' he said to the occupant, jogging alongside.

'A girl back there said you were the new IO,' said the driver in an accent that held out the promise of education.

'Where are you headed?' asked Turlough.

'To the road, of course, man!'

'Can you give me a ride?'

'Yes, yes, climb on!'

The buggy stopped so that he could clamber up between its two big spindly wheels. Its driver slid over and proffered a hand in greeting.

'Colonel Jones, on my way from a meeting last night with Lord Sligo.'

'Turlough Walsh, from Dublin.'

'Glad to have you with us my man,' said Jones, cracking a long, fishing-rod-like whip alongside the horse to urge it on again. 'We're going to need all the help we can get now.'

'What's going on?' asked Turlough.

'The word has gotten out somehow that the depot in Westport is empty. Trevelyan is beside himself, blaming everyone, and Routh won't stand up to him.'

Colonel Jones's own words drove him on, and he urged the horse to a speed that convinced Turlough they would both be thrown clear of the little two-wheeled conveyance at any moment. He gripped the seat, afraid to talk now in case he bit his tongue. Looking across at the uniformed stranger he saw that he was a middle-aged man with the weather-beaten face of a lifelong soldier set amidst bushy white sideburns, perhaps sufficiently overweight to have heart problems in years to come, but certainly, to judge from his quick movements and fiery temperament, in the best of health now.

'It's not right!' the Colonel continued, 'The relief committees did what was expected of them, and more! What did they think it would come to? Look around man! More people per acre than China!'

The road now led them due south, climbing steadily uphill, until the great web of tiny farms gave way to boggy ground, with the usual banks and trenches left over from cutting turf. Even up here there were people, and Turlough saw that however poor looking Bríd and her family had been, they were by no means the worst off. Whole families huddled under makeshift shelters, smoke rose in grey puffs from fires of wet turf, and at the sound of the horse's hooves, beggars appeared on both sides of the road, far more emaciated than the people below, devoid of any real muscle tissue, and held out their skeletal arms to the passing buggy.

'This is the famine!' cried Turlough, smacking his forehead at the realization.

'Of course it's bloody famine country, man! Why else would we be building useless roads through it? Have you been abroad or what?'

'Yes.' This seemed like the best answer.

'India? The Americas?'

'America.' Turlough knew nothing about India, but he could answer questions on the United States.

'Army, was it, or trade, or what?'

'Well, trade, mainly.'

'You sound a well-educated sort. Wish we could find more like you.'

The road passed through a saddle between two dark hills and the view changed. Below, at first, the wicker tents and lean-to structures of the landless paupers gave way to close-packed farms like those of Erris behind them, but these did not continue on into the distance as before. Soon, the Colonel's horse was pulling them through acres of small cornfields with their neat lines of green shoots, and here and there were even larger fields with cattle grazing on them.

'This looks a lot more prosperous,' said Turlough.

'And that's the curse of the whole scheme!'

Colonel Jones looked over and saw the puzzled look on his passenger's face. 'Well, I suppose you're a Board of Works man now, so you may as well know my view. Routh and his two cronies don't know what they're doing. You may say I'm bitter that I didn't get a place on the Relief Commission, and I am, but God blast it, man, what is the point building more roads where the land has already been improved, will you tell me that?'

He whipped the horse onward, venting his anger on the sweating beast, until they rounded a few more bends and came on a long line of men, who cleared a path for them, doffing their caps, those who had them, to the red-coated officer and his curious looking, bareheaded, though otherwise well-dressed, companion.

CHAPTER SIX

Again, it was all too dreamlike, and instead of freeing Turlough to challenge the madness around him, it was this feeling that held him back from protesting. He was unwilling, even in sleep, to reveal himself, was possessed by a fear that he might shout out the wrong thing, that Nuala might hear the other woman's name, or that someone else, he could never say who, might use whatever they heard him say to their own advantage.

'This is outrageous!' cried Colonel Jones.

As he watched the Colonel he understood what was troubling him — it was the sheer number of men in line. Walking past these dour unwashed peasants, it seemed to Turlough that they had stumbled on some hideous, everlasting dole queue.

'Why are they all here?' he asked.

'Well put! Why indeed? We can scarcely employ a tenth of them.'

'There must be five thousand of them,' said Turlough, his mind busy estimating as it was trained to do.

'Ah! There's poor Pendleton now. Let's hear how you can assist him.'

Colonel Jones hauled in the rein as he made this remark, and would have had to do so anyway, since the road now became a flattened rockpile sure to break the buggy's wheels if they tried to ride on over it. He and Turlough climbed down on opposite sides and the crowd of men that formed the front of the long line parted to let them through to Pendleton.

'Colonel Jones!' cried Pendleton, rising from behind a small makeshift desk, removing his top hat and bowing as he came around, 'This is a wholly unexpected honour, sir!'

'Thought I'd take a gander at things myself, Pendleton. I do read your letters, you know, and I am not indifferent to the situation.'

'But...but you came all this way without so much as a single soldier to escort you?'

'When the day comes that those of us, those few of us –' he grasped Pendleton's shoulder, 'actually doing something to alleviate the suffering, have to resort to armed protection, then I think we may give it up.'

'Indeed,' Pendleton replied, though he didn't sound convinced to Turlough. 'And who is this?' he asked, coming over.

'Aahhh!' said the Colonel, 'See, now, here's proof of our good intent. You said you were swamped with paperwork, and I bring you a new assistant, Mister, eh, Walsh.'

Pendleton held out a hand. 'Oh, thank God! Glad to have you here.' He turned again to the Colonel. 'I've received no correspondence about this, sir.'

'Not surprising,' the Colonel replied, his voice taking on an even gruffer tone, 'I'm ashamed to admit it, but things are completely out of hand. Imagine your own problems here, Pendleton, multiplied a thousandfold, and that'll give you an idea. I'm not exaggerating when I say that we may well have upward of half a million of these beggars employed as I speak.'

'Of course, sir!' Pendleton twisted his top hat around by its rim and turned once more to Turlough.

'Will you be looking for lodgings, Mister Walsh? Where are

your bags?'

'Well, eh, no, actually I have a place.' Turlough had no idea why he said this. It was as if, right then, he knew he would have to return to the mausoleum that was the once and future Uncle Bernie's cottage, whatever else happened. He chuckled coldly at the thought of it and shook his head.

'Yes, well, I'm sure it's not what you're used to in Dublin,' said Colonel Jones, 'but come on then, we'll make a quick tour of inspection, then I'll get on for Westport. The Relief Commissioners want me to make a report on the state of things there.'

He took off, one of the men falling in on each side of him.

'What do you make of the change of government?' asked Pendleton.

'Hard to say,' said the Colonel, 'What's your view Walsh?'

Turlough had no idea even what kind of government they might have had in 1846, let alone that one had come and gone that year.

'I've never known it to make any difference which lot are in power,' he replied.

Colonel Jones clapped him on the back, very taken with this response. 'Absolutely right! A man after my own heart! Yes, Russell will have no more effect on all this than Peel. Less, I should say! Trevelyan is as much in charge as he always was. More so. By God, I had dinner with Sligo last night and he read me the last reply he got. "The peasantry must not learn to become dependent on low-priced meal...those in the workhouses should expect some discomfiture...mill it only once...." All the usual remarks, and more, and of course finishes up with his "laissez faire", not interfering with the laws of supply and demand and that the merchants who do bring in food must make their profit!'

They ambled on across the broken stones, evidently the foundation for a new road, though not one that appeared to follow any clear design, varying wildly in width and direction; in some places no more than a single layer of rocks over turf, while in others great piles of rocks sank slowly into the black ooze below, and here and there the work had actually blocked the courses of streams which had now risen up to flow across it.

Colonel Jones left for Westport, apparently untroubled by these quality problems, telling Turlough to take his orders from Pendleton until further notice. Other than attempting to walk to Dublin, this was his only alternative, so he took what had been Pendleton's seat and went on with the hiring process, while the other man went about with his foremen giving instructions to the various gangs already hired.

'Look for heads of household who are in the most need,' Pendleton had said and after an hour or so Turlough became adept at this, though it seemed to him an incredibly stupid course of action, since these men were invariably in worse shape than the others. Surely they should hire the fittest labourers, finish the road at minimum cost and distribute the profit they made to the poor, if that's what this was all about, keeping, say, ten per cent for themselves as a management fee?

Pendleton had told him to stop when he had another two hundred and he was just coming up to this number when he asked the name of the next in line and heard, 'Tomás Kernen.' He looked up and saw the resemblance right away, not so much in the man who had spoken, but in the younger man next to him. He was Bríd's brother alright. They were both gaunt, with ragged collarless shirts and ill-fitting britches hanging off them, but still, they were as healthy looking as any he had spoken to that morning, tall, big-boned, bright-eyed, products of a strict diet of unlimited potatoes, until recently anyhow.

'And why do you want a job on a relief project?' he asked the elder man while he was still scrutinizing them.

'Oh, sir, I have a wife and five children to feed!'

Turlough shrugged. Everyone in line had a story that morning and he pondered whether he would have believed this fellow if he hadn't already known he was telling the truth.

'And don't you have a farm?' he asked, his next question to those he didn't dismiss after the first one. Turlough was amazed that the man had answered his first question truthfully since he had no way of knowing he would be found out if he lied.

'Oh God, you wouldn't hold that against me, would you, that I have a tiny bit of land?' Tomás replied.

This was annoying. Why didn't he just say he had nothing? Do what he had to do to get the job?

'And haven't you a hen or two left on it?'

This time Tomás Kernen was stumped for a reply. He and his hungry son stared down. Surely they would come up with some new story now. But the older man just shook his head.

'Is that the way it is?' he asked quietly. Then he put his arm around his son and they began walking away. Turlough sprang to his feet.

'No wait, Mister Kernen!'

The two of them turned around.

'Eh, look, you can have a job!'

Tears welled up in Tomás's eyes and he shook his head.

'No sir, you were right. There's plenty more worse off than us and we can't deprive them of the chance.'

Turlough was flabbergasted. He put down the quill pen he had been using and went around to them.

'But I met your family this morning. Your daughter, Bríd, showed me the way here. Here, look, you can both have jobs.'

He gestured back to the roll book, but the older Kernen shook his head again.

'Dad!' said the son, 'The man is doing us a kindness. Think of the little ones! They'll never make it till the new potatoes come in.'

'I won't have it on my conscience that I took the food out of someone else's mouth for us. Come on, Mick-Óg.'

The older man began walking away again, but the son stood his ground.

'I'll work!' he told Turlough. If the father heard this he did not let it show, just walked on back past the others in the line, clenching a cap of sorts in one hand, dragging a spade behind him in the other.

'Your father's a bit of an idealist,' said Turlough, signing Mick-Óg on for the day.

'He'll be the death of all of us,' said Mick-Óg.

'Come back and see me at the end of the day,' said Turlough as he watched Bríd's brother go. Then he had an idea and wrote Tomás Kernen's name down in the next space of his book. He was so pleased with this stroke of genius that he wrote down under that, 'Séamus Kernen'. He would have written in Bríd and Nan too, but knew that any half-witted junior auditor would surely pick that up.

'Next!' he called, looking up again then.

Those who were not employed that day melted away into the laneways, the sun came out for a while, Pendleton came back over and produced great bundles of foolscap paper from a horse and cart, and he and Turlough went through various calculations of roods and perches and hundredweights of rocks until finally Pendleton nodded to the nearest of his gaffers that it was quitting time and the ragtag army of labourers stopped their banging and scraping and once more formed themselves into a long weary line.

A wagon that had arrived earlier in the afternoon pulled up closer to the desk and two constables of some sort manhandled a chest down from it and carried it over to the rickety chairs on which Turlough and Pendleton were seated.

'Nine pence to each of them, Mister Walsh,' said Pendleton opening the lid. Turlough smiled at the sight of the old coins, figuring out which were sixpences and threepences and using those up first, listening carefully until he heard, 'Mick-Óg Kernen!'

'Oh, yes,' said Turlough, 'I remember you.' Then he looked to Pendleton's list. 'Ah, yes, Mister Pendleton, that's his father and his uncle too, the next names there. Eh, Mick-Óg, would you take theirs on back down the line to them?'

Turlough produced two more wages and gave them to the boy, who stared down at the money in his palm, bewildered. Then at last the wild eyes rose to meet his own and Turlough winked slowly back, hoping that Pendleton wasn't looking at either of them, then jerked his head at Mick-Óg to go away.

The wind died and a mist came down. The Peelers, as Pendleton called them, put the mostly empty money chest back on their wagon, the gaffers loaded the furniture onto the other one, and Pendleton himself fussed over some paperwork, signing receipts and tallying the day's work.

Darkness was falling, the road all but deserted, when Mick-Óg came warily back up to Turlough.

'You could ride a horse at full gallop along here before we did any of this,' he said, evidently completely at a loss as to how to bring up the subject of the three wages.

'I'll walk home with you,' said Turlough, 'and make sure you give that money to your father.'

'What do you take me for?' asked Mick-Óg, unamused by this remark.

'Alright, I'm sure you're an honest lad, but I'm going that way anyhow.'

'Well, I'm not!'

'And where are you off to?'

'America.'

Turlough laughed at this and shook his head. 'Even if this is 1846, you can't go to America for twenty-seven pennies.'

'No, but there's a ship in Westport right now, a lumber brig going back, and he's taking those that are fit for ten shillings. He wants to set out without any more delay.'

'How soon?'

'Some of the men today said he might leave on the tide tomorrow.'

Turlough considered this situation. Mick-Óg was the oldest

son of a family of seven who were half-starved. He would have to leave anyway, so why not now?

'America's a great place, Mick-Óg. You could make a lot of money there.'

'And that's the very thing I'll do.'

'Do you have the fare?'

'I do now!'

Turlough watched as he fished a small satchel out of his pocket and held it up. Then he reached into his own left pocket and felt his keys and the metal flashlight and dredged out what coins he could feel in between them.

'Here!' he said, 'I know these are just foreign coins to you, but someone might give you something for them.'

Mick-Óg took them and looked up at Turlough.

'These'll be valuable alright.'

'Have you said goodbye to your family?'

Mick-Óg shook his head, and then a tear came into his eye, and he looked more than ever like his father. 'I'll send for them all, one by one, when I get there.'

Turlough nodded. 'You do that. These are very tough times. I'll go and see your parents tonight and tell them what you've done.'

'Oh, sir, that'd be very kind of you. And be sure to tell them I'm doing it for them.'

'They'll be very proud of you, Mick-Óg.'

He watched as the oldest son of Tomás Kernen walked away, down the famine road, a botched and senseless disimprovement on what had been there already; a brave young man, all alone, going to do the only thing he could that might help his family — emigrate.

Turlough waited till Mick-Óg was out of sight, then turned back to see if Pendleton would lend him some transport for the night, which he did, riding back to Ballina himself with the Peelers, and agreeing to meet in Westport the next day since there would be no work on this site again until another survey could be taken.

*

The screams from inside the Kernens' hut that night roused people from all over. Turlough stood by the wagon he had borrowed, aghast at the effect his news had had, and refused the repeated invitations by Tomás and his neighbours to come inside. He was convinced that the man's wife, and Bríd, and perhaps even Nan, were now in such a frenzied emotional state they might well set on him like a pack of wolves.

As more and more people came to join them the house filled up entirely with keening, howling women, so that Tomás and all the other men had now to gather outside anyway.

'Where did he get the money?' Tomás asked everyone, but he got only vague replies. Someone gave him a dark bottle with a long neck and he threw back a mouthful of its contents.

'Mister Walsh, will you have a sup with us?' he asked, passing it to Turlough.

It was poitín. The real McCoy. Make-you-blind firewater. And it was just what he needed to cope with this unreality. Two gulps and he was reeling.

'I think your wife should be very happy that he's going off to America to send you all back money,' he said. 'I think she should stop yelling like a banshee.'

'Oh, there's an awful thing to be saying!' cried someone. It was dark, and in the faint glow that came from the doorway of the cabin it was impossible to tell these people apart.

'That's all very well, Mister Walsh,' said Tomás, seizing the bottle once more, and swinging it toward what was now a chorus of crooning from within, 'but we might not be here when he sends the first of his wages over.'

'Why not?' Turlough shrugged, not about to turn maudlin with the rest of them.

'Why not?' Tomás repeated, and there was quiet laughter from those around him. 'Because that money he had could have paid the rent a little while longer. Oh God, isn't it enough of a curse to be living next to a man that died of the fever, God have mercy on you, Murkeen, without losing your son like this?'

This made no sense at all. Turlough took the bottle and drank again.

'You mean,' he said, 'that he stole the rent money to go to America?'

'Not at all! Mick-Óg would never steal anything! He'll send it all back!' This was a girl's voice. Turlough looked down to see Bríd next to him, shawl over her head now, her sister Nan inside it too, standing next to her, clinging to her arm. Bríd was hoarse from her contribution to the lamenting, which was still going on inside.

'And would you go to America after him if he sent you the fare?' asked Turlough. Not only was his voice slurred, but he was beginning to take on the local accent and idiom. He shook himself, trying to remain clearheaded.

'I would,' she said sadly.

'And what about you, Nan?'

She nodded defiantly up at him, and finally he understood the nature of their reaction. They had all lived together from the day they were born, and the thought of separation was identical in their minds with death. They were having a wake for Mick-Óg because he was gone, gone from their world as surely as if he had died, and died suddenly at that, and he was gone to a place so far away, and so impossible for them to picture, that it might as well be the very heaven above the clouds they all believed in.

'I've been to America, you know,' he said, stooping down to Nan's level. Everyone became quiet at this revelation, waiting to hear what he might tell them next.

'And your brother will do very well there, and so will you.'

The girl stared back at them with those same huge eyes that he had first seen that morning.

'You gave him the money to go, didn't you?' she said.

He nodded, which was a mistake, because it set him swaying, and he knew then he had overdone it on their illicit whiskey.

'I better get to bed,' he said and wandered round the side of the house and up the potato field.

'Where are you off to?' asked Tomás, following him.

'Eh...good question!' Turlough just wanted to get away from them. He swung around in a circle, walking backwards, and fell over. Tomás ran up and helped him to his feet again.

'Up there,' said Turlough. 'Over the wall.'

'What do you want to go there for?' asked Tomás.

'He came out of old Murkeen's house, Dad!' said Nan.

Tomás froze, then let go and backed away quickly from Turlough. 'Oh, God spare me,' he said, holding up his hands and staring at them. 'Is the child telling the truth?'

Turlough nodded, backing up the hill until he bumped against the wall, then slid over it and fell onto his back, and stared dizzily up at the cloudy sky until he felt himself drifting off into a drunken sleep.

He floated over the fields and cottages, turf smoke billowing from every chimney, and drifted on over silent hills, until he was over the ocean, and the sun began to creep up behind him, and he passed over the white spray to dark waves driven by the wind, and caught up on a sailing ship, a brig by its rigging, and at first it appeared to be pounding away through the surf on a broad reach.

Then as he got closer he saw that its gunwales were barely above the waterline, and one last wave broke amidships and its deck was gone and whoever had set those sails was gone, and everyone who had been on board, unless they were trapped below, and somehow he knew they were, and that it was their last drowning breaths that gushed to the surface, those streams of bubbles in all the white foam that surged in on itself as the spars followed the rest of the ship to the bottom, and then there was nothing below him but the ocean again. A tiny, distant murmur came to him over the wind, telling him, though he tried not to listen, that Mick-Óg was in their midst, and now he would never send for Bríd, or send the rent, or be heard of ever again.

CHAPTER SEVEN

'Mr Walsh?'

'What?'

'Mr Walsh,' he heard repeated, 'are you alright?'

Turlough came to, on the wooden floor of Uncle Bernie's cottage and looked around. It was daylight and he lay where he had fallen, in the middle of this disused one room building.

'Oh God, I was afraid for a minute you might be dead!'

The voice was somehow familiar. Turlough sat up, and saw, looking in through the half-door, the face of the man with the soft cap that Cohan had thrown out of the bar the night before.

'What time is it?' he asked, looking at his watch as he did so. It was half past nine. He stood up and rushed to the door, startling the other man into backing away. Outside it was misty, but he could see down the hill to the wall and beyond.

'It's gone!' he cried, undoing the bolt that held the door's lower half in place and staring down to where the Kernens' mud and stone hut had been.

'Oh no,' said soft-cap, 'your car's round the other side.'

'What? No, no! Listen, what's your name?'

'Muiris O'Toole, but you may as well call me Morris Minor, like everyone else.'

He held out a hand but Turlough ignored it.

'Morris,' he asked, 'was there ever a wall about halfway between here and the one at the end there?'

'Well....'

Turlough glared at him.

'I couldn't say,' Morris answered slowly. 'If there was it's long gone.'

Long gone. He had that right. Turlough shook his head and took a couple of deep breaths. He had been dreaming about something that had happened a century and a half earlier.

'Are you any good at fixing things?'

'Oh, I am,' said Morris.

Turlough took out his wallet. 'Well, look, here's forty quid. Would you ever put a new lock on that door and send me the key? My address is on this card.'

'Fair enough.'

Turlough left him and walked around to his car, this time using a side gate he hadn't noticed the night before. As he pulled this closed he looked down and saw that his shoes and the bottoms of his trousers were all covered in mud.

It was a dream, he told himself, getting into his car, and then, with the door closed, he got a whiff of poitín from his own breath. Startled, he saw clearly the faces of the different people: Nan, Colonel Jones, Mick-Óg, Bríd, Tomás Kernen, Pendleton. All their names and faces came back to him, parading past, as clear as ever, when they should be fading away, like all dreams.

He started the engine and reached down to shift it into reverse, meaning to manoeuvre it around on the narrow road and go back the other way, but as he did so he was all but overwhelmed by the feeling that he was doing something wrong. An irrational urge came over him to go on to Westport in the hope of stopping Mick-Óg from getting on that ship that he had seen sinking at the end of his dream.

Why? The two dreams might have nothing to do with each other. And they must be just that: the wanderings of his drunken mind. Forcefully, he jerked the car back and forth until it was pointed the other way and took off, still pondering his night's imaginings when he sped back into Killala.

He looked at his watch again. It was after ten. MacCarthy was having a staff meeting at two and he could not be late. O'Gorman and this cottage thing would have to wait. Fuck him anyway! He was in cahoots with Cohan, and it would do neither of them any harm to cool their heels for a while. He would get his own solicitor to fire a warning shot across O'Gorman's bow lest they come up with some new and even murkier scheme to get around him.

'Turlough!' said his secretary, doing a crossword puzzle at her desk during lunch break when he arrived, 'Everyone's been looking for you.'

'Who?' he asked as she gave him all the message slips.

'MacCarthy. Mulholland. O'Brien. Your wife....'

'Yes, okay, eh, I'm in time for this bloody meeting, amn't I?'

'Just about. You look like you've been up all night.'

Turlough felt his face. He had not shaved. He wanted to go home and crawl into bed. But he couldn't. This meeting was a follow-up on previous ones and if he wasn't there they would be sure to make decisions he couldn't live with.

'Family emergency,' he said, and she nodded, meaning everyone would be told this.

Turlough wandered into his office and gathered up what notes he thought he would need. He had wiped his shoes clean, but there was nothing he could do about the mud on his trousers. Would anyone notice? His wrinkled jacket he had simply left in the car.

'One more thing,' he said passing his secretary again, 'Who was the Prime Minister in 1846?'

She frowned, wondering if this was something she was expected to know.

'Of Ireland?' she asked.

'No, no! We didn't have one. Call some history department and find out! The British Prime Minister. 1846.'

He hurried away, leaving her to write this down, hoping to be seated at the table with his legs hidden before everyone else got to the conference room.

'Then it looks as though we're back to your suggestion, Turlough,' said MacCarthy three hours later.

'I'm afraid I still have to disagree,' said Mulholland, throwing down his pen for dramatic effect.

Turlough smiled at him. He wanted to say: got you at last, you useless evil arselicking whining Corkonian reptile! But instead he nodded sagely.

'I know,' he said, 'that this is tough medicine for all the young talent we're grooming....'

'No one is going to want to work for us,' Mulholland declared, folding his arms now that he had no pen. Turlough narrowed his eyes. Did he not know this was over? Feigning more antagonism would change nothing. Universal greed had triumphed over parochial cronyism, at least for now.

'You'd better summarize this again,' said MacCarthy. 'I think the benefits are clear, but I want a commitment from all of you before we proceed.' He swivelled his bony face around, taking in the tight-lipped stares of all the men down each side of the table.

Turlough watched them: O'Brien, complacent, unaffected; Finucane, sheeplike, ready to salute any plan that emerged; O'Toole, intent on the game now in play, and Mulholland, ill at ease, realizing too late that he had failed to keep up with MacCarthy's thinking, and itching now to be allowed to talk, to backpedal.

'Everyone,' MacCarthy continued, 'listen very carefully to what Turlough has to say, and no one,' he raised both voice and a scrawny finger, 'no one is to sit here and agree to this and then say outside of this room that they did not agree when it comes time to act!'

Turlough cleared his throat and flipped through his untidy notes. There was a page missing — and if he went back to his office they would all notice him. He would have to wing it.

'Go on,' said MacCarthy.

'Far from being a drastic plan,' said Turlough, 'what I'm proposing is a gradual, but systematic reduction in payroll. The only layoffs will be all those who really could use the time off to study for their next exams anyway....'

He got some nods for the way he had put that one.

'...the eleven month year for everyone below manager level rids us of any holiday pay, sick leave, all those kinds of entitlements, and keeps us flexible against any future unexpected boom and bust cycles....'

Everybody was taking notes.

'Do you want me to do this up as a memo?' he asked, looking down to MacCarthy for a response. He got a shake of the head and was just about to continue when Mulholland said: 'Why don't you just write the main points on the board, with the numbers and the timing?'

MacCarthy nodded at this. Double whammy. Now he had to get up anyway and he didn't have the figures. MacCarthy didn't usually favour that kind of presentation because he was nearsighted. Say nothing, thought Turlough, and maybe he won't notice.

He walked up to the board and pulled the top off a marker, but he realized even before he started how he had underestimated his own dishevelment. He actually heard a buzz of muttered comments.

'Up all night working on this,' he said. It was a mistake.

'Looks it!' said someone.

'Where?'

'Girlfriend threw him out the window,' added Mulholland.

There was no way he was getting away with that.

'Actually,' said Turlough, 'I was pursuing a nocturnal activity common to your part of the country, Terence.'

He continued scribbling the main points of his plan on the squeaky board until Mulholland took the bait.

'And what's that?' he asked.

'Fucking a few sheep.'

'Turlough!'

Should he pretend he didn't hear? Just keep going until he reached the elevator and jump in?

'Turlough!'

There was no ignoring MacCarthy's second command. The meeting over, he had bolted for the door but been too hemmed in by the other doddering fools filing out to escape for the day.

'A moment of your time.' MacCarthy beckoned and slipped into his own office. 'Don't sit down,' he warned as Turlough followed him. 'Whatever muck you were rolling in I don't want it on my furniture.'

'Oh? Ah yes! Eh, a puncture on the way in.'

'I see. So you decided to pour whiskey all over yourself, grow a beard and crumple up your shirt while you were fixing it?'

'Ah, well, no, you see....'

'I don't see! And I don't want to see any more. Turlough, stories have reached my ears, just vague rumours, but nonetheless it's only fair to remind you that all of this cutting back will reach into every level of the organization.'

'Of course.' This was a direct threat. Very rare. Not to be taken lightly. Turlough put on his gravest face, nodded at MacCarthy's wisdom and began to back away.

'Don't blow it, as they say, Turlough! You made partner at a very young age. You're full of brilliant ideas. Next week we'll have some corporate consultants wandering around. Be sure not to let them see you like that.'

'You can count on it.'

He was almost at the door when the last salvo came.

'And I never want to hear another Cork joke out of you, least of all one on bestiality.'

'No, no. Just very tired. Bad taste. Sorry.' Turlough mumbled the words as he exited into the corridor again. He wanted to say what a bastard Mulholland was, but that might remind MacCarthy of the girlfriend joke, and that might prompt him to listen harder to his rumour-mongers. No, let it go.

He trudged back to his own desk, sat down wearily and started sifting through the day's accumulation of paper, mostly reports from his many subordinates.

'There were two.'

He looked up to see his secretary, coat and hat on, about to leave and join whatever bus queue brought her to wherever she lived. He ought to tear her a new asshole for leaving him short of a page of notes like that, but right now he just wasn't up to it. 'What?' he asked.

'Two of them. Prime Ministers. Peel was in power at the beginning of the year, but he was ousted by a fellow called Russell.'

'Aahh.... Thanks!'

'Did you win?'

He thought she was referring to the meeting and was shocked that anyone at her level knew already what they were discussing.

'What? Eh...'

'I mean did you have a bet on as to who the Prime Minister was in 1846?'

'Oh! No, no, just something I've always wondered about.'

She shook her head at this reply and left. Turlough scratched at his growing stubble. It was uncanny. What she had said fitted exactly with what Colonel Jones had said to him. For a long time he went back over the events in his strange dream, which was doing anything but fading.

He looked at his watch again. It was too late to call Caitríona at work and he was not up to calling her at her flat and having to make up some lunatic story if someone else answered. Lunatic. Why had he thought of that word?

He stood up and walked slowly out of his office, brooding all the way home on the year 1846.

*

'Well?' asked Nuala, 'How did it go?'

'Not very well,' Turlough replied.

'Hi Dad!' said Emily, actually rising from wherever she had been nesting to come out to the hall and greet him. 'Are we going to make a bundle out of this farm?'

Turlough shook his head, huffed loudly, glared at Nuala for infecting Emily with her own avaricious outlook, and clambered up the stairs.

'Dinner's ready any time you are,' said Nuala after him.

'Fine. Let me have a quick shower and I'll be down. This suit will have to go to the cleaners in the morning.'

'So I see.'

'Where's Gearóid?'

'I don't know,' said Nuala.

'In his room studying, of course,' said Emily.

Turlough showered, a ritual to cleanse the mind of the day's layers of half-finished plans and thoughts-in-progress as much as to remove the grime from his unusual trip. And there it was again, a whiff of poitín on his breath. Had that bollocks Cohan laced his pints with the stuff? That must be it! He shook his head. You just couldn't be up to the antics of these rednecks. But at last he had an answer that explained the whole night.

Reinvigorated by his shower and the solution it had yielded, Turlough whistled as he pulled on some casual clothes, combed back his hair, and was halfway down the stairs when Emily shouted up: 'Dad! Call Gearóid!'

'Right!' He swung round and went back up to his son's room, musing on the fact that no two of them pronounced the boy's name the same way. They had christened him that before they had gotten over their 'Irish names' phase and now he was stuck with it. He knocked on the bedroom door.

'Yes?'

'Your mother wants us for dinner,' said Turlough, swinging the door open. Gearóid had indeed been studying, the desk they had given him cluttered with open books and writing paraphernalia.

'I'll be down in a minute.'

'Okay.'

'Dad?'

'Yes?'

'I was just wondering....'

Turlough raised his eyebrows, sensing a request for money. His fifteen year old son was less of a drain on the family purse than his younger sister, but still there were things he absolutely could not possibly live without, such as sneakers that cost more than everything else he wore combined, the kind they shot each other for in American schoolyards.

'Go on,' he said.

'Any chance of going to the match in Paris with you?'

This was unexpected.

'Oh, come on! Do you think we're made of money?'

'You always go.'

'I didn't when I was your age.'

'I saw cheap flights advertised in the paper.'

'Well, look, it's too late to be asking about this year now. It's just not in the budget....'

'What about all the money from this farm?'

'Jesus! Come down and I'll explain to the lot of you what's going on!'

Turlough left and wandered down to the kitchen, where Nuala had left a bottle of wine and opener on the table. Gearóid and Emily sat down while their mother bustled between cooker and sink, watching him as he tinkered with the multi-purpose gadget.

'I want to clear up this whole farm thing right away, now that I've been down there.'

They were all attention. Turlough poured wine for Nuala and himself, mind racing for the best story here.

'I'm afraid,' he told them, standing by the fridge door, wine glass in hand, 'that your great-granduncle Bernard, far from leaving an inheritance for any of his distant relatives to squabble about, died owing a lot of money, to the home in

Ballina, to the nuns, and, worst of all, to the Revenue Commissioners.'

Nuala shook her head as she carried over a couple of plates. 'Then it was a waste of time going over there?'

'Well, I wouldn't say that. No not entirely.' He did not want to cut off the possibility of future trips. Killala was off the radar screen, a good cover for trips elsewhere with Caitríona, and anyway he would probably still have to go back to cut a deal with Cohan and O'Gorman, those venomous bastards.

'Emily, get the other two plates!' ordered Nuala, sitting down. 'Then he did leave something, but maybe not enough to cover all his debts, is that it?'

'That's about it. The house is a wreck, but someone might buy it, and when all the bills are paid we might get the price of a holiday out of it.'

'A ticket to Paris,' said Gearóid.

He startled Turlough, still tense, and always edgy about anything that might be a reference to one of his secret trysts.

'Next year,' he said, recovering. 'Do they teach you kids anything about the famine in school?'

Emily shrugged and shook her head.

'Just that there was one,' said Gearóid, 'because everyone lived on potatoes. They were too dependent on one source of food.'

The image of all those tiny tilled fields came back to him and filled him with foreboding. They had all been growing a new crop of potatoes, putting the previous year's failure behind them, but the blight would come again. He had known that and he hadn't said anything. Even if it was only a dream, shouldn't he have said something, warned the people to make other plans?

For a while, Turlough's life trundled along under its own momentum as it usually did, every waking minute filled with some task or thought of family, business or social agenda, hidden or otherwise. Only once before he boarded the plane for Paris did he reflect again on the events in Erris.

He was at Mass, on the intervening Sunday, and the priest was giving an unusually enthusiastic sermon.

'It is expected of all of us,' said Father O'Connell, 'that we will give, not some pittance on the plate every Sunday, but...but a tithe!' The words reverberated around the church's nave, coming simultaneously from loudspeakers fixed to each pillar, assaulting the listeners from above with equal force no matter where they sat.

'And a tithe is one tenth of our incomes. If everyone in this parish were to contribute half that, we could build the new church with no loan at all.' He paused and there were a few coughs, and then a baby cried out in some far corner of the crowded church. 'If the congregation a hundred years ago could make the sacrifice necessary to build this beautiful building that we're celebrating Mass in here today, then surely...surely you...you can do as much and more today!'

Once again he paused and Turlough took it on himself to study the architecture Father O'Connell had just praised so highly. True, it was an enormous edifice, in shape and size much like a medieval cathedral, with stone-arched stained-glass windows and two rows of carved granite pillars and rows of oak benches, each with a brass plaque naming someone who must have given the money for it, or some amount like a life membership in the yacht club.

'Two hundred years ago there were no Catholic churches! Have you forgotten that?' continued Father O'Connell. 'The people risked their lives to hear Mass on a rock. And even in the time of the famine....'

Turlough stiffened. It was as if he were suddenly being addressed directly.

'...even then, faced with starvation, the people gave what they could, and willingly. So, once again, we will be calling on every home in the parish and leaving envelopes, and the rest is up to you! We desperately need a second church for our growing congregation, and only you, the parishioners of today, can give the priceless gift of a new church to your own children and all the faithful of tomorrow!'

The rest of the Mass flew past and they were all driving home before he snapped out of the re-run of his dream brought on by the mention of the past.

'So, what do you think?' he heard Nuala ask.

'Of what?'

'This new church! Are you listening to me at all, Turlough?'

'Eh...what? Oh, it's the most stupid thing I ever heard. What's the point? By the time it's finished no one will go near it.' He looked in the rear-view mirror at his two children. 'Am I right?'

Both nodded, but then looked quickly out the windows when their mother turned round.

'Of course people will go,' she said.

'Ah, they will not! Half that crowd weren't under the age of twenty-five. It's all dying out. We only go to be seen....'

'Turlough!'

'Well, it's true. It would be bad politics for me not to go and you just want to be seen arriving in the big car by everyone, and it's an excuse to dress up....'

'Don't listen to him!' she warned, looking back at Gearóid and Emily again. 'He's in one of his moods.'

'Oh yes, two up-and-coming vocations back there,' said Turlough, knowing this would incense her more.

'You can't go through life with no religion, you know,' she said.

'Millions do!' he replied, shrugging.

Nuala smoothed her skirt, crossed her ankles and looked out her own window.

'Not in Ireland they don't,' she muttered.

True, he thought, that's perfectly true, and then it came to him that he had been given a glimpse, in a way and for a reason that he could not yet fathom, as to why her words were so ringingly accurate.

CHAPTER EIGHT

The following Friday Turlough hitched a suitbag over his shoulder as he left his office, checked the time of his ticket once more, and decided that, with the dramatic announcements of cutbacks and layoffs that had gone on all day, he could do a lot worse than mingle with his staff across the road for an hour. He would still have plenty of time to get a taxi to the airport.

The street was cold and dry, not yet fully dark. In the twilight, passing by the much repainted spiked iron railings, and looking up at the Georgian facades behind them, he felt for the first time a brooding, even menacing quality about these old buildings, as if perhaps they should all have been demolished to make way for an entirely new city, instead of being preserved and then rebuilt on the inside, complete with plastic pillars and double glazing, a puzzling memorial to times otherwise forgotten, a sort of perverse Irish theme park.

The bar was thronged. Everywhere he saw faces he recognized, vindicating his decision to be here, all the more so when he saw Mulholland, O'Toole and several other partners, who rarely if ever sank to such proletarian depths; all of them sombre, sympathetic, highly visible, there in the fray to be seen by the troops.

'My God! Is there anyone not here?' he asked, passing by.

'Like Christmas Eve,' said Mulholland. 'Look, let me buy you a drink, Turlough, bury the hatchet?'

'Sure.' There was no sign of O'Brien, so Turlough shoved his suitbag out of the way and joined the enemy.

'Off to the match?' asked O'Toole.

'Yes, and yourself?'

'Ahhh! Doesn't really interest me. Might watch it on TV. Any money on the game?'

'No, but I'll get some frog to give me odds over there.'

'You know,' said Mulholland, clearly tacking into the troubled waters of the events at work, 'it all went down very badly, at least with anyone I talked to.'

'Bound to,' said Turlough. 'They didn't see it coming. Any real anger?'

'Yes, but who's going to let it show?' said O'Toole.

They were irritating him already, intentionally and with malice. He was sorry he had accepted Mulholland's offer of a pint.

'So, you never told us what the story was there the week before last,' said Mulholland.

Turlough put on a perplexed look, as if he had trouble remembering so far back. 'There's no story, Terence.'

'You had us going there for a while,' said O'Toole.

'We thought it must have been a lovers' quarrel.'

Mulholland exchanged glances with O'Toole as he said that. The bastards knew about Caitríona.

'I see Jim O'Brien over there. I'd better rescue him from the mob,' said Turlough, pushing a way through the crowd. What did it matter what they thought? Unless they caught him screwing someone on the job, which they never would, there was no way they could act on their suspicions.

'Jim!'

The tax adviser excused himself from the younger crowd he was with, Desmond and the others, all of them standing since there were no seats to be had, and sidled over.

'They're gunning for all of you, you know,' he said.

'Oh, and they hold you blameless?'

'Hey, listen, white man, I'm not a part of this.'

O'Brien was right. He was a loner, an individual contributor with no subordinates. His was a seasonal business and he simply borrowed from the main partners when he needed help. He could run with the hare and hunt with the hounds.

'So what are they saying?'

'You're not going to like this.'

'Go on.'

'They think it was all too severe, that it amounts to a breach of promise since there's no way any of them can change horses in midstream; that they should have been given some warning that it was coming....'

'Did it not dawn on them that every week lately there's been more of them sitting around scratching their hairless arses and that something would eventually have to be done about it?'

'Apparently not, but let me finish.'

'Sorry, I thought you were.'

O'Brien paused and took a drink. 'And they think you're behind it all.'

Turlough's grip tightened on his glass. 'Suffering Jesus, where did that come from?'

He knew he wouldn't get an answer to that, but once again his friendship with the neutral and thus well-informed O'Brien had paid off.

'Let's socialize,' he said.

Turlough bought a round of drinks for about twenty people, some of whom did not even thank him, just gave him surly looks when they thought he couldn't see them. He ignored that and for the next forty-five minutes gave forth on the economy, the US dollar, rugby, the possibility of an election, the need for more women in the practice, the latest trends in computer networks, and the benefits of air travel, finishing with this as a lead into taking out his ticket one more time and asking the barman to call him a taxi.

'You know,' he began slowly, watching as Desmond, three

of his cohorts, and a couple of female trainees leaned slightly closer to catch what he was about to say. All had declared they were drowning their sorrows at the distinct possibility of what might well prove to be prolonged unemployment, and were being helped to the first destination, if not the second, by yet another round of drinks Turlough had ordered just now. 'I feel very bad about taking off on a skite like this right now, and if I hadn't bought a non-refundable ticket I'd cancel it.'

'Well, Turlough, you're not affected by any of this,' said Desmond.

'No, but that's the worst of it. I mean, I was back on the first rung of the ladder like you once too.'

'I suppose,' said Desmond sympathetically, 'you had to do it. That's what management is all about.'

Hooked. Reel this in carefully. The timing was perfect, most of the other partners had left, leaving the juniors to settle into their own cliques and discuss this without their enlightenment for the evening. There would be no dilution or revision of what he was about to say; indeed, it would only be exaggerated and embellished.

'How do you mean I had to do it?' he asked, raising his voice, as if offended.

'Well, I didn't mean you personally, of course,' Desmond stammered, the others also freezing up at his faux pas. Even O'Brien shifted his feet.

'You're right, of course,' Turlough continued. 'At times like these we all have to be team players, even at my level. But I have to tell you....'

He shook his head.

'I think I'd better be going,' said O'Brien, looking at his watch, clearly telling his fellow partner in code to shut up.

'Well, they might as well know, I suppose, although it's too late now. What's done is done.'

They all looked at him.

'I was dead set against this,' said Turlough. 'Oh, I know people are crediting me with dreaming all this up, but this isn't what I had in mind at all!'

Their eyes were riveted on him.

'No,' he went on, 'I'm afraid we have some very spineless people involved in these decisions. Afraid to raise prices or offer new services more aggressively, just always trying to cut cost.'

No one said anything. No one wanted to stop this flow of priceless information, except Turlough himself.

'Mr Walsh!'

He looked around.

'Your taxi is outside,' a barman told him. He nodded and put his glass down on a table.

'I shouldn't really say any more, so don't repeat any of this,' he said, pausing for conspiratorial glances, 'but I want you to know that neither Jim nor I agreed readily to this plan. Certain partners got enormous kudos with our international affiliate at your expense.... Now I can't name names, but...let's just say that they come from the same part of the country as our leader.... Must fly. Have a great weekend everyone!'

He turned away, followed by a chorus of well-wishing, and picked up his bag. In a last sidelong glimpse as he pushed out through the door he saw they had already dispersed, all of them eager to spread the news, the real scoop on who had been behind it all: Mulholland and O'Toole, of course, wasn't it obvious? Hadn't they been the first to rush in with their denials, a bit too enthusiastic to place the blame elsewhere? Weren't they always plotting together and didn't Turlough Walsh spend more time socializing with his staff than any of them? Yes, he was a people person alright, the only one of the whole lot deserving any loyalty! By the time he reached the taxi he was laughing so hard he could barely say 'airport'.

The plane was full and they made no effort to put anyone in their proper seats, which, he conceded, would have been impossible anyway with the mob involved. He and Caitríona filed on separately and stayed apart until they emerged from the terminal at the far end and got into the same taxi together.

'Now that was really infantile!' she cried, laughing as he closed the door.

'Hey, people know about us, people who'd like to knife me at work.'

He read out the hotel address to the driver, then put his arm round Caitríona. She swung around on him, coiling her legs up under herself, pressed her lips so hard against him that she pinned him against the headrest of the seat, and, as the taxi careered round the ramps and out into the fast lane, she felt for the belt of his trousers, slid her hand forcefully down inside it and seized hold of his genitals.

'My God! What are you doing?' he asked, the words muffled by the presence of her tongue in his mouth.

'I want it, right now,' she replied.

'The driver's watching us!'

'So who's he going to tell?'

'Well, eh, we'd only be at the hotel before you came.'

'Want to bet?'

Turlough shook his head at her. Caitríona was part of the next generation alright, shameless, outspoken, individualistic, focused on the moment, capable of instant gratification, all the things he felt he could never be. But would she stay like that?

'The taxi's too small for you to really let go in,' he declared.

She backed off, smiling, scraping her nails along his scrotum as she withdrew her hand.

'It's all very well for you,' she said, 'you get to hump wifey whenever you like, but it's been a whole two weeks for me!' She pouted at him, then broke into a broad smile again. Being away like this exhilarated her far more than he had expected.

'I told you, Caitríona, there's not much left of our marriage in that area....'

She laughed. 'Well, of course, any married man would say that. At least you weren't blatant enough to put on the sad dog face and say you hadn't had any since the last child was born.'

He would have said that if he thought it was what she

wanted to hear, but there was no lack of self-confidence in that
area in this young lady. Nor of ability. He doubted she would
be around for long, just wring what she could out of the
situation, then move on. But she was worth it.

The hotel was a claustrophobic old building with an elevator
that barely held the two of them, and a room whose white
duvet-covered bed took up the whole floor, but it was within
walking distance of the Latin Quarter.

'Let's go out!' she said as soon as they dropped their bags.

'I thought you were in heat.'

'Oh, I am!' She wrapped her arms round his neck, and
caressed his leg with an inner thigh. 'But when we get into the
sack I want to stay in it. Come on, buy me a bottle of French
wine and turn me into your French lover!' She reached up and
licked his ear. 'Mon amour.'

'Okay, let me get out of this accursed suit.'

They walked along dark streets toward the Seine, both lost
in their own thoughts, until they came on one of those Parisian
intersections with roads leading in all directions, and cafes
with tables outside them.

'Take your pick,' said Turlough.

'How about this one?' She walked in amongst the nearest
tables and sat down where she had a view of the street.
Turlough followed, sitting opposite, so that all he saw was
Caitríona and the Gitanes ad on the wall behind her. She was a
vision though, dark hair extravagantly swept up into an
off-centre tail, long geometric shapes for earrings, the metal
flashing as it reflected the lights strung along the awning, the
same gold cross at her throat, focal point of a parabola made
by the scooped neckline of a black top that accentuated her
paleness...and then it came to him. He must tell her about his
dream!

They sat there until the early hours, until they were the only
ones sitting outside, and he recounted every detail to her, all
the names, everything they had said and done.

'That wasn't a dream, Turlough,' she said when he finally finished, 'that was a vision.'

'You mean you believe in all that stuff?'

'I don't keep crystals by my bed, or consult a star chart, or whatever, if that's what you mean, but I'm open-minded about, well, psychic phenomena.'

'You're the only person I've told.'

'The American Indians believed in visions,' she said quietly.

'And look where it got them.'

But she was not put off by his cynicism. 'Sitting Bull had a vision, just before he defeated Custer,' she said.

They were both pensive, Turlough because the accuracy and persistence of this memory troubled him, and Caitríona – well, whatever Caitríona's reasons were he would rather not know. He already felt obligated to her for having listened to him, and her taking it so seriously just made it worse. Could she not have just laughed and made a mockery of it? Everyone else he knew would. He paid the bill and they walked more slowly back the way they had come, she with her arms folded, he with his hands in his pockets.

'I suppose that's why I'm drawn to you,' she told him as they neared the hotel.

'How do you mean?'

She rocked her arms from side to side. 'I don't know how to put it. You're not exactly a stray cat, but...I just feel, well...you're not all bullshit.'

They both laughed. Turlough used the front door key and listened to her footsteps echoing toward the elevator. He leaned over and kissed her as they ascended, but, responsive though she was, he noticed her earlier passion had cooled. In the room, he watched from the bed as she busied herself in the tiny bathroom with the door open, panties shimmering as she shook her hair free, swabbed away eye make-up, then turned out the light and clambered quietly across him.

'Are you upset about it?' she asked in the dark.

'Hhhmm?' What was she talking about? He just wanted to

be a mysterious stray cat that needed her affection.

'Your vision!'

'Oh. Not at all. I just thought you'd be the best person to tell, and you were.'

He swung toward her and stroked her hair. 'So where's all this uncontrollable pent-up lust gone?' he asked.

'Keep searching around and you'll find it,' she whispered, and for a while he did, caressing her everywhere. Then suddenly he stopped. He had to, because he was somehow sure they were being watched, and he felt too embarrassed, or ashamed, to go on.

'What is it?' she asked.

Turlough said nothing, but slowly turned around, toward the window, and his heart stopped.

Bríd Kernen and her younger brother, Séamus, were standing there, staring at them. His heart started again with a thud and he shot up into a sitting position. They were so close if he reached out he would touch them. He held out a hand, but his whole arm shook uncontrollably, and just as he touched the end of Bríd's ragged shawl they vanished.

'Oh Christ!' He was nauseous, wanted to get to the bathroom, but he couldn't move, was rooted to the spot with fear.

'Turlough? Are you alright?'

'Didn't you see them?' Even his voice had no strength.

'See what?' asked Caitríona, sitting up and fumbling until she turned on the bedside light.

'They were there!' he said, pointing, 'Right there. The girl and her brother.'

He felt her gaze on him, a stare that held a mixture of disbelief and fear, not his irrational fear but an understandable one at being alone in a hotel room, in a foreign country, with a madman.

'Are you on medication of some sort, Turlough?'

He shook his head.

'You look awful,' she went on, sliding to the far end of the bed. 'Let me get you some water.'

While she did this some of his terror passed.

'What does it mean?' he asked.

'It means the wine was bad,' she answered.

'I thought you believed me!' He was angry now that she was making light of it.

'I do. I mean I'm willing to believe in your vision, but I draw the line at ghosts in the bedroom with us.'

'You don't! You don't believe any of it! You're just humouring me because I brought you here,' he shouted, the sound of his own voice reassuring him, somehow making it less likely that these phantoms could still be near at hand.

'Is this some kind of game, Turlough?' She looked up at the roof, untroubled by her own nudity, but visibly baffled by the evening's course of events. 'Is that it? You get off on this stuff? A whiff of the supernatural to really get the libido going?'

'No, no!' He shook his head frantically.

'Well, I take back what I said in the street!'

'What?'

'That there was something in there, something about you I liked? Remember? Well, maybe I was half right, but Jesus, get past the facade and you're really sick!' She swung her legs off the bed and fumbled in her hold-all, shook out another folded garment, a cotton tee-shirt, which she pulled on.

'Look....' Turlough wanted to explain, but what was there to say?

'I must have been out of my own tiny mind,' she went on, sitting with her back to him, 'to go out with a married man.'

'I thought I was one of many.'

'Yes, well, we can all play games.'

They sat there in silence, Turlough knowing that each passing moment must strengthen her belief in his perverse nature. She had revealed a little of herself and now she was sure she had been duped. And it was beyond him to invent any explanation that would undo this. He turned to her and put his hand on her shoulder.

'Caitríona, nothing like this has ever happened to me before. I mean it.'

He did mean it, but she just pulled away from him, saying nothing, just watching intently over her shoulder to see what he would do next. He lay back down on the far side from her and stared at the ceiling for a long time, and was still looking at it when the dawn arrived.

Caitríona had dozed off, coiled uncomfortably across her pillow at the edge of the bed, but she was in a deep sleep nevertheless. He smiled at her. Yes, she had been worth the trouble, but now he had blown it, and it was entirely, if involuntarily, his fault. He splashed water on himself, glared at the tired, middle-aged face that looked back at him, dressed, packed, placed all the money in his wallet on the bedside table by her jewellery, and left, pulling the door quietly behind him.

The streets were deserted and he had walked all the way to Boulevard Saint Germain before a taxi came along. Even the cool air hadn't revived his spirits, nor did coffee in the basement of Charles De Gaulle airport, where, if he even momentarily lost interest in the surrounding trivia, the two pauper children returned inside his head. To his relief, there were seats on the first flight to Heathrow, from where he connected on the next flight to Dublin, which was all but empty.

He sat by a port window, putting up with the dazzle of the ocean below so that he would have a view of the east coast of Ireland as the plane approached Dublin airport, heading north-west. The spectacle of the Wicklow hills, the morning sun on their wooded flanks, stirred in him a feeling he could not explain, as if he shouldn't have left and these mountains themselves were glad he was back. Then they drifted back from view and were replaced by Dublin, a great flat expanse of discoloured rooftops wrapped around a bay, cloven at its centre by an estuary that protruded into the sea.

As they crossed high above it, he was reminded again of Caitríona, Howth Head her right knee, Bray Head her left, spread apart so that he could go up that river, which zigzagged between the city's rooftops, and feel the quays pressing in on either side of him, all the way to her falls at Islandbridge, to send his sperm up the salmon leaps to the fresh water beyond, and all the way in, in, inland to her hidden source. And as the view of the city fell behind, and the aircraft banked and descended, he realized for the first time that he could not be sure that she had ever really had an orgasm with him and now that it was over that fact, for the first time, troubled him.

CHAPTER NINE

He thought of calling Nuala to come and get him from the airport, but he hadn't the energy to come up with a story that would explain why he was back, let alone a second one to cover up the fact that he was going back to Erris, to Uncle Bernie's cottage, so instead he rented a car, took the back roads round the edge of the city, then followed the familiar chain of towns across the midlands – Mullingar, Longford, Carrick-on-Shannon – and arrived four hours later, about mid-afternoon.

The back door had been fixed and everything else looked the same. The rainbarrels were full; the tiles on the north facing roof slope each held a tuft of green moss; the weeds were coming along on what had once been potato ridges. He walked all the way down to the stone wall at the bottom, pausing halfway to imagine passing through the one that had been there in 1846, then turned left toward the corner where the Kernens' hut, of which there was no trace either, had once been. Perhaps the stones had been re-used in the wall here.

Beyond was what remained of the old road, an all but overgrown track between two sets of stone walls, so he vaulted over and began following this as he had done with Bríd. In places the brambles and gorse plucked stitches from his jeans, and there was the ever-present threat of nettles, but he kept going, until he judged he had reached the spot where the girl had left him. 'Bríd!' he yelled, cupping his hands to his mouth. 'Bríd! Where are you?' There was only silence, which relieved him, and he walked on, feeling more like his old self, thinking to find some other way back to the real, paved road up the hill on his left, glad that the land did not resemble his dream, when, as if in some way the past had once again seized hold of his mind, he came on it.

Yes, it was the very church he had passed just after Bríd had blessed herself and backed away from him. Now it was disused, all the graves long overgrown, crows sailing through the space that had once been the roof, the surrounding walls crumbling, eaten away by the roots of the ivy and lilac that grew on them; yet it was, undoubtedly, the same place.

Turlough tried vainly to push open the rusted metal gate, is lower reaches now buried in fifty years or more of humus. He scrambled over the broken wall, afraid to blink, sure that at any moment he would find himself back in 1846. He had never been here before, he was absolutely certain of that, and yet he had visualized it exactly the way it was.

He was stunned by this proof. Caitríona had been right: he had had a vision. And those two children really had reappeared; for some reason that only they knew, they had reached out to him from beyond the grave.

There were graves all around him, and he checked every one. None had the name Kernen chiselled into it. Most were from the early nineteenth century, a few seemed much older, but their inscriptions were worn away. He checked and rechecked the names and dates, finally ending up in front of the most recent one again. It read:

In memory of Lorcan MacCurran,
1814-1850.
May God have mercy on his soul
and forgive us all.

There was something unusual about the wording. Turlough read it again, but he was too perturbed by the very existence of this place to figure it out. Again he felt he was being watched and his back shivered as though a cold wind were blowing on it, no matter which way he turned. The light was failing when he left, throwing his shadow out in front of him as he crossed a wide field, the grass just beginning to grow again after the winter, a herd of black and white cattle in the far corner. At the top of this he met the real road, turned left, and after a mile or so was back at the cottage.

He sat at the wheel of his rental car, squeezed his eyes shut and felt for the first time since he was a young child a frustration so intense he wanted to cry. He was sick, sick in some way he couldn't understand. Some door, or half-door, in his mind had swung open and these images had gotten in, and now they wouldn't leave. Why had this happened to him? He started the car, his self-pity changing quickly to annoyance at his failure to resolve any of it, and was just about to turn it around when another thought returned to him.

Once again, he wanted to go on to Westport, and this time there was no reason not to, so he pulled out and followed this narrow lane, choosing at each of the many junctions of the country's dense web of minor roads whichever one headed south. Eventually he came to a wider road, one that was actually on his map of Ireland, and had a dotted line down its centre, and twenty minutes later he was in Westport.

Turlough parked, walked down the street of two storey, slate-roofed shops and turned into the first bar he came to. It was a foul-smelling little place, half the size of Moran's, with a low nicotine-sticky roof and warped shelves behind the high counter.

'A pint of stout.'

There was no verbal confirmation from behind the bar, but the publican went through the motions of preparing this drink. Turlough paid, watched the drink settling out, then reached for the glass and finished half of the stout in two long gulps.

Was there no way out of this? Why could he not simply get away from this place, throw this nightmare over the transom and get on with his life as it had been? He put the glass down and as he did so a ringing came into his ears so that he could no longer pursue these or any other thoughts. He squeezed his eyes shut and pressed the lids with his fingers. The sensation went away again and as it did it seemed to him that the sounds in the bar, and beyond, had changed somehow.

The light too was different and even the air had a quality to it that he couldn't place, as if... as if this was now a much, much older room, in which peat burned, unventilated. Slowly, Turlough stood up and made for the door, even smaller now than it had been. He heard a horse clatter by outside, and even before he stepped out into the street, his suspicion became a certainty.

There was a smell of horse-dung, the cobbled street smeared with the stuff, and it was no longer night, but a bright, if overcast, day. There were still two storey buildings here, but smaller, built of uncut stone, with no great skill, and Westport, if that's where he still was, had a tiredness to it, as if it could only have seen better days before now.

He had returned to the past. Mick-Óg! Turlough could not see the bay from where he stood so he sought out any street that might lead downhill. The second turn he came to did so, and he swung left into this narrower lane. There were people everywhere, some ragged and sticklike, others a little better off carrying bags of belongings, but they paid no attention to him, and seemed even to want to avoid each other.

He splashed through a fetid green pool that blocked the whole road, and then came to a point where the right-hand houses ended so that he walked out onto a market-day square, thronged with these emaciated, unwashed folk. To his right the street that led away from this open space fell away steeply, and looking down it over the knotted, matted hair and the caps of the crowd, he saw the grey-green surface of Clew Bay.

'Good heavens! Mister Walsh? Is it you?'

There, in front of him, stood Pendleton.

'Yes, yes, indeed it is.'

The other man did not remove his hat or offer his hand in greeting.

'I hope you got your wagon back alright,' said Turlough, at a loss in this ridiculous situation, and thinking the other man might have been put out by that.

'Oh, yes, yes, but I heard the strangest story, and in truth I was sure you had perished,' he shook his head, 'like so many.'

Apparently, some time had elapsed since the last visit to this accursed time.

'What's today's date?' asked Turlough.

'Eh, let me see...I believe it's the fourth.'

'I see.' Turlough was no wiser.

'Yes,' said Pendleton, 'September fourth, 1847.'

A year later. Would he be able to find any of them?

'How are the relief works going?' he asked.

Pendleton shook his head. 'I'm afraid there won't be any this year. The whole attitude of the government has taken an appalling turn for the worse.'

'I see. And you? What have they got you doing?'

'Do you really want to see?'

Turlough nodded and Pendleton led the way out into the square, pushing through an ever thicker horde, until it became apparent that all of these wretched people were waiting around for some reason, too numerous to be organized in any way.

'There!' said Pendleton. 'There's what we do now for what I'm told may be upward of three million destitute!'

Some policemen stood by here while the people formed a queue for the last fifty paces or so of the approach to a cluster of large cast-iron cauldrons. Each person in line held a pot, cup, bowl or glass jar and when they came to the end of the line they were ladled out a portion of watery looking soup.

Pendleton brought him up to the cauldron in use and they both looked in.

'There you are. That's what they get now instead of wages: stirabout.'

The steaming liquid gave off only the faintest smell, a pungency, like cut grass drying, that might have been from the water itself, rather than from the corn that swirled here and there, or the film of lard on the surface.

'These people are living on this?'

Pendleton nodded at him. 'That's the last of Peel's brimstone, as they call it, though it was really Trevelyan that organized it all. And now we have to pay market price just to get our hands on that, and they're shipping the last of it back as we speak.'

Turlough looked around, aghast at the realization of what he was witnessing. These people were all starving, and would all starve, eventually, to death, if they were not overtaken by disease first. He looked into every face, searching for one of the Kernens, but he saw no one he recognized.

'And the potatoes? Have they failed again?' he asked.

'No, no! It looks like being one of the best of years!'

'Oh, well, that's good news,' said Turlough.

'Not for those already dead, or dying, or who've lost everything. There isn't a landlord in the country that hasn't used this potato blight to his advantage. The best of them paid for the emigration of their surplus tenants, and the rest,' he gave a jerk of his head, 'just got on with it.'

The mention of emigration brought Turlough back to what he had been doing.

'You remember the day we worked together on the road?'

'Oh yes!'

'There was a ship about to set sail the next day from Westport. Do you know anything about it?'

'No, no. You mean did it make it?'

'Yes.'

'Who knows? You might ask down by the harbour.'

'I don't suppose you'd consider lending me your wagon again?' asked Turlough.

Pendleton smiled at this. 'It wasn't really mine you know. Belonged to the Board. But I do have a horse I could let you have....'

They agreed that Pendleton would send a servant with the horse an hour later, down to the waterfront, and parted, each making his way in the opposite direction from the spectacle of debasement that was the outdoor soup kitchen.

Turlough was more conscious than ever of the misery all around him now. What must once have been shops were boarded up all along the street, and before he reached its end he passed a corpse, a woman, he reckoned, lying propped against a doorway, where she must have sat down to die.

He had seen pictures of famine before of course. Somalia. Ethiopia. Bangladesh. He was even old enough to remember Biafra, and the jokes they told as schoolboys about the fastest thing in Africa being a Biafran chasing a bread truck. But this was different. He had never imagined his own country as being anything other than a pastoral landscape on which, from time to time, wars had been fought, and from which people emigrated when they got fed up with their lives on small farms or because they were one of too many children.

How had it come to this? When he reached the quay the scene was even worse. Hundreds of people swarmed around and there were arguments going on at both sets of stone steps that led down to the water. When he got closer he saw that people were begging to be taken on rowing boats to a three-masted ship that floated with furled sails out in the bay. A woman clung to the leg of one of the sailors, while another knelt by her bags, hands clenched together, face turned skyward, praying. There were children around too, as weary and listless as the adults. It would be hopeless to ask here about something that might or might not have happened a year ago.

Then, while he waited for Pendleton's horse another horde, a couple of hundred people, came mooching slowly up from the south, like some macabre funeral procession.

He watched as the leaders of this band presented a scroll of paper to one of the sailors. This fellow hailed what Turlough took to be his superior, who was arguing with all comers at the head of the nearest steps.

'This is them!' he yelled. 'Palmerston's lot.'

'You mean Lord Palmerston, blaggard!' said his boss, coming over and taking the document. 'Very good! Yes, this is them, all named. Sort them into bunches of thirty and we'll get them into the boats and be away from this plague ridden town.'

'Sir, this one's got dropsy!'

Two of the sailors now busying themselves with these arrivals singled out one wretch whose rags showed all the signs of incontinence.

'You won't make it, you know, old man!' shouted the boss, coming up to him. 'Your fare's been paid I'll grant, and ye're lucky to have had such a generous landlord, and we'll put you on board if you insist, but the sharks'll have you before you're out of sight of land!'

They were obviously making an example of this poor creature in the hopes of dissuading some of the other wasted spectres, many of whom looked even more ill, but not one of them was put off. Turlough watched from the edge of the quay as the sailors filled one of their launches with this human cargo. Even if the ship made it to America, how many of them would survive? And what must they have endured already that they were willing to do this? Did they understand the risks? Or care? Clearly, they were of a mind that to stay was certain death. No matter the perils of sailing the Atlantic, they would all go.

A servant of Pendleton's arrived with the horse.

'Tell your master thanks,' said Turlough climbing onto the beast, a lot bigger than the ones he and the kids went pony-trekking on in France.

'He won't be needing it much longer,' the youth replied.

'How's that?'

'You didn't notice? The fever, God have mercy. Better he goes quick before he gives it to us all.'

Turlough took a last look at the boat full of emigrants from his new height, one small platoon of the vast army of destitute fleeing the country, clinging to their last few belongings as they bobbed across the water, and to the hope that there was some way, other than death itself, out of this living hell.

He took the only road north out of Westport, travelling for over an hour before meeting a fork of any significance. He stayed left, following the bay out west, and now, where he had been passing small fields of crops before, he was surrounded by what was mostly wilderness. There were beggars on the roadsides and paupers watched from the hills, but no one troubled him, or made any real effort to seek charity from him. He knew he was passing now through a place and time where all kindness from the outside world had been wrung out, and the people were scraping out whatever existence they could, devoid, justifiably, of any further illusions of help.

The autumn twilight deepened as he cantered on north, until the land again took on a familiar look and then the horse had to slow and pick his way carefully over rough patches of broken stones. Turlough dismounted, and in the gloaming realized that he had come to the very stretch of road where Tomás Kernen had refused work.

Leading the horse by its reins he walked on, embittered by the memory, knowing that he was to blame, that it had been his fault for having asked those questions, for pricking the man's conscience like that. He was to blame, not just for depriving the Kernens of those wages, but for sending their oldest son to perish at sea, with all their savings.

He wandered on, and was about to remount where the old, unimproved road led up the hill, and then down to where the Kernens lived, or had lived, when, from all sides, men's faces popped up and they climbed over walls, yelling, and surrounded him.

'We'll be having that horse,' said their leader, distinguished by the fact that he wore an outsized white shirt over his other clothes.

Turlough looked around at the group, mostly young lads, with some older men on the fringes. A couple had muskets, more had forks and spades, one even had a pike.

'What do you want it for?' he asked.

'Well, he won't be needing a blacksmith again!' said the leader, drawing a laugh from the others.

'Is this some sort of uprising?'

They closed in around him.

'Are you an agent?' asked someone, menacingly.

'Do you work for Sligo?'

'Or Montegrine?'

'No,' Turlough replied, 'Look, you can have the horse. I don't have all that far to go. I'll walk.' He let go the animal's rein and stepped forward, but white-shirt blocked his way.

'We'll have a better account of you before we decide if you're going anywhere!' he announced.

There were murmurs of assent.

'I've seen him somewhere before,' said another.

'Let's card him! That'll make him talk.'

'Well?' said white-shirt, 'What's it to be? Tell us who you are or we'll draw blood right quick!'

Someone nearby brandished a wicked looking steel brush still holding what looked like scraps of the flesh of a previous victim on its spikes.

'Alright! I'll explain!' said Turlough, mind churning. They grew silent, waiting for him to say something. He opened his mouth, but no words came. He couldn't understand it. He could tell them anything and they would probably believe it, but he just could not think of a thing to say.

For the first time in his life, Turlough Walsh was stumped. Never before had he lacked an answer, but now, with his life at stake, his imagination failed him. Even the most preposterous lie would work here, and yet he couldn't think of one.

'This fellow knows he's found out,' said a voice.

'He's an agent alright.'

'Come to watch the tumblings.'

Rough hands grabbed him, and he flailed around until he lost his footing, then felt himself being carried over to a wall and held spreadeagled, face down, across it.

'Pull down his fine trousers there, men!' ordered white-shirt.

'Arrah, Lorcan, do a bit of his leg first.'

Whoever said that was ignored and he felt the cold air on his behind anyway. Then there was a painful slap and he knew they had dug one of their woolcarders into his left buttock.

'You'd do well to tell us who you are and when you'll be going about your dirty work,' said Lorcan of the white shirt, 'else we'll leave your remains as a warning to them.'

He knew what they were going to do. The stinging was already intense, and when they pulled the tool down along him they would turn the whole of his leg to hamburger meat. And yet still he was stayed from telling them any kind of a lie. Then he thought he understood why he couldn't lie, not here in this place, and he cried out:

'If this is Tomás Kernen's revenge, I want him to know I never meant him any harm!'

CHAPTER TEN

'Mister Walsh! Oh Jesus, Mary and Joseph, oh good God of all Virtues, what have we done to him!'

'You know him, Tomás?'

'Let him up!' There was great urgency about this command. Turlough felt the spikes being pulled slowly back out the way they had gone in, and looked around as he raised himself, to see an array of small holes that was quickly becoming a rectangle of blood.

'Oh, Mister Walsh, are you alright?'

Turlough looked up into the concerned face of Tomás Kernen and smiled.

'I'm fine,' he said. 'Fine.'

He rearranged his clothes, heedless of the blood trickling down his leg.

'What brings you back? Are they starting up the roadworks again?' asked Tomás. He turned to Lorcan. 'This is the man I told you about gave Mick-Óg three wages one day to go to America.'

'I thought you said that fellow caught the fever?' asked Lorcan, rougher looking than Tomás, burlier, almost stocky by comparison with all the others.

'Well he went into the fever cabin up above and we never

saw him again.'

'Oh, well, I went back to Dublin right away,' said Turlough.

'And where are you headed now, Mister Walsh?' asked Tomás.

'I rode up here to see you.'

Tomás shook his head and backed away. 'I know what you must be thinking,' he said, 'about what's going on here, and sure, swear to me, you won't ever tell the children or their mother, will you?' He gestured to the band of men all around.

Turlough shook his head in agreement, glad to hear they were alive.

'We'll have that horse of yours for dinner anyway,' said Lorcan, sneering at this exchange. 'There's men here haven't eaten for a week.'

Turlough glared back at him. If this fellow could remain unmoved having inflicted an innocent man with pain, then why should Turlough show any gratitude at his own reprieve?

'But you haven't ever gone a week without food, have you, Lorcan?'

This brought a laugh from the others.

'If everyone rose up against this tyranny, no one would go hungry,' stated their leader.

'Murdering passersby, and taking pleasure in it, is hardly going to drive the British away,' Turlough replied.

'It's not them that are the problem,' said Lorcan, 'it's Irish landlords and their Irish agents that are driving us out!'

'Ah, but they wouldn't get away with it without the British there helping them,' said someone else.

'They won't get away with it anyway!' said Lorcan. 'Come on, we mightn't have another night like this before the threshing's over!'

The whole band of them began marching up the road Turlough would have taken anyway, until they came to the wheat fields on the south face of the hill that he had first noticed riding with Colonel Jones. On both sides of the road the crop had been harvested and set up in stooks to dry and the men now leaped over the walls and set fire to the nearest of these.

'What are they doing?' Turlough asked Tomás.

'Burning the whole lot of it!'

'Why? Why not take it and feed it to their own families?'

Tomás shook his head back. 'How? You could count the number of mills in this county on one hand, and if you had flour itself there isn't a village for twenty miles that has one oven to make it into bread.'

It was now completely dark so that the fires were like bright yellow flares in the night, more and more of them crackling to life, sending red sparks showering up into the black sky as Lorcan's men made their way through field after field.

'Whose crop is it?' Turlough asked Tomás.

'It belongs to a man that's never seen it, nor ever been to Erris, or any part of County Mayo, and who doesn't even live in Ireland. Sir Montegrine. Has a mansion outside Killala.'

The burning excited Lorcan's younger followers to whooping and cheering, but left Tomás unmoved. His face, lit up by blazes on both sides, had that same hopelessness about it now that Turlough had seen on so many others earlier that day.

'Why don't you go home? I'll go with you. I'd like to see your family again.'

Tomás nodded at him and they began walking purposefully away.

'Kernen!'

They turned to see Lorcan's white shirt.

'Will you not stay and have a bite of this fellow's horse?'

As he said this they saw the horse being led into one of the burning fields, surrounded by the young arsonists. Then a shot rang out and it toppled over, and immediately they all fell on it, and began hacking with what tools they had at its flesh.

'I haven't sunk that low yet!' said Tomás.

Lorcan laughed, the sound of it carrying up to them as they continued up the hill.

'Who is he?' asked Turlough as they tramped on over the dark wild hill.

'Lorcan MacCurran. Leader of the local Whiteboys, who think they can frighten the landlords into leaving us alone.'

Lorcan MacCurran. That was the name on the tombstone in the old church. He would die in three years' time, having done all this to survive the potato famine. Who else would die between now and then?

'How's Bríd?' asked Turlough.

'She's a strong girl, but she loses heart, as we all do, when she sees the others failing.'

'The others? Young Séamus?'

'Oh God, how well you remember us, Mister Walsh!' His voice quivered. 'And do you remember Nan?'

'Of course.' He hadn't asked about her because she hadn't been a part of the apparition in Paris. Now he was gripped by a dread so intense he had to stop walking. 'Is she...?'

'Not yet,' Tomás whispered, 'but she's beyond our help.'

They continued walking on more slowly.

'Has she caught the fever?' asked Turlough. The other man's head nodded in the darkness.

'We put her up in that cabin you came out of that day.'

Tomás broke down at his own words. Sobbing fitfully, he clutched at Turlough's arm. 'What else could we do? If we kept her with us till the end we'd all get it from her. Oh God forgive me but I was only trying to keep the rest of them alive!'

They moved on in silence after that, passing the church that would see MacCurran's remains buried in it when this great dying season ended, and finally came to the Kernens' home, the tiny hovel that was the centre of their world. Turlough ducked in through the entrance with Tomás and in the glow of the turf embers saw his sleeping family, huddled together on the mud and straw floor.

There was his wife Sheila, with the toddler, Maura, in the crook of her arm, and then Séamus, lying on his back with his bony knees raised, and against the wall furthest from the door,

Bríd. None of them woke as the two men slipped in and lay down on what floor space was left.

Turlough dozed a little between then and dawn, but he was afraid to fall asleep, thinking he might wake up back in the present and, for reasons he could not explain to himself, he wanted to stay here with these people, at least for a while.

'Mister Walsh? Is it you?'

Daylight filled the smoky room from the doorway and Turlough looked up to see Bríd crouched over him, little Maura in her arms.

'Come on out,' she said, and he got up and followed her out into the cold morning air.

She had grown up in the intervening year, losing any sign of plumpness. Her hair, still sleek, now hung down both sides of a face that was far too gaunt, far too pale, with no colour left in the cheeks. Bríd too was starving, and the same dress and shawl that had fitted her so well once now flapped loosely from bony hips and shoulders.

'You look very well,' he said, lying, but drawing an embarrassed smile from her. 'You're turning into a real beauty.'

'Ah, Mister Walsh, stop, would you!' She rocked the child in her arms back and forth.

'How's this little one?' he asked, and by way of reply Bríd stepped forward and handed her to him.

'She has the good sense to cry whenever she's hungry!' said her sister, but even still the child felt impossibly light to Turlough. Had his own kids ever weighed so little? This child was now two years old, and should be toddling around.

'Bríd,' he said abruptly, handing the child back, 'listen to me. You've got to get away from here. Do you understand? If you stay here you'll die.'

'Any day now,' she replied, 'we'll hear from Mick-Óg in America, and he'll send me the fare to join him.'

Turlough shook his head. What should he say? He had no

idea whether her brother was really alive or dead, but even if Mick-Óg had made it, what were the chances of him getting on his feet so fast? And how would he remit money to this wilderness? And if he did, what was the likelihood of the Whiteboys or some other bandits stealing it?

'Bríd, that would be great, but you can't wait for it to happen. You might....' His words trailed off and both he and Bríd turned their faces up the hill behind them to the cabin with the sack cloth that hung limply in the mist.

'I must bring her something,' said Bríd. She went back inside with the young child and came out with a crockery cup that held some milk and both of them started up a trough between leafy green potato plants that showed no signs of blight.

'See?' she said, 'We won't be so hungry this winter!'

Part of the wall that separated the two fields was now missing and he followed the girl through this gap and on up through more potatoes to the fever cabin.

'Who was the dead man in there last year?' he asked.

'Old Murkeen, my grandfather.'

'Ah, then he left you this patch of land too?'

'Arrah, don't you know the landlord's man had someone else working it right away!' She lowered her voice. 'But no one will go near the cabin, not even to tumble it....'

They both stopped in front of the door. This was where they brought fever victims to die. No wonder it was haunted forever after. No wonder Uncle Bernie and all the rest of them had lost their minds, living in a place that had such a hideous past.

'Every morning I'm afraid to go in,' said Bríd softly.

'Here, give me that,' said Turlough.

'Oh God, no Mister Walsh! Why should you risk getting the fever for my sister? When I said I was afraid, I just meant of finding her...dead.'

Turlough looked at the doorway and considered the possibility of his getting the fever in this possessed state, or whatever it was that he was going through. His arse still hurt and now it was bleeding again, making his clothes stick to his skin. If he could feel this pain could he also catch the fever and die from it?

'Aaahh, this is bloody ridiculous,' he said out loud and plunged into the cabin.

He must have woken Nan, because she swung her head round to him as he entered, slowly, as if it hurt even to do that much. She was too far gone to smile or speak, but he knew by her eyes that she recognized him. He knelt down on the ground beside her, remembering what she had looked like that first time he had seen her, holding up the egg. He had thought her a ragged urchin then, but now, thinking back on it, she had been in perfect health by comparison.

The fever had ravaged her nine year old body, far beyond any hope of recovery. Nan held out a shivering hand to him, and instinctively he took hold of the dark wrinkled flesh. Then he picked her up, almost weightless in his arms, and carried her out into the morning air.

'Bríd, give me the milk!' he ordered. 'And don't come too close! I'm going to stay here with her until the end. We won't let her die alone.'

The older girl handed him the cup, then burst into tears and ran back down the hill.

All that day, all that night, and all the next day Turlough stayed with Nan, swabbing her, talking to her, trying to coax her to drink water, until sometime during the second night, he could not be sure when, her little body gave up its struggle and grew cold.

That morning, he carried her body to the top of the hill that continued rising behind the land, followed by the Kernen family, until they found a dry patch of turf that overlooked the whole valley. Turlough and Tomás dug a grave, sharing the one spade between them. Then Tomás and Sheila and the children recited the prayers they knew by rote, a decade of the rosary, and Turlough picked up Nan's body, and as he lowered her into her grave a gust of wind blew the fever infected rags from her face, and the wisps of what had once been fine black hair fluttered about, as if feeling the air in one last attempt to find out why this fate had befallen her, but there were no answers, none that a child could understand.

Turlough let her drop to the bottom of her resting place and when he shovelled the first dirt in on her, Bríd and her mother rent the air with their keening, and it began to rain, and they finished and left the hill, Tomás helping Sheila who limped on emaciated legs, Séamus clinging to his sister, scurrying to their cabin in their ragged garb for fear they would catch cold and lay themselves open to infection and death like Nan.

Turlough cared nothing for any of that and stood by the little girl's grave, crying, glad that it was raining so that his tears mingled with it, glad that the valley was hidden now by the great silvery sheets of water that were whipped along by the wind, and felt, in the pit of his heart, for the first time, the same helplessness as all these people, as if he too were sinking into a dark, pitiless bog of despair.

Worried that he might now be infected, Turlough stayed up in the fever cabin for the next couple of days, being brought milk and potatoes by Bríd or Séamus once a day. The weather did not improve much, the land lashed by equinoctial gales, but on the third night there was a lull in the wind and Turlough looked out from his doorway to see a half moon coming and going from behind ragged clouds.

The valley was in darkness, everyone asleep. The stone walls cast their shadows on the potato crop when the moon came out, and then the fields became square black pools again when it disappeared behind a cloud. Suddenly, Turlough thought he saw a movement down on the road, something flitting along by a wall. The moon hid itself again and it was hard to make things out, but he went on watching. Then he was sure he saw the dark shape rush into the Kernens' home, and as quickly dash back out again.

'Hey!' he shouted, taking off down the hill, but if whatever it was had heard him it showed no sign, and the moon went in again as the phantom figure fled down the road.

Then he heard a shriek, and knew it was Sheila, and then she and Tomás and Bríd and Séamus were outside.

'Oh God spare us!' she said, falling to her knees as Turlough ran up. 'A pooka has just taken the child!'

'Maura!' shrieked Bríd, 'Maura! Come back!'

All four of them began to cry. Turlough shook his head, confused, then took off at a run down the road. He was in luck, the moon came out again and he could pick his way along, and he caught sight of the kidnapper taking off down a side road. He closed the distance and plucked a rock from the top of the wall on his right.

Getting closer still he let fly and hit the black cloak from behind, sending the man sprawling. The child howled momentarily, but the man was getting to his feet again and two white sleeves reached out, grabbing the little child roughly.

'MacCurran!' shouted Turlough. It was a wild guess, he couldn't see the face, but the man hesitated, and then another cloud sailed across the moon, the land darkened and Turlough ran into a rock, twisting his ankle, which sent him flailing for the support of a wall, whose loose stones fell away around him.

They never saw Maura again. Turlough did not tell the Kernens his suspicion as to who the kidnapper was, reluctant to start a feud between them and the local revolutionary leader who, either way, innocent or guilty, might retaliate with some other atrocity. Anyway, it would have been almost impossible to shake them from their belief that only some supernatural being, some evil horror from the pagan past, would steal a child.

Besides, an even more far-reaching disaster was about to overtake the Kernens and everyone else around them. After Maura's disappearance Turlough took to sleeping with the Kernens again, worried about Séamus, but the next few nights were uneventful. Then one morning they awoke to the sound of horses passing by outside. Turlough stepped out and watched as a detachment of red-coated soldiers rode past, two by two, followed by a wagon filled with poles and chains, and then a second one with a man who looked like some kind of merchant riding in front, wearing a top hat and a black coat with tails, and a dozen or so grim looking characters in the back.

They stopped a little way down the road.

'Is this where you want to start, Mister Kincaid?' shouted the lead soldier.

Kincaid, clutching his hat in one hand and some papers in the other, jumped down from his wagon, followed by the others, and walked up to the bend in the road where it wound on past the church and up the hill.

'This is it,' he said, consulting a map. 'All to be cleared out down both sides. Start up this end and work your way back.'

Crowds of people were gathering now, streaming out of the little huts or converging from further away, and a swarm of pedestrians that had been following this horse-drawn convoy earlier was now catching up.

'Oh, dear God, don't say it's come to this!' said Tomás coming up beside Turlough.

Sheila burst into tears and fell to her knees blessing herself. 'Oh God in heaven above let them stop before they reach us! Holy Mary, Mother of God save us!' Her two remaining children joined her.

Turlough, still not understanding, pushed through the crowd until he was up with the soldiers.

'Back!' they shouted. 'Stay back!'

Kincaid walked on ahead to his chosen starting point.

'Oh God, Mister Kincaid, you wouldn't do this to us, would

you?' Turlough heard the head of this household say.

'It's been a year and a half since we've had any rent out of you!' he snapped back.

'Oh please!'

They were a family much like the Kernens, man, wife, some kids, an older man, and they all fell to their knees in front of Kincaid, grabbing at his coat as he passed.

'Do you have the rent?' he asked.

'If we had wouldn't we have paid it?'

The agent swatted at them with a big notebook and signalled to his crew who ran up to the hut, the first two ducking in and throwing or kicking out anything in there, some clothes, a metal pot, a few implements. Then they stood back while some more of them used their long poles to prise away the roof, sending the thatch and its stick frame sliding off to crash in a heap behind. A hen took to the air and a couple of mice scurried away. The family screamed and the man, losing his temper, attacked the nearest of Kincaid's thugs, but they beat him with shovels until he gave up, his head a bloody mess.

In a few minutes it was over, the mud and stone walls levelled with sledgehammer blows, the hearth trampled out, any usable piece of timber splintered into firewood. And then Kincaid took five steps across the road and it all began again. Some of the houses were harder to level than others, the stones held in place with mortar, but for these they erected a battering ram on a tripod and pushed the walls inward from all sides, leaving just rubble anyway.

Eight soldiers, a wizened little landlord's agent, and a dozen thugs. Turlough marvelled at it. There were hundreds of people watching them, but they were too frightened and too weak to do anything about it. And if they did, what good would it do them? Eight hundred soldiers would be sent to hang them all.

Had any other people in the world been so cruelly destroyed? Even the American Indians had come out of it all with some dignity. But there was no Sitting Bull here, the empire had no need to send out any ambitious general like Custer to test the people's resolve. Their spirit was now as blighted as their food had ever been. Perhaps the Jewish experience was equally horrifying, but they had been the knowing victims of a hateful regime, not one that made a pretence of saving them while allowing their monstrous fate to run its course. And, albeit far too late, they had been saved....

'Now do you believe that England is the problem?'

Turlough turned to see Lorcan MacCurran beside him, indistinguishable this grey morning from any of the other peasants.

'What did you do with the Kernens' little girl?' he demanded, ignoring this political question.

MacCurran's eyes narrowed. 'We'll stay alive any way we can, long enough to settle with these bastards anyway,' he muttered.

'Fuck you, what are you saying?' Turlough shouted, grabbing hold of MacCurran's clothes.

'What difference does it make now? Look! They're all as good as dead. We knew this was coming!'

The wrecking crew had reached the Kernens' house, and as the roof collapsed one end of it caught fire. Sheila, still kneeling in the road, beat the ground with her fists. Tomás tore at his own hair. Bríd and Séamus just stood there, barefoot, with the smoke billowing past them, she clutching her shawl with one hand and holding onto her brother with the other.

Turlough threw himself at MacCurran, desperate to take out the rage he felt on someone. 'You animal! You fucking animal!' he shrieked, then smashed his fist into the other man's face, and their scuffle drew the attention of the soldiers.

'You ate her, didn't you?' Turlough roared, pushing MacCurran backward onto the ground.

'Look around you, Walsh! They'll all perish this winter anyway! All of them! And what are you going to do about it?'

The righteousness in the man's voice enraged Turlough

still more. He tried to punch him again, but he was wrestling back now.

'Some of us have to live through this!' MacCurran went on.

'You cannibal!' Turlough yelled.

Then, hoarse from this roar, he raised his fist for another blow. But a soldier on horseback cantered up behind him and swung his musket, two-handed, like a club by the barrel, sending the heavy wooden butt into the back of his head. Turlough felt his skull crack and toppled forward. The last thing he saw was Bríd holding onto Séamus the way she had in the hotel room, the two of them frozen by the horror of what was happening to their lives, watching him as he fell.

CHAPTER ELEVEN

'Walsh? Walsh!'

The insistent voice repeated itself until he grunted an acknowlegment.

'Come on, wake up! You can go.'

The room came into focus, filing cabinets with papers stacked untidily on top of them, a calendar, a notice about licensing bulls, and a young man in a blue shirt shaking him.

'How did I get here?' Turlough asked.

Fully awake he saw he was in a police station, the man had gold numbers on his lapels, and there were a couple more of them talking quietly behind him. A sergeant came into view, dark blue jacket on and looked down at him.

'You had a fair few on you alright, Mr Walsh.'

'What? I only had one drink!'

They laughed. Turlough stood up out of the wooden chair. His head hurt and when he put a hand to it he felt encrusted blood.

'I'd get that seen to if I were you,' said the sergeant.

'Really,' said Turlough, clutching at the other man's sleeve, 'what happened? I...don't remember.' He did, but he was back in the present and he could hardly tell them what he did remember.

'Well, you picked a bad choice of drinking establishments. Apparently you got into a fight with a couple of tinkers and they followed you outside. You're lucky it was a Saturday night. They only clobbered you the one time, then they were seen and ran for it.'

'So why was I brought here?'

'Ah well, you were making a disturbance the whole time and we were coming around for you anyway.'

'What? Oh, I'm sorry, I must have really gone off the deep end. Eh...are you charging me with anything?'

'No.'

They said nothing else then so he made for the sliver of daylight that was hurting his eyes.

'Come back to Westport again sometime, Mr Walsh, we're glad of the tourism, but go easy on the hard stuff!'

He nodded at the sergeant's words without turning back.

Turlough crisscrossed the town a few times in his rented car hoping to recognize the spot where the soup kitchen had been, but he couldn't find it, so he followed the signs for the Dublin road, as anxious now to get away from this whole place as he had been to come a few days before.

On the outskirts of the town the road had been straightened, leaving an arc of disused asphalt to one side. Parked all along this were caravans fitted here and there with conspicuous chrome trim. Smoke drifted up from a flue in each one.

Were these his assailants of the night before? Should he stop and ask them what had happened? He slowed the car, and across the dank weeds that separated the new and old road saw a dirty green shelter between two of the caravans, and in it a woman and some children. None of these latter-day dispossessed looked back at him, nor did the few men hanging about look familiar, so, as always when he passed one of these itinerant camps, he was relieved not to be noticed, looked away again and accelerated.

*

He brought the rental car back to the airport, turned it in, and called Nuala to come and get him, saying he had caught an earlier flight.

'My God, you look like death warmed over,' she said when he got into the passenger seat next to her.

'Well, the wine's so cheap I suppose I overdid it.'

He had brushed his hair as best he could over the cut left by the soldier's rifle, and when they got to the house he vanished into the bathroom to shower away the rest of the blood. When he came back into the bedroom Nuala was there, sitting on the bed, absently filing a nail.

'You timed this well,' she said, cocking her face around at him, 'home too late for Mass and too early for dinner.'

'Where are the kids?' he asked.

'Gearóid is off playing a match and Emily is horseriding.' She paused and swept her hands out. 'We're all alone.'

He might have been tempted if she hadn't mentioned the word 'horse' but that brought back the hungry men tearing Pendleton's horse apart, and then the sight of MacCurran running away with the little girl, and then the eviction and the soldiers' horses.

'I, em, really don't feel up to it,' he said.

She gave him a curious look, said 'Oh!' very shortly, and stalked out of the room.

What did she think? Was she suspicious of him? My God, he thought, what if she asked who won? France or Ireland? Or what the score was? He had better get downstairs and read a Sunday paper.

He dressed quickly and had just reached the head of the stairs when a new idea came to him. Why not tell her everything? For a while he stood there attempting to figure out an opening statement, the way he did for meetings, but it was impossible. She would say he had lost his mind. And she might be right.

'Turlough, MacCarthy wants you.'

It was his secretary on the intercom. He stood up, contemplated putting on his jacket, decided not to, thought about bringing pen and paper, declined to do that too, began deliberating all the things MacCarthy could want to see him for at no notice, gave that up before he reached the door of his office, and ambled down the corridor, preoccupied with the history book he had been reading the night before.

1849 was the year of William Smith O'Brien's uprising, if you could call it that, but that was still two years in the future. And before that the last rebellion had been 1798. And who exactly had that lot been rising up against? Their own middle-class had put them down, brutally. Tomás Kernen wouldn't even have been born then. Why hadn't the French done more? And why hadn't they all risen up again five years later against the Act of Union? Because they were all dead, you moron, some fifty thousand of them, flayed alive, pitch-capped, raped by the Hessians, boiled, hanged, beheaded, disembowelled, or, on the bright side, sold off as Prussian slaves or transported to Australia.

MacCarthy's door was open.

'Turlough come in, sit down!'

He was ushered in with a hearty wave and MacCarthy even went through the further ritual of standing up and closing the door himself, a rare and positive portent.

'How was Paris?' he asked, reseating himself.

'Not one of our better games,' said Turlough.

'Ah, well!' MacCarthy clapped his hands. 'You got away for the weekend anyway, got your mind off all this, and that's the main thing.'

Turlough nodded. If only the old buzzard knew what an understatement that was. There was a pause, both of them looking at each other.

'Still doing some sailing?' asked MacCarthy.

'Oh, yes. I have that half share in the J-24.'

'You see, these are all the things that are really important.' MacCarthy leaned forward to emphasize this. 'When you get to your level, or above, Turlough, it's a given that you know your job like the back of your hand, so that's what makes the difference.'

Turlough was finding it difficult to follow him. What did he mean, 'your level or above'?

'What I mean is,' he continued, outpacing his listener's deeply divided attention, 'that in order to be in a position to provide leadership, you have to have all the different aspects of your own life in order.'

They nodded at each other, then MacCarthy slowed, approaching some important point.

'This whole cost reduction exercise is a lot more than just that, you know. It's easily the most traumatic thing we've ever done here. You have no idea how impressed London is with our moves...they want to talk to you, have you tell them how to implement the same thing! How's that for praise?'

Turlough smirked involuntarily but if the other man caught it he said nothing. So this was why he was beside himself with joy! They had gotten one up on the Brits. That generation just couldn't get past the Black and Tans...the War of Independence...1922. The old history trap. But wait.... Gearóid's history book just skimmed over the famine period, but surely there was more information somehwere.... Ah, of course, the local library! Turlough nodded his head to himself at the thought.

'Now, of course, you'll have to go over and advise them once the dust settles here. But it's the results right here that impress me. And I have to tell you Turlough, I thought our staff would be making voodoo dolls of you by now, but they're not, and by God, I call that leadership ability.'

MacCarthy pounded his palm down on the desk, startling Turlough, intent now on the whereabouts of the nearest library and what time they closed on Wednesday nights.

'Thank you. I appreciate that,' said Turlough, vaguely aware that he had just been complimented.

'These things often get watered down, or even lost sight of

after the fact...'

Turlough nodded, thinking how true that was about the past.

'...but really it was visionary.'

'Visionary?' Turlough was baffled now. 'You mean me?'

MacCarthy laughed. 'Come on Walsh, there's no need to put on an act like that with me!'

Did he know? Did they all know? Turlough shook his head.

'Oh now that's just false modesty!'

'A vision? Yes, I suppose that's true.'

'And that's what this organization needs, Turlough.' MacCarthy picked up a couple of legal sized sheets of paper, stapled together. 'You know what this is?'

Turlough shook his head, entirely at a loss as to how this document might relate to events.

'It's in effect my will, at least as far as the practice is concerned. And they make me update it every two years and...'

They had discovered that he had some uncanny paranormal ability, and now they wanted to make use of it, was that it?

'...we have to look to the future.... I've named you my successor...given my age...this should be announced....'

'The future?' asked Turlough.

'Yes.' MacCarthy's face darkened. 'You hardly expect me to step down now do you? I'm in good health, looking to be here for quite a few years yet!' His voice had grown strident.

'Oh no, no, that's not what I meant!' said Turlough, alarmed.

'I certainly hope not. Nice try, Walsh, but you'll have to wait it out, and longevity runs in my family, I'll have you know.'

'No, no! What I meant about the future is that I don't in fact have any visions about the future. Only the past.'

It was out before he could stop himself. The office was deathly silent. MacCarthy stared at him. The fifteen hurlers in the black and white photo on the wall stared at him. Nobody moved until eventually both men cleared their throats at the same time.

'It's alright, Turlough, don't explain. "Genius sure to madness is close allied." Donne, or Bacon, I'm never sure. Just keep up the good, I mean excellent, work.'

Turlough stood up, nodding. MacCarthy held out a hand.

'And congratulations, you're now the heir apparent!'

They shook hands and Turlough left, bothered by his own misunderstanding, as if somehow, unknowingly, he had cast off from a last familiar pier and was being blown out to sea by an offshore breeze, away from the life he knew. His secretary reached out and handed him a yellow message slip as he passed, but he didn't bother to read it until he was seated at his desk again: 'Caitríona says she knows someone who could definitely help.'

He groaned, crumpled up the paper and flung it in his waste-basket. That's all he needed, an ex-lover's pity! Why didn't she just find herself another businessman to brighten up her monotonous life? What kind of help did she have in mind? A shrink? An astrologer? The intercom buzzed.

'Turlough, it's your daughter. She says it's an emergency.'

Emily? She never called him at work. As far as he knew she didn't even know the number.

'Put her through.'

'Turlough?'

This wasn't Emily's voice. 'Who is this?'

'It's me, Caitríona!'

He jerked back in his chair. 'What do you mean impersonating my daughter?'

There was a pause and he was sure she was laughing on the other end.

'Look,' she said, 'I realized my message was very vague and that you probably wouldn't call back.'

'No, no, I was just about to....'

'No you weren't. I'd never have heard from you again.'

'Well, you know, after Paris, I didn't think....'

'I know. I know. But listen...this person, she's a friend of a friend, is doing a PhD in history, and it's on that very period.'

He hadn't expected that. 'That's very interesting.... I was just about to thrash about in a library trying to find out more.'

'Don't!' said Caitríona.

He frowned at this command. 'Why not?'

'Instead, why don't you meet her, and see if she's heard of any of these characters. If you've never read about any of them before then you'd know,' her voice dropped, 'how they got there.'

'Okay.' She made perfect sense, even though she knew nothing about his second experience, and he had an urge to apologize for the way he had been thinking about her, but he couldn't do that, not over the phone.

'So, eh, where can I meet her?'

'I imagine she'd go for a gourmet meal. You know, living on grant-aid....'

'Verdi's? Tomorrow night?'

'I'll set it up.' Caitríona's voice trailed away, followed by an awkward pause. 'Turlough?'

'Yes?'

'Would you mind if I came too?'

'What? No, no, of course! I meant you...too.'

They hung up and he stared at the phone. Verdi's. Caitríona and her friend. Everything had its price. 'Aaaahhh!' he roared at the ceiling, in the hope of dispelling some of the conflict inside him. He stood up and stretched out his arms as the roar subsided. Why did he have to think badly of everyone, even when they were trying to help him? The door flew open and his secretary stood there.

'Are you alright?'

'Absolutely! Fine. Just thinking out loud.' He shouted the words at her and she backed away quickly, pulling the door behind her.

Caitríona and her friend arrived together, and he waved to them across the unusually crowded restaurant.

'This is Bronagh O'Herlihy,' said Caitríona, peeling off her jacket while the other two shook hands.

'How do you do, Mr Walsh,' said Bronagh, withdrawing a hand that had been both cold and limp.

She too shook off a heavy woollen jacket, revealing a ludicrously demure shirt and skirt, something a woman twenty years older might wear.

'Wine?' asked Turlough and both women nodded.

'So, you're an expert on mid-nineteenth century history, Bronagh?' he asked, pouring.

'Actually, I did my Masters on pre-Darwinian feminism, but that was too narrow to build on for this, so I had to choose a related starting point.'

Turlough poured wine for Caitríona, who stared blankly back at him, studying him, as if he were the subject of some caricature she were about to draw.

'I see,' he said, nodding to Bronagh.

'So then I, if you like, moved back and across, and what I'm working on now is the development of women's values in Victorian Ireland.'

'Ah! Fascinating.'

Reassured by the sincerity of this response, Bronagh took a sip of wine, seemed to like it, and drank half the glass.

'Did you two go to school together?' asked Turlough, thinking that was likely from their accents and not wanting to leave Caitríona out of the conversation.

'Oh no,' said Bronagh, shaking her head. 'We were just talking about that on the way in. I went to the Ursulines, Caitríona's family all went to Holy Child.'

'Bronagh,' said Caitríona, 'went to UCD with one of my sisters.'

'Oh! An excellent background.' He had no interest at all in this trivia and was glad when they were handed menus and ordered, judging that to be an appropriate end to the preamble.

'How much has Caitríona told you about my problem?' he

asked.

His erstwhile paramour placed a gentle hand on his arm. 'Just that you've come across an amazing story about the famine in Mayo, and wanted to verify a few things,' she said. They smiled at one another then, and he wanted to thank her, for everything really, but instead he turned back to Bronagh O'Herlihy.

'Yes it's, well, a sort of family legend,' he said. 'I suppose you could say it's my granduncle's legacy, and I've no idea whether there's any truth in it.'

'Most of our history is wildly distorted by myths, people bending things around emotionally,' she replied.

'Well, in this tale, there is a Colonel Jones, who was in charge of all relief works in 1846.'

'Oh well, that's true,' said Bronagh calmly. 'Yes, Colonel Harry Jones. Quite a character. Lot of friction between him and Routh and the others, because he wasn't on the commission itself and he thought he should be....'

'Routh!' said Turlough, 'He mentioned that name!'

'Who did?' asked Bronagh.

'And there was someone else, begins with a "t", Trevor, or Trifle-something....'

'Oh yes,' she said, nodding and picking up her wine again, 'you mean Trevelyan.'

Turlough looked at Caitríona, shook his head and drew his hands down along his face.

'What about Pendleton?' he asked next.

'Never heard of him. What did he do?'

'Relief. Inspecting Officer. Soup.'

'Aah! Well, if he wasn't a bigwig there's probably no record of him. There would be locally, since he was most likely Protestant.'

'Apparently he caught the fever and died.'

Bronagh shrugged at this. 'That's quite likely. The fever was actually typhus. Highly infectious. You get it from a bug in the excrement of lice, so even if you were clean yourself, just being around the great unwashed was very dangerous. A lot of these relief people picked it up. In fact, more people died of typhus than of hunger itself.'

As she droned on, deadpan, he saw once again the ruined face of Nan, and just for an instant he was back there, shovelling clumps of peat in on her.

'Was there a cure for it?' he asked.

'No, not then.'

'And the blight itself?'

'You mean is there some way to prevent that?'

'Yes.'

She twirled her empty glass and he refilled it while she answered.

'Well, I'm no biologist Mr Walsh, but I understand it was some sort of fungus, and the problem they had then, apart from never having heard of pesticides,' she tittered, 'and if they had they might well have started by using them on their hair, apart from that, they hadn't selectively bred the potato to be resistant to, well, anything.

'They were always having famines, you know,' she continued. 'The one that started in 1845 was just worse than most.'

'Right, let's talk about that then,' said Turlough. 'The potatoes failed in '45 and '46, is that right?'

'Yes, partially the first year, and totally, everywhere, the second year.'

'Then why did they have relief works in '46 to alleviate the failure in '45, and none in '47 to alleviate the one in '46?'

'That's quite complex,' she began. 'First there was a change of government, then they changed tack on the laws a few times, then the landlords didn't cooperate, well they couldn't, because the only way to pay the rates was to collect the rents, which the people couldn't pay, and the rates anyway were assessed based on the number of people in the area....'

'We're getting off the point. Why did the government do nothing?'

'Governments at that time didn't do very much other than fight wars. There was a huge underclass and no such thing as income tax.'

'And after all it was only Ireland, right?'

'Well, now you're getting into the area of myth again, Mr Walsh. If you hadn't interrupted, what I was going to say is that the answer, as far as the landlords were concerned, was to reduce the numbers of destitute in their districts, and they were right. These places were drastically overpopulated, and the only solution was, finally, to clear them out.'

'I can't believe I'm hearing this!' Turlough raised his voice, oblivious to the intimate dining taking place all around. 'That's what the Nazis did! And Stalin! How can you advocate anything like that?'

'Mr Walsh, please! Everyone is staring. The fact is, if there hadn't been a famine the same thing would have happened, just more gradually, and if it hadn't happened, we'd be a third world country today.'

Turlough folded his arms and the three of them sat in awkward silence until the main courses arrived. Nouvelle cuisine. Carefully arranged baby carrots and Chinese peas. Fillet of trout. Sprig of dill. Thin sliver of lemon. Still life on white china. Food as art. Turlough wanted to hurl it against the wall. Instead he said, 'Bon appetit', and the three of them started eating.

'Do I take it then that you're telling us that the famine was a good thing, Bronagh?' If she answered yes to this he would stab her.

'To be honest, I hadn't really given it a lot of thought, not from a moral perspective,' she replied, tempting him but not going far enough for him to act. They went on with their meals then, Turlough glowering across at Bronagh, who tried to avoid any eye contact with him. Caitríona said nothing, apparently judging the silence preferable to whatever might come up next.

'I don't understand,' he said eventually. 'I thought you were writing a whole fucking PhD on this period.'

'Turlough!' said Caitríona, glaring at him.

Bronagh was taken aback, but only for an instant. 'No,' she said, 'my thesis, and the book I'm also working on, will open in 1849, with Queen Victoria's visit. So my interest in the wretched period preceding that is only by way of contrasting it with the tremendous development that took place in the second half of the nineteenth century.'

'And what about all the people who died? Millions of them!'

She shrugged. 'We don't know exactly how many people died then....'

'You mean whether it was two, three or four MILLION!'

'Shhhh!' said Caitríona. 'Turlough, there's no need to shout!'

'Most of those emigrated,' said Bronagh, voice edgier now.

'They did in their arse!'

The history scholar shook her head emphatically, and continued in a shrill voice: 'Half of all the people born in Ireland in the last hundred and fifty years have left and died somewhere else. That's a well known statistic.'

'That's true,' added Caitríona.

'How do you know where they died?' asked Turlough, jerking his head at her, irritated by this attempt to smooth things over.

'There are seventy million of us out there,' said Bronagh, reaching for her wine glass, but it was empty.

Caitríona wrapped manicured fingers around the bottle and picked it up, but it too was empty. She cleared her throat, but Turlough ignored her.

'I'm telling you,' he said slowly, leaning forward, glaring, 'they all died. Whole villages, parishes, that starved, caught fever, or were evicted, without the money to emigrate, or the shoes to walk to the next town.' He knew by the faces of the two women that they did not believe him. 'I tell you what I'll do: you come to Mayo with me, both of you, and I'll dig up the remains of a child that died then, who's buried in an unmarked grave!'

'My God, Turlough,' said Caitríona, her own composure vanishing at this suggestion, 'this thing has really taken hold of you....'

'I don't know why you're so emotional about this, Mr Walsh. It all happened a very long time ago, and –' she paused, '– by definition, your ancestors didn't die, did they? Or mine, or Caitríona's, or we wouldn't be here, would we?'

Her words rang in his ears, over and over, and he sat back without replying, to brood on them.

Bronagh O'Herlihy banged down her fork at this last insulting behaviour. 'Yes, you just think abut that Mr Walsh,' she whined, then stood up. 'Thank you for dinner!' Her voice shook as she picked up her jacket. 'And for giving me a whole new perspective from which to view things!'

She swung around, knocking over her wine glass with her sleeve and fled, and before he could say anything Caitríona had picked up her own bag and jacket and was chasing after her.

CHAPTER TWELVE

'Do they teach you anything about the causes of the famine?' Turlough asked Emily over dinner a week later.

'My God!' said Nuala, 'Not again, Turlough.'

'No,' said Emily.

'My history book says it's because the people were entirely dependent on the potato,' said Gearóid.

'I know what your history book says!' Turlough shouted, turning on him. 'I've read the whole bloody thing! I was asking Emily to see whether the female population is likely to have any greater insight into it all a generation from now....'

'What is it? Will you tell us why you're obsessed with this one period of history?' shouted Nuala.

'Obsessed? I'm not obsessed!'

'You certainly are.'

'Don't you want me to take an interest in what they're learning at school?'

'Yes, but that's not what this is about.'

Nuala stood up, signalling an end to the meal, and both children disappeared from the room. Turlough watched his wife busying herself, her back to him, still trim enough to fit into the latest off-the-rack jeans. Was it aerobics or some manifestation of mind over matter? A triumphant combination of vanity, idleness and luxury? Poor women never kept their figures for so long. A pampered life and easy childbirths...and only two of them.

'Why are you being so secretive about this?' She asked the question without turning around, shaking her head in frustration.

He mused over an answer to this, but once again he was stumped for a credible lie. Still, at least she wasn't about to rip him open with a woolcarder. Why not just explain it to her?

'I've been having strange visions,' he began slowly, 'of things that happened then.'

'What are you talking about, Turlough?' She swung around now and folded her arms, defying him to look for any kind of sympathy.

He told her anyway, about both of his 'visions', and as he did so her haughtiness gave way first to incredulity, and then to dread, as he pressed on into what he knew she would regard as the supernatural. When he finished she went on staring at him for a long time.

'This isn't some kind of joke, is it?' she asked quietly.

'No. No, it's not.'

'And these people, the ones whose names are in those history books you've been buying, you're sure you couldn't have known about them any other way?'

'No. I mean yes, I'm sure.'

'But why you, Turlough?'

'How do you mean?'

'Why have you been haunted, or possessed, or whatever you'd call this?'

'I don't know.'

They lapsed into silence again. Evening turned to darkness and Nuala got up and went out to the hall. He heard her making a phone call but couldn't make out what she was saying. And anyway, as usual of late, he was too far lost in the labyrinth of his own thoughts to stay tuned into the real world for long.

Was he haunted? People talked about houses and cemeteries being haunted. Was there some curse on Uncle Bernie's cottage because it was built on the site of a cabin where fever victims had died? The eviction came back to him. At least he knew now why there was no house down the far end of the field any more.

Was the place haunted because it was the site of so much suffering? But that didn't explain why the ghosts of the last two remaining Kernen children had followed him to Paris. Or why his second episode had begun in Westport, forty miles away. And what about MacCurran?

He had no answer at all as to why it should be him. He didn't believe in ghosts. He scoffed openly at every kind of superstition. He was not at all convinced that an afterlife of any kind existed. But he was certain everything he had witnessed, and been a party to, had really occurred. He had no doubts at all about that.

It wasn't just the names, the corroboration he had gotten from Caitríona's odious friend, or all the reading he was doing now about that period. He had real, undeniable, heartfelt feelings for the people he had met. And that, to him, as he sat there in his dark kitchen, was all the proof he needed.

How could you feel anguish for people who weren't real? And if they were real then it was all true. And knowing it was true he ached all the more to do something for the last of the Kernens. But how could he? If he were ever somehow transported back again they might well be dead. How much longer had it taken, after what he had seen, to depopulate the whole of Erris?

He stood up, determined to go back over there again, unable to picture the landscape clearly in his mind, then or now, when he was startled by the lights coming on. It was Nuala returning.

'My God, you're so jumpy,' she said. 'I just spoke to Father O'Connell, and I arranged for you to go over and see him tomorrow night.'

'What? This isn't a religious thing!'

'Then what is it?'

He shrugged, unable to answer that.

'I'm going to get an early night,' she said, 'Are you coming?'

'I'll be up soon,' he mumbled, and heard her steps retreating back down the pine floor of the hall. He did not follow her, and wouldn't for many hours, going through the other door into their formal dining area, where the table was covered in detail maps of Erris, stacks of paperback history books for which he had scoured every bookshop in the city, and as many hardback ones from various libraries.

He sat down and flipped back through the pages of one of two notebooks he was keeping. Here he had summarized what he had read so far. Then his eyes drifted to the other one in which he had to-do lists, questions, cross-references, dates and statistics. It lay open at the page where he had drawn the Kernen family tree. Sheila Kernen had told him that she had lost four children in infancy, but he had not put in those lines. Only the five children whose names he knew were there, and sure now of what had happened, he picked up a pen and struck a line through Mick-Óg, then Nan, then Maura.

Drowning. Fever. And most horrific of all, cannibalism. His hand trembled and a lump came into his throat, but he shook it off and began reading again where he had left off: *The Great Hunger* by Cecil Woodham-Smith. The single major opus about an event of such magnitude that the volumes written about it should themselves fill whole libraries. He would straighten out that PhD O'Herlihy bitch one day. He would do something, he did not yet know what, but that might come to him when he was back over there again.

It was drizzling when he pulled into the empty churchyard, stopping the car right up against the railings that separated the parking lot from the priest's house. Turlough looked up at the stone facade, the big central oak door that was never opened, and the two smaller ones on each side, also closed and locked at this time of day, then high up above these the huge circle of segmented stained glass, whose meaning was hidden from outside, revealing itself only to those who went inside and looked back at it. Was it the resurrection or the last day?

He got out and walked up to the porch of the house, regretting the lack of an umbrella when no one answered after two rings of the bell. Had Nuala got this right? He looked at his watch again. Eight pm, as agreed. He stood back to see what lights were on when the light in the porch itself dazzled him through the door's rippled yellow glass. Then a dark shape blocked out most of it and the door swung open.

'Father O'Connell? Turlough Walsh. I believe you were expecting me?'

'Oh, yes! Come in out of the rain!'

The parish priest was a portly man, a fact not well masked by his black suit. The original shape of his face had long since given way to fattish jowls accentuated by a purplish darkening of his cheeks, as though the skin had been lightly sanded.

'An awful night out, isn't it?' he said jovially, leading the way into the first room on the right. Clearly, this was his study, or living room. It had masses of books piled on everything, and a TV in one corner that was off. There was a coal fire burning, and Father O'Connell, as if out of habit, picked up the poker and prodded it before sitting down in a dark red padded leather armchair on the far side of the cast-iron mantelpiece.

Turlough sat down in a lesser seat, still with his raincoat on and a silence ensued.

'Will you have a drink?' asked the priest.

'Oh, ah, no, better not, I'm driving.' He did not want any suspicion to arise that the descriptions he was about to give were coloured by alcohol.

'I'll have one myself if that's alright.'

'Oh of course, Father, go ahead.'

The priest reached over to the table and lifted up a mostly empty whiskey bottle, twisting off the cap and splashing some of the contents into a glass on the floor by the chair.

'Visions of some sort, your wife said?' he asked, leaning down to grasp the drink.

Turlough nodded, then, taking this as a cue to start, he related exactly what he had told Nuala. The man listened without interruption, saying nothing for the twenty minutes this took.

'Most extraordinary,' said Father O'Connell when he finished. 'And are you related to any of these people?'

'No. At least I don't think so...' Turlough shook his head. He hadn't considered that before. 'No, no, I'm sure they all either died or emigrated, Father. There's hardly anyone over there now.'

Just Cohan, who was married to the last Moran, and Morris Minor and the others. And Uncle Bernie, who was now dead.

'As I'm sure you know, Turlough,' the priest continued, 'the Church looks on all reports of supernatural goings-on with great skepticism.'

'Then you don't believe me?'

'Oh, well, I didn't say that. Can't just discount it, it's all very precise, very detailed, but we have to look for every other possible explanation.'

'Such as?'

The priest put down his drink and leaned forward.

'Tell me about your personal life,' he said.

Turlough clasped his hands together. How far should he go here? He had hoped to be the one asking most of the questions, but, he reminded himself, the Catholic Church had a long tradition of one-way communication — the other way.

'Can I tell you a few things in the strictest confidence, Father?'

'Nothing you say will go beyond these four walls.'

'Well, the second time, when I came back from Paris...these ghosts in the room...I wasn't actually alone.'

He watched the priest, who seemed to be focused on the front window, glistening with condensation where the curtains failed to meet.

'I, eh, had a friend there, a woman....'

'Aaahh!'

'She didn't see anything.'

'I take it this was not your wife?'

'No, Father.'

'Well, that sheds an entirely different light on everything.'

'It does?'

'And were you and this woman in the act of committing adultery?'

'We were, yes.'

'A prostitute?'

'Oh God, no! Just a friend I met along the way.'

'She must be very promiscuous.'

'What? No, no, I was speaking metaphorically! I mean I didn't just meet her there and then. No, no, she's not that sort....'

The priest picked up his glass and shook his head.

'Ah, don't you see, Turlough? It's all very clear now.'

'Not to me it's not!'

'Your conscience is troubling you. You knew that what you were about to do with that woman was sinful, and in some mysterious, marvellous way, you conjured up these appalling thoughts of other people's suffering to save yourself.'

'But I don't feel saved. I feel worse than ever.'

He should have brought a bottle of whiskey. Father O'Connell poured himself the last of it.

'That, I'm afraid, is because you've lost the gift of faith. But you are a Christian, a Catholic, baptized and confirmed, and God will restore this to you if you so desire.'

'Oh.'

'I see you at Mass on Sundays with your family, Turlough. You can overcome this weakness.'

His conscience? What part of the brain was that?

'You know, Father, I have to say there was absolutely no religious significance in any of these events. I mean no stigmata, or images of saints, or voices, so I'm not sure....'

'There you have it: you're not sure. You must try to become sure. Rid yourself of these doubts! Will you let me hear your confession and try to mend your ways?'

'Alright.'

Where was the harm in that? If the priest was right it might work, it might all just fade away, and he no longer felt any adulterous or other carnal inclinations, so that would be easy to agree to.

Father O'Connell went over to a sideboard and from one of its drawers took out the thin strip of cloth they wore, and a crucifix, and returned to his chair.

'Kneel down and begin,' he said.

Turlough knelt in front of the fire.

'Bless me Father for I have sinned.' He remembered the words from childhood. 'I don't know how long it is since my last confession, years anyway, and in the meantime I've, eh, told a lot of lies...I embezzled some money once...I gave misleading evidence at a trial...and I've been unfaithful to my wife.'

'How many times?'

Turlough stared at the fire.

'We've been married sixteen years Father, so I'm not sure. Maybe a dozen times.'

'And all with this same woman?'

'No! I meant with a dozen women, some of them once, others a lot, this one maybe....' He was surprised when he thought about it at how few times they had actually made love. 'Ten times, about.'

'Are there any other sins?'

What was a sin any more? Masturbation? Using contraception? Oral sex?

'I've missed Mass a few times.'

'Try not to let that happen again. Is there anything else?'

'No Father.'

The priest cleared his throat. 'Here is what I want you to do to reconcile yourself with God. Pray every night, no matter

how little. Bring up your family as good Christians. Stay away
from this adulterous woman who has caused you this
suffering. Tell her to seek help herself before it's too late. And
make a significant offering, one that represents a real sacrifice
for you, to the building of our new church. That way you'll be
helping others to adhere to the Faith while you repent.'

For the rest of the week Turlough mulled over his penance.
The prayer part was easy, since he was constantly imploring
God to look after the four remaining Kernens. Bringing up the
kids as good Christians was at least as much Nuala's
responsibility as his, but he would keep after her on that one.
Not only had his adultery come to a complete halt, but he
could not now remember when he had last made love at all, or
to which of them. And he would get around to having words
with Caitríona, eventually.

That left only the donation to the new church. He did not
view himself as a selfish person, was willing to support
worthwhile causes, and reminded himself that he was
sponsoring that idiot Mooney's attempt to demonstrate that
the Irish were a maritime super-race at the next Olympics. He
did not, however, believe that his or any other parish needed a
new church.

Still, he felt that if he didn't do this, and if Father O'Connell
had been right about his visions being brought on by guilt,
then he wouldn't really have done anything with the real sting
of penance to absolve himself and would not be able to move
on.

'Do you make any contributions to your parish?' he asked
Jim O'Brien the next Friday evening over drinks.

'Well, we do what we have to, like everyone else, I suppose,'
said O'Brien.

'So, how much would you give them in a year?'

O'Brien looked wildly from side to side at this question.

'That's a very personal question,' he replied quietly.

'No one's listening,' said Turlough.

'Even still, it's like asking someone who they voted for.'

'But you never stop telling me who to vote for, and why you're going to vote for them....'

'Yes, but if I didn't tell you I wouldn't like you asking, would I?'

The two men lapsed into silence, surrounded by the babble of a hundred conversations.

'Well, alright then,' said O'Brien. 'I've no idea what that Gordian knot of a brain of yours is driving at, but we do give regularly. Always send them cheques, by the way, so they have to go to the trouble of cashing them, then they know where the money came from, and you know they know. Besides, I wouldn't trust some of the characters I see passing the plate around on Sundays. Take that robber of a greengrocer....'

'Jim, what I asked is how much. How much do you give them?'

O'Brien's hair dislodged itself as he swigged back the remains of his drink. He put the glass down and swiped it back into place.

'Another one?' asked Turlough.

'No.' His friend looked at his watch. 'I have to go.'

Turlough grunted disapprovingly at this decision to flee rather than tell. O'Brien had taken his first step away when he stopped and glared back.

'We give them ten or twenty, every week or so,' he rasped. 'You do the fucking arithmetic and figure out how much that is.'

He turned away and pushed on forcefully through the crowds, leaving Turlough to brood on what per cent of O'Brien's income that was, and what per cent of his disposable income, and why he had been so reluctant to divulge this, and why, if the whole reason for giving the Church money was to have a clear conscience, he seemed so put out at having been called to account about it.

When he got home he called Mark Flaherty who was predictably enthusiastic about getting together next morning to step the mast on their boat, so they met at Dun Laoghaire harbour, to find it was a windless day, the water flat calm, perfect for the task. For two hours they busied themselves at this, tying up the hull next to a section of the long granite pier, spreading out the rigging, tinkering with the bottle screws and shackles, then lowering the mast with the aid of a few passersby to its vertical position and fixing it in place with its wire stays.

This done, the boom took only minutes to secure in place. There was still no wind, so they puttered out to their mooring with the boat's small engine and secured it in place, swapping it for the inflatable that would take them and their toolboxes back to shore.

The sea mist had thinned to a haze, the surface of the calm water now bright enough to dapple the white undersides of the other yachts around them, all the rigging clinking merrily, most of the fleet now back in the water, a sure sign of spring, of the promise of long summer evenings racing in the bay, of regattas up and down the coast, the best of times.

Mark Flaherty pulled at the two paddles, steering the rubber craft slowly between the moored craft, pointing them back in to the slipway. Why not ask him? He might be more forthcoming than O'Brien.

'Does Veronica drag you off to Mass on Sundays?' They were sitting facing each other, so Turlough could see the frown forming on the other man's face.

'No.'

'Oh.'

'I go if I feel like it, which is about as often as she goes herself.'

'I suppose your kids are old enough to decide all this for themselves?'

'So are yours! Which way are we going?'

'Port a bit,' said Turlough in reply. 'Okay.'

'Emmm, look,' said Flaherty, 'since you mention churches and Mass, I heard about these visions of yours....'

'What?' yelled Turlough.

'You know how Veronica and Nuala like to talk....'

'Christ almighty! I'll strangle her!'

'Turlough, I wasn't going to say anything, but you bringing up religion...I guessed that must be what was on your mind.'

'Well, no, it wasn't. I was going to ask how much you contribute to the Church.'

'I contribute fuck all to the Catholic Church, in money or in any other way.'

'But you said you go now and again.'

'So?'

'So why do you go?'

'What do you mean why do I go? I'm entitled to go! They baptized me, so now they're stuck with me! You don't have to pay to go to Mass! You pay for weddings and baptisms and funerals, for services rendered. And that's it!'

Behind the yacht clubs that fronted the harbour rose terraces of plastered three and four storey houses. They were not as old as the buildings that surrounded his office, dating only to the last century and not to the one before. They had not been built by the ascendancy that had cleared out the Kernens and a million others from the land, but by the people who had, as Bronagh O'Herlihy put it, benefited from the new economy that had grown up after that time, from the rise of the British empire under Victoria.

Aptly, they faced to the east, were huddled here on the east coast, where every day their owners could be reassured by the sight of the mailboat that plied back and forth to the 'mainland'. In that direction lay everything they craved, industry, prosperity, and above all, order. To the west, behind them, lay only a dark, frightening hinterland, stubbornly clinging to the past, but dying away nonetheless, a place whose importance in the great scheme of things had now waned, and whose people would eventually flicker out, an occasional hindrance perhaps, but really just a curiosity, pages in a book on strange customs, more reminiscent of the aborigines to be found in the furthest reaches of the empire than of its enlightened provincial participants, faces in old pictures between covers that could always be slammed shut, easily, and best, forgotten.

CHAPTER THIRTEEN

'Who else have you told?' Turlough bellowed the words across the dining room table at Nuala.

'Stop shouting! Emily has friends in the front room,' she replied, closing the door to the kitchen and folding her arms in a gesture of defence.

'I want to know who else thinks I'm a fucking basket case!'

'Just Veronica. I have to talk to someone....'

'Yes, well that's the bloody problem. So will she. You can bet she's told Philomena, who's told Larry. The whole of Dublin must know by now!'

'Oh don't blow it all up out of proportion. It's not that fascinating.'

'Jesus, couldn't you at least have kept it in until I figure out how to end it?'

'End it? Is that what you call this?' Nuala's right arm shot out and she banged it down on top of one of the books that were scattered over the maps that covered the table. 'There's no end in sight, is there?'

Turlough looked out the window. The day had continued as it had begun, cloudless and calm, and now the blue sky was still pale in the west, a few stars high up, starlings wheeling in the distance over the neighbours' rooftops.

'The truth is,' he said, 'maybe there isn't. I don't know.'

'The truth? Hahhh!' She looked up at the crystal light fittings as she shrieked this. 'You wouldn't know the truth if it fell on you!'

'Oh? And are you all that different?'

'Oh, go on, Turlough, go on the attack! That's always been your best ploy. But I'm not the one seeing banshees.'

'Alright! Alright! Look, you sent me to see a priest, and I've done everything he told me to, so maybe this thing will end now!'

'You've done everything? What did he tell you to do?'

'Ah, the usual, penance, prayer, a donation....'

'Oh, that's good. So what did you do? Bless yourself with holy water and throw a few bob in the poor box?'

'No.' He was enjoying this now. 'I wrote out a cheque for a thousand pounds and stuck it in the parish offerings slot.'

'Oh, Mother of God in heaven, tell me you're not serious.'

'I am.'

'Where do you think we're going to get that kind of money?'

Turlough shrugged. 'If they cash it quick it won't bounce.'

'No! But we won't be able to pay another bill this month, or next!'

'We'll manage.' He looked out the window again. The lawn was like a putting green from all the weedkiller, fertilizing and mowing. A triumph of state of the art chemicals.

'You know,' said Nuala, 'you're doing this to punish me. I can see that.'

'No I'm not. I'm following the cure prescribed by the authority you recommended.'

'You want to hurt me, don't you? Isn't that it?'

The argument had taken an unexpected turn. Nuala did not usually resort to self-pity at times like this. Maybe he had been unreasonable in expecting her to tell no one about it; after all, he hadn't told her not to. And he had, really, if he thought about it honestly, made his payment to the church on the way home at least partly with a view to shocking her now, and, yes – punishing her.

'Why would I want to do that?' he asked, hoping she might give something back, some little admission of her own flaws. But no.

'Why don't you answer that for me yourself?' she replied, a cold anger in her now.

'I don't know what you're getting at.'

'Don't give me that! This whole charade...,' she indicated all the papers on the table between them again, 'this pretence at being mad, or possessed, or whatever the word is, you had me going there for a while. It was really brilliant!'

He was speechless. The strains of the CD player came through from the other room, and above it the laughter of young girls, silly repetitive tittering.

'Who is she?'

At first he didn't understand his wife's question. He thought she meant who was doing the laughing. Then he realized she wasn't tuned into that at all, that this was a follow-on to the conversation they were having, and he was going to say the ghost of Bríd Kernen. And then finally he understood.

'There's no one,' he said, his voice unconvincingly weak as he grappled with all the different goings-on in his head at the same time.

'My God, you must really think I've turned into a cabbage over the years, Turlough.'

He shook his head, bared his teeth, and leaned forward, supporting himself on clenched fists that thumped noisily onto the table.

'You're barking up the wrong tree, Nuala!' he roared.

'Oh, I don't think so.'

'This is not about another woman!' Vigour returned to his voice, and the table wobbled under him as he growled out the words, but she was ready for this.

'Don't think you can intimidate me into backing away from

it this time. Whoever she is, this one's got a hold of you alright.'

'You are absolutely wrong!'

'Hah! Listen, Turlough.' Nuala's eyes danced as she gesticulated with splayed fingers. 'Don't you think that after all this time I can read you like a book? But for this I don't even have to,' she screamed, 'because you have never, not since you first found out where to put it, gone without sex for this long! So I know you must be doing it with someone else!'

Her logic was perfect. Her words were right on, or at least they had been until this last month.

'Look,' he said, straightening up, voice calmer. 'There, eh, was someone, but it's over.'

Tears welled up in Nuala's eyes.

'Who?'

'You don't know her.'

'What's her name? Tell me!'

'Caitríona.'

Nuala walked to the window and looked out.

'I'm not crying,' she said swinging back around, 'because you've been unfaithful to me. It'd be a bit late starting that now. In fact, I don't really know why I'm so upset.' Her voice spiked up in pitch on every word she emphasized. 'Well, yes, yes I do. I know that this is the end for us and I just can't handle the devious way you went about it.'

'Nuala, I'm not trying to end anything.'

'Oh, stop! It's finished for us in the bedroom, and once that's gone we're just pretending to ourselves, which is really stupid, because we never had much else, and I don't want to go on with it.'

He walked over to her.

'Get away from me,' she said, backing off. 'Stay in the spare room tonight, then get out of here and go and live with this little floozy, Kathleen, or Katerina, or whatever you call her!'

Nuala's cheeks were two streams of tears. She fumbled for the door handle, pulled the door open, vanished into the kitchen and pulled it shut again behind her so hard that it shook all the Waterford glass in the sideboard.

'Turlough, it's a Mr O'Gorman.'

'Okay.'

He pressed the button that disconnected the intercom and the other one that brought the speakerphone to life.

'Turlough Walsh here,' he said, swinging himself side-on to his desk so that he could look out the office window as he spoke.

'Ah yes, Mr Walsh, Thadeus O'Gorman here in Killala. Sorry I missed you when you came over a few weeks ago.'

'Not half as sorry as I am.'

'Oh well, I did wait for you as long as I could, but I had another appointment.'

'Yes, well, anyway, things have changed since then and I'm not sure I want to sell the property now.'

There was a pause as the Killala solicitor digested this. 'I see,' he said. 'May I ask why?'

'What do you know about my granduncle, Mr O'Gorman?'

The practice of answering one question with another was one Turlough detested. He hoped O'Gorman found it just as irritating.

'Nothing. As I told you, my client is someone else who wants to buy the place.'

'A Mr Cohan, of Moran's Bar, am I right?'

'I'm not at liberty to say.'

'Well what do you about the place itself?'

'Eh, very little.'

Once again he had paused. He must know something.

'Are there any stories about that particular house or the land it's on?'

'Well, there's the one about a Dublin man that knocked himself out there one night.'

'Very amusing. I mean older stories, going back, say, to the time of the famine.'

'There isn't a piece of land west of here that doesn't have some yarn or legend about it.'

'But this particular site....'

'I'm sure it does, Mr Walsh, but can we get back to the matter at hand? If you'll just come over here and sign these papers I'll make you a firm offer.'

'No.'

'You might never be rid of the place if you don't act now.'

Get rid of it. Was that the way to end this? He wanted to say yes, but something inside held him back. Some dread came over him so powerful that he began to shiver, his hands shaking on the armrests of his chair.

'I can't,' he said.

There was silence on the other end.

'Mr O'Gorman, are you still there?' Even his voice quivered and his face flushed hot and cold. Saliva welled up in his throat.

'Yes, yes.'

'What I mean is....' Turlough didn't know what he was going to say next until it was out. 'I want to find out how the land came into my family's possession before doing anything with it.'

'Oh, I see. Well, as I told you in my original letter, the records are very incomplete. You could say really that you own the place more by way of long-standing occupation, at least legally, though I dare say someone must have paid something for it long ago for it to be debt-free now.'

'Could you help me there?'

'How do you mean?'

Turlough wasn't sure about that himself.

'Find out how long...how long we've had it?' he suggested.

'Well, we could do a sort of ancestral search for you. County marriage records, that sort of thing. How far back do you want me to go?'

'To the famine. To the 1840s.'

'Now, that could be very time consuming. And people lived

and died back then without ever signing their names to a piece of paper. Of course this will cost you a bit....'

'Fine. Do that and get back to me.'

They both hung up and Turlough sprang up out of his chair, breathless. He pulled at his silk tie and unbuttoned his collar, but already the feeling had passed. What was happening to him? Had they been listening? He looked frantically all around the office, expecting to see Bríd and Séamus Kernen standing in a corner, but there was no one there. Still, he had to get out of here, outside into the fresh air. He grabbed his jacket and left.

It was early afternoon, the streets full of traffic, but there were never many pedestrians about in this office district, and he walked unimpeded as far as St Stephen's Green, entering the square park by its south-east corner. He had fed the ducks here as a child, had once come across a brass band playing in the ornate covered bandstand on a summer day, and remembered, long, long ago, being brought here by his parents to see people skating on the pond.

The winters never seemed to get that cold now. They were warmer, and the summers cooler, everything overcome by a cloying mediocrity, his own life included. Somehow, in the intervening years, innocence and wonder had given way to guilt and cynicism. How had it come to this? Where was he going? Having no answer to this last question he slowed down, shuffling along until he came to the humpbacked bridge over the duckpond, where he stopped and looked down at the brackish water.

Should he go back or should he go on? Would it make any difference and would anyone care? If he threw himself off and smashed his skull on the shallow bottom, who would be sorry? He would be doing Nuala and the kids a favour. She would cash in the insurance and pay off the mortgage. Gearóid had taken her side, glumly avoiding him until he left. Emily had at least cried when she saw him carrying his suitcases out to the car but cheered up when he told her she would see even more of him now.

He had been two weeks in a bed and breakfast, living on a diet that alternated between expense account meals and fast food, or just no dinner at all. He decided this would be another of those nights. He would walk to a bar where nobody knew him, drink himself senseless, and take a taxi back to his digs. He turned from the parapet, dug his hands into his trouser pockets and pondered the great selection of drinking establishments between where he was standing and the river Liffey.

Two nights later, Friday, he was surprised when Jim O'Brien invited him across the road for a drink.

'I'm sorry about quizzing you like that last time we were here,' he mumbled, unsure of himself, when they met at their usual standing space at the bar.

'Ahhh, don't mind that,' said O'Brien. 'That was ages ago.'

'Was it?'

'Turlough, look, I'm not sure how to say this, but I have to.'

He had been in dozens of bars since then, but not once had it occurred to him to come to this one, where he was sure to meet someone he knew. He wanted to drink alone and he wanted no one to know about it. He could not even remember where he had been all those Fridays.

'Go on,' he said to his friend.

'Everyone at work knows you and I are very close, so they've been coming to me, asking me about you. People are talking, Turlough. You're a partner and everyone watches you.'

'What do you mean "talking"?'

'Jesus, you come in late every morning. Sometimes you don't shave, sometimes your face is cut from shaving. You smell of drink. You spend half the day in your office with the door closed, and nobody knows what you're doing in there. You miss meetings. You don't return phone calls. Will I go on?'

'I return all my calls!'

'That's not what your secretary says.'

'What?'

'The girl's demented leaving messages for you at home. She doesn't know what to say when people are looking for you in the mornings.'

'Oh, God!' Turlough looked up and shook his head. 'I suppose I might as well tell you. I'm not living at home. Nuala and I have split up.'

'Eh...yes, well, that rumour has been going around too. Is that what it is?'

'What what is?'

'Oh, for God's sake, Turlough, you're falling apart! Is that the reason?'

'Have fallen apart. Past tense. I didn't know it was so obvious, but no, Nuala's not the reason.'

'Then what is?'

'It's eh...it's all inside my head, but it'll sort itself out.'

'Turlough, whatever it is, it won't fix itself. You won't get well without help.'

'Help? What kind of help?'

'Well, maybe a psychiatrist?'

'No. I actually thought of that, but there's no way this can be analysed. This is something that came in from outside of me. Not childhood stuff. Too sudden.'

'I don't know what to tell you then. You really need to get back on the rails soon though. There's a lot of people out to get you.'

'Get back on the rails?' Turlough felt himself growing angry. 'Get back on the fucking rails? Is that it? Don't you think I should know where the fucking train is going first? You're a religious man Jim, you give your bit to the church! How do you think God feels about us?'

'There's no need to shout.'

'Why not? Why should we all mutter away here, telling lies about each other? What do you think God will say when you finally croak?'

'Turlough you're really losing it....'

'No! No, I'm not! I never had it to lose! And neither had you! We don't have any souls, we choose not to, so we probably don't have anything to worry about...but what if...what if all that money you give them actually gets you to the front gate of heaven? Hhhmmm? What then?'

O'Brien looked at his watch. 'I really need to get going....'

'You do in your arse! God's going to have a big fat file on you, old friend, and all these stupid lies will be in it! But he might forgive all that and just ask one simple question: Tell me James O'Brien, what did you do with the life I gave you?'

Turlough raised both arms to make himself look more Godlike, but O'Brien misunderstood the gesture and stepped back, flinching, and bumped into the man behind them, sending his drink slopping onto the shirt of the next person.

'Ah for Jesus sake!' said someone.

'Sorry!' said O'Brien.

'You're going to have to tell God,' said Turlough, 'that you spent your whole life showing rich people how to pay less tax, how to keep and hoard more than they should have! And do you think that will please him?'

'You owe me a pint!' said the man whose drink had been spilled.

'He owes me a new fucking shirt!' said the other man.

'I was pushed!' said O'Brien.

'No you weren't!' shouted Turlough. 'You could have done anything you wanted with your life! You chose to live like this! Free will, remember! We all did!'

O'Brien began walking away.

'You could have lived a better life, but you didn't!' Turlough shouted after him. 'That'll be the judgment of God, and everyone else that comes after us! You're a Pharisee, O'Brien! Oh yes, but the truth will out! We won't be able to go on covering everything up after we're dead! All this idiocy will be nigh!'

'Sir,' said a young barman, reaching over and tugging

Turlough's sleeve, 'sir, I'm going to have to ask you to leave.'

'It's alright,' said a familiar female voice, 'we're just going.'

Turlough turned around to see Caitríona, her face right in front of his, smiling at him.

'Come on,' she said, linking his arm, 'let's go somewhere quiet where we can talk. This bar's too noisy.'

CHAPTER FOURTEEN

'I never knew you were so profound,' she said, laughing, when they were outside.

'Just making a spectacle of myself, I suppose,' said Turlough. 'Where did you come from?'

They were walking up the street, away from the city, toward the Grand Canal.

'I was looking for you. Maybe I'm the one making an idiot of myself?'

'There you are then, we do have something in common.'

'Turlough, you ignore all my calls. I'd almost given up on expecting to find you back there. It's been weeks since you've been in. I ask about you and I'm told you're not well....'

'Jesus! Does the whole city know everything about me?'

'No. They don't know what you're going through. It's them isn't it? The famine people that you saw in Paris?'

Turlough sighed. 'It got much worse after that,' he told her, and went on describing his second excursion into the past, finishing as they reached the canal. They turned right, continuing across the narrow street to the bank, and sat down together on a bench whose wooden planks had graffiti carved into them everywhere.

'You should have told me all this before,' she said, tucking one leg under herself and digging her fingers deep into her thick masses of hair as she propped her elbow on the back of the seat.

'Well, I really thought it was over back there in Paris. I mean, I was sure you were finished with me. And I'd rather walk away from these things than put them to the test. I'm sorry, Caitríona, when it comes to anything emotional I'm a coward.'

She reached out and touched the back of his hand. 'See! There's something else we have in common! I'm such a coward I only want to go out with married men so it'll never go anywhere.'

'Ah, well, that leaves me out now too.'

'What?'

'Nuala threw me out.'

Caitríona's eyes widened. 'For good?'

'How would I know? It's never happened before. I suppose so. I certainly don't feel inclined to try to patch things up.' He chuckled coldly. 'Funny. She became convinced I was having an affair, with you, after it ended.'

'Oh God, oh Turlough, I'm sorry.' She stared at the glistening black surface of the canal. 'Do you want me to write to her, or something? Tell her it was my fault? Oh my God, I never wanted anything like this to happen. Oh Jesus, what kind of bitch am I?'

He watched her, saw her biting her lip, fighting back tears.

'Takes two to tango,' he mumbled, but her composure was now gone. She was no longer the sassy young lady, sure she could have whatever she wanted in life. She was distraught at the consequences of what she had done. She was not a bitch at all, or a slut; he had misread her. No, that was giving himself credit for having made some attempt to understand her, which he had never done. He had simply interpreted her the way he wanted, and, for as long as she could, she had done the same.

'Is that where we went wrong?' he asked out loud. 'Making things up? Pretending things are different to what they really are?'

'What do you mean?' she asked.

'I'm not sure. I just have these strange thoughts, as if there's something horribly wrong with all this.' He waved his arms, indicating the buildings all around them. 'But then maybe it's just me.'

'Well, you do look awful,' she said. 'Come on back to the flat and I'll make you dinner.' She reached for his hand to get him to stand up.

'Emmm, no...look, I look and feel like shit. What about tomorrow night? Want to do something then?' He stood up, she following him.

'Okay.' There was apprehension in her voice, as if she only half believed him.

'I'll be there. I promise.'

'You better be. I don't take cooking lightly.'

'I'll take you out if you like.'

'No, no. I want to do this.'

'See you then.'

They parted, Caitríona returning the way they had come, Turlough watching her for a few minutes, then wandering up the canal to loop back down the next street to where his car was parked, confused, as he was most of the time now, but more so with Caitríona's sudden appearance, like a breeze from nowhere, that might just carry him to the edge of this Sargasso sea of doubt on which he saw himself becalmed.

'I can't explain it,' he said to Caitríona, sitting at the metal table in her flat, its top concealed by a white tablecloth, which, to judge from its sharp creases, she must have bought that morning. 'I'm as confused as ever, but meeting you has somehow given me the hope...that I might get through this.'

Candles. Long-stemmed glasses. She had gone all out. All the more impressive from this girl who scoffed at domestication of every kind, an artistic feminist who, if she wasn't lobotomized along the way would surely shrivel up and die in suburbia. He watched her in the kitchenette, carefully arranging the pasta and then the seafood sauce on top, hair up, pale shoulders exposed, then swinging energetically around to smile down at him as she carried the two plates in.

'So what will you do?' she asked, sitting down.

'I was hoping you might suggest something.'

They went back over all that had happened again while they ate. Turlough had brought his notebooks and paced around after dinner while she browsed through them, coiled up on her faded old sofa.

'My God!' she said shaking her head, 'You'll soon know more about the famine than anyone, including that twit Bronagh O'Herlihy!'

'I already know more than her.'

'Alright. Look, I think you know what you want to do next. I mean you're very logical....'

He nodded and sat down again on one of the chairs opposite her.

'You tell me. That's what I need, to hear it from another human being, not from my crazy self.'

Caitríona stared at the fireplace, the grate hidden by a lacquered screen. Downstairs, a door slammed, followed by silence, someone leaving from one of the other flats. She closed the notebook she had been reading and placed it on top of the other one beside her.

'You have to go back there again,' she said softly. 'There's no other way to find out what happened, and finally put a stop to this torment.'

She was right. 'But how do I do that?'

'Well, both times you were in Mayo, so I suppose you'll have to go there...and wait.'

'I know. I'm just terrified of doing it.'

'I would be too,' she replied.

'Come with me!'

The words were out before he could stop himself. Caitríona

sat there for a moment without saying anything, and he watched as she grappled with the idea. Was it an invitation to madcap romantic adventure, or the pathetic final appeal of a gibbering demoniac? Did she hear a bold proposal of cohabitation or the wild urgings of a dangerous psychotic? Whatever she thought, she shook her head slowly in reply.

'No,' she said, 'this is something you have to do yourself.' She stammered over the words and he knew that, whatever else she might feel, she too wanted above all else to avoid being drawn into some unknowable realm of dark terror and finding herself, like him, altered in some irredeemable way. After all, she had not been sought out.

There was no point prolonging the visit after that, and though she invited him to stay the night he refused and she did not press him. They kissed briefly like old friends at her door and she said she would always be there for him, that he was unlike anyone else she had ever met, that there was no one else, that she would be waiting to hear what happened, and to be careful and not let any of this harm him.

Turlough met his two children at the yacht club next day, where he had taken to buying them Sunday lunch. Emily handed him the week's mail, mostly bills which Nuala could just as easily pay herself, out of the same joint bank account into which he lodged his salary, but she was not about to let him lose sight of his financial responsibilities.

As he flicked through them a bulgy envelope caught his attention. It was postmarked 'Ballycastle, Co. Mayo', and when he tore it open two shiny door keys held together by a wire ring fell out.

'What's that?' asked Gearóid.

'An omen,' he replied.

'Have you bought a house?' asked Emily.

'No. These are the keys to Uncle Bernie's place in Mayo.'

'But you said there was nothing there,' she replied.

'I know,' said Turlough, 'I lied. And I'm sorry.'

'Then we own a cottage in the west of Ireland?' asked Gearóid. 'Cool!'

'Far out!'

'When can we go there?'

'It needs a lot of work,' he told them. Only a half-truth, but he didn't want them involved in any of this.

He stared at the keys. He had been summoned.

He checked out of his bed and breakfast next morning and called his secretary telling her he had strep throat. Then he bought a sleeping bag, camp bed, propane stove, propane light, fuel, mantles and flashlight batteries and took off for the west, stopping in Longford for lunch and buying a kettle, mug, tea, coffee, milk and toilet paper.

It was dusk when he reached Uncle Bernie's cottage, sunless, with a low grey mist over everything, the slates, stones, brambles and grass all slick from this cold watery air. He could barely make out the wall at the end of the field when he went round the back and unlocked the upper half of the door with the new keys Morris Minor had sent him. He unbolted the lower half, swung it open and walked into the gloomy dwelling.

The ancient wallpaper peeled away at its top edges, where it met a ceiling of dull paint, all cloudy patterns of mildew where it hadn't yet blistered away. Even the windowpanes had a grey film of dirt over them, every corner arched over by long defunct cobwebs. The small ceramic tiles of the fireplace were the only material in the place impervious to this decay, gleaming pale squares that surrounded a well-blackened cavity, its iron grate all but scoured clean of ash by whatever wind and rain had come down the chimney in the years since Uncle Bernie had last lived here.

It was not a one-roomed dwelling as he had earlier thought. Opposite the fireplace there was a door in the wall, and when Turlough pushed against this it opened stiffly to reveal a small bedroom, with a window in the gable wall. There was even what remained of a bed here, a dank mattress on a metal frame, and behind it a small dark crucifix nailed to the wall. He backed out of the room and pulled the door closed again.

The main room itself was no bigger than his children's bedrooms. He would sleep here, close to where he had fallen the first time, and see what came of it. He tried opening the front door, but it had long since swollen into its frame, seldom, if ever, used. That brought back a memory, of the time as a young child, thirty years earlier, when they had stopped here to visit.

They had used the back door even then, but there had been a neat gravel path leading around to it, with narrow flowerbeds of pansies and snapdragons against the house, the soil surrounded by rows of red clay bricks, stood on their ends and half-buried. He saw no sign of these as he walked back around to the car, and the overgrown privet bushes prevented him from getting close enough to kick around in the long grass.

He did not sleep at all that night, just sat on his camp bed with the propane light hissing away on the floor beside him. Once, he thought something was happening. A broken windowpane behind him rattled and there was a groaning sound from the chimney, but it was just wind, the first gust of a breeze that whipped away the mist next morning.

Turlough walked out the back with a mug of tea in his hand to see the fields lightening in the valley, but they were empty fields, and it was hard, unbearably so, to know that every one of them had supported whole families, for generations, and to know how violently it had all ended. And yet the sight was reassuring too, as though he was always meant to be looking at this, that he should stay here and not leave at all.

He drained the tea and put the mug on the windowsill, walked round the house and onto the road, immediately leaping a wall on the far side rather than following its steep descent. His shiny blue and white yachtsman's Wellingtons squelched uphill through the grass until it gave way to gorse and he picked his way through this with difficulty and out onto the heather of the higher ground beyond.

Everything had long since grown over and they had left no marker on her grave. The hill lacked any distinguishing features, and when he looked down into the valley trying to remember what he had seen the day he had buried Nan Kernen, he could find nothing in the pattern there to help him either. There were far, far fewer fields now out in the middle. Kincaid and his crew had been thorough. What had once been hundreds of tiny potato farms was now a few dozen cow pastures, mean ones at that, with tall brown weeds and dark clumps of rushes overtaking the grass in places.

Where was she? Surely he had not forgotten where he had buried her that day. He was close. If only he could recall a few landmarks that were still there, he could triangulate his way to her. The mist was entirely gone now, the breeze sending higher clouds northward across the sky, so that the rising sun lit the valley in spots, patches of brightness that also drifted north.

He followed one such movement, watching the light pass across wall, field, hedge, field, high wall...and then he saw it. 'Yes!' he shouteed, and scrambled further up. And there it was: in front of him and to the right was the roof of Uncle Bernie's cottage, and beyond it the lower wall where the Kernens' cabin had been and, in front and to the left, what had shown him he was in the right place – the old church where Lorcan MacCurran was buried.

The irony of it pummeled at him. The bones of an innocent child lay under his feet, bogwater seeping through them, a forgotten outcast, while this barbarian who had stopped at nothing to survive had his place in the parish cemetery. He cried again, as he had done the day they had brought her here, and began walking slowly back down, but this time, inside him, some resolve hardened. He would not languish in a corrupt present brought about by a cruel past, accepting the inevitability of it all. No, somehow, he would do something, he would make a difference.

Nothing happened the next two nights either, but Turlough had now spent three nights alone with his thoughts and was formulating a plan. Why depend on some idiot like O'Gorman to do the work for him? He drafted up small ads for the local newspapers, left his survival gear in the cottage, then drove back toward Dublin, stopping in Ballina to phone in similar ads to the national papers, to be placed in the personal columns, and calling his secretary to say he felt better now and would be in to work tomorrow.

Jovial as he had ever been, he was at his desk before eight, showered, shaved, in clothes fresh from the dry cleaners, hair a little longer than usual, but well groomed to sit behind his ears. There was a mountain of correspondence and even when he had trashed the various magazines, junk mail and computer printouts that were out of date he was still left, after four days' absence, with a formidable pile.

He spent the morning dictating letters, scribbling replies to subordinates on the edges of their own memos, pausing from what he was employed to do only long enough to order a series of large scale maps from the Government Stationery Office. Yes, they said, if he sent his secretary down with a cheque before five they would mail them to his Mayo address.

There was a two o'clock staff meeting, to which he arrived completely ignorant as to its purpose. He chided himself as he sat down for his lack of interest in his work over the last few weeks, or was it now months? He resolved to do better, though he was completely at a loss as to how he could do both: research in detail what had become of his ancestors in Erris during and after the famine, and maintain his position as a partner here. Maybe he should ask for a demotion?

'Alright,' said MacCarthy, 'get on with it, Terence!'

This was ominous. No introductory chitchat. No agenda. Mulholland took his place at the overhead projector and coughed. He looked haggard, as if he had been working hard on whatever was now about to be revealed. He glanced over but looked away quickly again.

'Our last attempt at cost reduction has not yielded the benefits promised,' he began. 'In fact I think it is fair to say it has gone disastrously wrong.'

Turlough looked around the two rows of faces to see who might be nodding agreement, but they were all sullenly unresponsive.

'Our best juniors,' said Mulholland, 'have either left, or we know they're looking for other jobs....'

'That doesn't make sense,' said Turlough. 'The best of them know they'll survive, unaffected. That's the beauty of it. It weeds out those who repeatedly fail their exams....'

'But everyone knows,' said O'Toole from across the table, 'that the exams are on a quota system, and sooner or later you're going to get tripped up. We've all failed one or two.'

'Not me,' said Turlough.

'Well I have,' said O'Toole.

'Then maybe you shouldn't bloody well be here!' Turlough leaned forward, gripping the table with his hands.

'Gentlemen, shut up!' said MacCarthy. 'Go on, Terence.'

'Apart from that it's proving impossible to schedule the work, and we're getting complaints from customers who don't like to see new faces all the time.'

There were murmurs of assent for this last point.

'Look,' said Turlough, 'that's a huge exaggeration. They still do business with the same partners and managers.'

'Well, Mr Walsh, that may be your opinion, and I suppose we know it is, since it's your scheme we're talking about.'

'Mine? We thrashed it out for hours, no, days, here, and you all agreed it was the way to go! Didn't we, Jim?' he asked turning to Jim O'Brien.

His old friend shook his head and looked down at the table.

'Et tu Brute,' muttered Turlough.

Finucane cleared his throat, surprising everyone. He never said much, particularly at acrimonious meetings, indeed would usually be the last person to wade into this kind of conflict.

'The fact is,' he said, blinking nervously, 'that we all chose not to allow margins to drop, which may have been a mistake if we're to grow this practice long-term, and we all went along with Turlough's proposal.'

Turlough looked wildly around, even gesticulating, but no one backed up Finucane's comment. The straw floated away.

'I always had my doubts,' said Mulholland.

'It hasn't worked, Turlough,' said MacCarthy. 'Our margins are down, we have lost a few people, and we have serious discontent at all levels.'

'But....'

'Perhaps,' said MacCarthy, raising his voice and cutting Turlough off, 'if you'd been here yourself to champion it, if you'd provided a better example to all of us, it might have gone some other way.'

'What do you mean? I have been here.'

'Hah!' MacCarthy snorted and O'Toole and Mulholland shook their heads.

Too late, far, far too late, Turlough saw what was going on. He folded his arms and turned back to Mulholland, saying nothing as the other produced a new series of foils, advocating higher fees, a reduction of clerical staff, more car pooling for site visits, and a lower subsidy for the Christmas party.

The meeting lapsed into silence then and MacCarthy looked at his watch. 'We'll take a twenty minute break, then resume. Turlough, could I see you in my office please.'

The walls glided past him until he was seated in front of MacCarthy's desk.

'I doubt that what I'm about to say will come as much of a surprise to you, although your behaviour has certainly been a shock to me.'

'You're firing me?' asked Turlough.

'Not exactly. You're being made redundant as part of this downsizing.'

'Why me? My department has always had the highest margins, and growth, in the practice.'

'Ah, don't throw numbers at me, boy!'

'Then you tell me, Mr MacCarthy, why me? Why not those two singsong assholes who went to the same school as you?'

'Oh, savour that one, Walsh! That's the last Cork joke you'll make around here!'

MacCarthy's wizened features darkened, his eyes dancing around.

'Well, with those two gobshites helping you to run the place you won't be here much longer yourself.'

'You don't know when to shut up, do you?' He was shouting now. He leapt to his feet and picked up a piece of paper that had lain face down on the desk. 'Do you see this?' he asked. Turlough shrugged. 'Six months' pay in it for you! A redundancy package you don't deserve. Wouldn't have even considered it but the other partners insisted.'

'Ah! So my demise is the result of a conspiracy!'

'Don't be so bloody righteous! You've been your own undoing. I stuck my neck out for you, put a dent in my own credibility, and with foreigners. You ungrateful pup! Just tell me this: why did you do it? Hah? It's as if promising you the top job unhinged you!'

'That had nothing to do with it.'

'Well, what was it then?'

'If I told you, you wouldn't have the faintest fucking idea what I was talking about.'

'By Jesus, you're a queer fish!'

'Tell me, MacCarthy, do you ever think about anything except money, religion, and this half-baked nationalistic politics?'

'What are you talking about?'

'You. I'm talking about you. We'll never meet again, we've worked together for years, and I still have no idea who you are, or why you're that way!'

'Get out of here, Walsh, you're full of shit!'

'No I'm not. I was, just like you, but I'm not now. Half-full maybe, but I've found some good in myself.'

'I don't have to take these insults, you know!'

'This is just the truth. You hang a photo of a hurling team on the wall and convince yourself that you're the captain of a team here, all honourable sportsmen, whereas the truth is there isn't a partner here who wouldn't stab another one in the back if it suited him. And why are we all like that? Because we know that's what it took to get this far, and if we get really good at it we'll get a shot at your job! You're a charlatan, MacCarthy, everyone working here knows it, and you know it yourself.'

'You'll take that back, Walsh!'

The little man was dancing behind his desk with rage. Then in a fit of frustration he tore the redundancy agreement in half, crumpled the pieces up and threw them in the air to flurry back down around him.

'Have it your own way then, you...alcoholic! Adulterer!'

'And have you never been unfaithful to your wife?' Turlough's own calm amazed him. For years he had feared this man, had lapped up every word he said, had squirmed at the least innuendo, had kowtowed in every possible way, and yet now here he was, the object of MacCarthy's open rage, and it had no affect on him at all.

'Go!' shrieked MacCarthy, 'before I call the police!'

He reached out a badly shaking hand for his phone and Turlough stood up and left without looking back at him.

CHAPTER FIFTEEN

Mistakenly, he went across to the bar, but it was still too early, and no one was off work yet.

'Are you going to be quiet tonight?' asked one of the barmen as he slid onto a stool. He nodded and they accepted, without further qualification, his money. By the time anyone he recognized came in he was on his fourth pint.

'Desmond, is that you?' he asked as he recognized the face amongst the younger crowd.

'Mr Walsh, is it true?' asked Desmond.

'Is what true?'

'About you being ...,' he hesitated, 'asked to leave?'

'No!' said Turlough, 'I wasn't asked to leave. I wasn't laid off and I wasn't made redundant. After sixteen years, I was just fucking fired!'

'I'm very sorry....'

'That'll tell you the kind of bastards you're working for. Will you have a drink?'

'Oh, well, I'm with some people.'

'I'll buy all of you one!'

'Emmmm, well, we're waiting for someone.'

'Who?'

'Emmm, ahh, there he is.'

Mulholland sidled through the throng, followed by O'Toole, and both ignored Turlough.

'Well, congratulations, Desmond,' said Mulholland, 'you're one of the youngest managers we've ever appointed.'

O'Toole also shook Desmond's hand.

'Christ almighty!' said Turlough, 'You didn't even wait till I cleared out my desk to carve up my department, you malicious shitheads!'

Mulholland turned slowly toward him.

'I'll take that as a compliment, coming from the evil genius himself,' he said quietly, then swung away again to meet O'Toole's smirk with one of his own.

Turlough looked into his half-empty glass, swirled the liquid around a few times, then stood up and approached the little gathering. Mulholland turned to him, about to say something, but he never did, because Turlough flung the remaining stout into his face before he got the words out. The others froze, leaving the Corkman to blink in surprise. He let out a roar and lunged, but he was far too slow, and Turlough had time to drop the empty glass and deliver a punch into his cheek that sent him staggering back to fall over the nearest table, scattering drinks and stools as he went.

Bar staff ran from everywhere, but no one tried to continue the fight, so they stood around, nonplussed, as Turlough dug his hands into his pockets and left.

Mark Flaherty and Larry Kent arrived at the yacht club at nine as they had promised, but by then Turlough was too drunk to say or do anything. With difficulty they manhandled him out again, but he flailed around in the lobby reading the names of the club's founders from the brass plaques beneath their oil portraits, calling them murdering Protestant bastards, and spitting at them, and then refused to be driven anywhere, calling his two friends a pair of apologist lackeys, and threatening them when they tried to take the car keys from him, saying as he left that he was ashamed to have had anything to do with them and that he hoped he never saw either of them again.

He slept in the back seat of his car that night and the next, sure that the company was out to repossess it, and too drunk to care where he spent the night. Then on Sunday he returned to the yacht club to meet Gearóid and Emily, only to be told that his membership privileges had been suspended, and would be reviewed at a committee meeting, and did he know he had tried to urinate on one of the paintings?

He bought his two teenage children pizza somewhere on Dun Laoghaire's main street, said goodbye and that he would call them when he was in Dublin again and to tell their mother that it was true that he really had been fired and she had better put the house on the market and left once again for the west.

For three days he stayed inside the cottage, mulling over it all again and again. The curse of the Kernens, as he called it now. Every time he visited this place something worse happened. And yet he was certain that they were completely without malice toward him, that all of the wrong was on his side.

He should call O'Gorman. Better still, why not drive to Killala and see him? It was Thursday morning and the alcohol was well out of his system, so he knew his thinking was as clear as it was going to be. He sprang up out of the camp bed and pulled on his jeans and boots, then went out the back and plunged his head into one of the barrels of rainwater.

He shook his head, blinked and looked around him. It was still the twentieth century. Was the milk still fresh enough to make a cup of tea? He went back in and picked up the carton on the mantelpiece, sniffed at it and decided it was. The kettle was just beginning to make boiling sounds when a green van pulled up outside.

A hand struggled vainly with the metal flap in the front door, now as rigid as the door itself.

'Just a minute!' shouted Turlough, and ran out the back and round the side. 'Hello,' he said, recognizing a postal van and its semi-uniformed driver, 'I'm Turlough Walsh. Are those for me?'

The postman handed him a thick bundle of envelopes. 'Well, they're all addressed to you anyhow,' he said.

'Thanks.'

'Are you living here now?'

The fellow had a passion for the obvious.

'Just getting away from it all for a while.'

'Doesn't look like it.'

'What?'

'Well, they've all found you out quick enough!' The postman chortled at his own observation, got back into his little van and drove away.

Back inside, Turlough found that the biggest of the envelopes contained the maps, and all of the others were the first replies to his advertisements. He made tea and sat down on the camp bed to read them. The first read:

Dear Sir, I don't know of any Walshs or Kernens in that part of the country, but my mother's people were Rattigans who all went to America after the famine. Do you know what happened to them?

'Bloody idiot,' he muttered to himself and tore open the next one.

Are you sure you spelt Kernen right? There are Kiernans and Kearnans and of course that fellow Kearney, who went off to Californy...

'Fucking hell!'

The next three announced that they were Walshs or Welshs from other parts of the country and would like to know what he found out. Number six read:

Cad as atá tú? Nach bhfuil sé ar eolas ag gach aon amadán go raibh an phobal go léir ag caint as Gaeilge ansin? Sé an clann Breathnach atá i gcómhair duit!

He was tempted to reply to that one. Though the people preferred to speak Irish, and would revert to it in those remote places where the empire abandoned them entirely, Daniel O'Connell had spent the generation leading up to the famine persuading Catholics to learn English so that their language would not be yet another obstacle to them gaining their rights. But why bother? He had placed the ads to get people to help him, not the other way around.

All of the letters proved irrelevant, either about people with different names, or people with the same names who lived somewhere else, or asking other questions about the famine. What kind of a country was he living in? He was just about to leave when another car pulled up. Whoever they were they made no attempt to come in so he walked around to find one of them sitting in the driver's seat of his BMW.

'Hey! What the fuck do you think you're doing!' shouted Turlough, coming up to him. A second man got out of the other car and came over.

'Mr Walsh?'

'Yes!'

'I'm afraid we've been sent to repossess this vehicle as it was leased by your company, where we understand you're no longer employed.'

'What? Get out of there, you!' He tugged at the seated man's shoulder.

'I wouldn't do that,' he said. 'Technically this is a stolen vehicle, so if you give us any trouble we'll just have to come back with the guards.'

'Now, sir, you don't want that do you?'

'Be much better if you just handed over the keys....'

Turlough took his key ring out of his pocket, twisted off the car keys and flung them on the road, then stood there and watched as the men drove away with both cars.

'Now what?' he asked himself. This first crop of replies was absolutely useless. Maybe he was wasting his time. Maybe there was no one out there who could help him discover how the Walshs had come to possess that same land from which the Kernens had been evicted. Now here he was, stranded forty miles from Killala, without a phone, and it seemed O'Gorman's efforts would be critical after all.

Where was the nearest phone? Probably Moran's Bar, two good Irish miles away. He went back inside, pulled on a sweater, closed the door and took off on foot back toward the crossroads, rehearsing what he would say when he got there, hoping that Cohan himself would be out, or still in bed, or off buying cattle, or selling them, or whatever pub farmers did at this time of year.

May. Almost June. Growth everywhere. What were those little white flowers that peeped out amongst the other weeds along the roadside? Or those blue ones? Were they bluebells? He had grown up in a city. No, even that sounded vaguely romantic. He had grown up in the grey margin they call suburbia that surrounds cities. Thus, he had neither the streetwise ways of a city kid nor the understanding of nature that country kids possessed. He had neither the wit of a Dubliner nor the quick turn of phrase of a culchy.

There were those two worlds and writers described one or the other. The country's literature did not concern itself with the halfway-house lifestyle of the middle-class, and yet, astonishingly it seemed now, this was what the rest of the people aspired to. Everyone wanted to be within that wide comfortable norm by which the everyday lives of all others could be made to look funny or tragic. Could they not see what was missing? As he strode on he realized that every book or play he had ever read or seen was about a world he did not inhabit. But then, why should even the least of wordsmiths trouble himself to describe such an artless, ignorant, self-centred, myopic, mediocre, dishonest existence?

The whitewashed walls of Moran's Bar peeped out from beyond an ash hedge, with no cars parked on the street outside. Would it even be open? He reached its double doors and pushed one of them in. There was only one other customer, one of the same men as last time, sitting in the same place underneath the window, reading the newspaper.

'Excuse me,' said Turlough, 'I wonder is there a public phone around that I could use?'

The man lowered his newspaper and raised his face. 'Oh! It's yourself,' he said. 'We were wondering would you ever pay us a visit.'

'Well, I didn't think I was welcome, having made such a fool of myself the last time.'

'Oh, well, you may be sure that's all forgotten about now.'

Turlough was sure it would never be forgotten.

'A phone?' he repeated.

'Tell me, are you settling in up there? Will you be coming here every summer? Is that it?'

How much of his life story would he have to trade for the whereabouts of a phone?

'Ah, young Mr Walsh!'

Turlough whirled around to see the burly face of Donal Cohan behind the bar.

'Oh, yes, Mr Cohan, hello again.'

'Will you have a drink?'

What should he do here? It was a bit early to start drinking, especially having eaten nothing but cheese and crackers for two days. An empty stomach had been his downfall last time. He was, however, being given an invitation back in here, an unexpectedly warm one.

'Emmm, a cup of coffee would be fantastic.'

He caught Cohan glancing quickly past him to the newspaper reader.

'Let me see if the wife has any,' said the publican, vanishing once more.

'I thought your ad was very well worded,' said the reader, face once more masked by newsprint.

'Oh, thanks. But I don't think it'll be very successful.'

'Well, that goes without saying.'

Turlough slouched onto a high stool and folded his arms. 'It does?'

'Well, if no one from around here remembers any Kernens

ever being here, then how would anyone who's not from around here know them?'

'She has no coffee,' said Cohan from behind, 'Will a cup of tea do you?'

'Eh, what? Oh, yes, thanks! That'd be great!' He swung round to Cohan, then back to the reader. 'Look,' said Turlough, 'they were evicted, see? So they must have ended up somewhere else.'

'Ah sure that's nonsense, man,' said the voice from behind the paper.

'Well where did they go then?' asked Turlough, straining to control himself with this ignoramus.

'They didn't go anywhere!' There was a rustle as he turned the page and straightened the sheets out again.

Turlough glared at him until he heard Cohan returning, turning to see him laying out a cup, saucer, spoon, bowl of sugar, miniature jug of milk, and a large steel teapot covered with a well-singed tea-cosy.

'They took your car?' asked Cohan.

'How did you know that?'

'Ah, well, not much happens that we don't know in an out of the way place like this.'

'Yes, I walked down here....'

'Sure, that thing was far too wide for these roads,' said Cohan, bringing a smile to Turlough's face for the first time in a week.

'That's one way of looking at it,' he replied.

'The poorhouse!' said the newspaper. 'If they didn't die by the side of the road, they ended up in the poorhouse in Killala.'

Turlough screwed his eyes shut and bowed his head at this remark. It was almost certainly true and yet he desperately wanted it not to be. None of the three of them spoke for a long time until at last Cohan poured the tea into the cup and said: 'Do you want to tell us what this is about? Maybe there's something we can do.'

He shook his head. No doubt O'Gorman had told Cohan

that it would be in his interest to help resolve this as then he could have the property, but he was not about to brighten up their existence with a few ghost stories.

'I really just wanted to use the phone, in fact, to call our old friend Thadeus O'Gorman,' he turned to the newspaper and raised his voice, 'in Killala.'

'Oh, by all means, come on back here and I'll get him for you myself.'

I'm sure you will, thought Turlough, following Cohan into the mostly dark-wood-stained interior of the house, what light there was in the hallway almost entirely blocked out by the two of them.

'Where's his number?' mumbled Cohan. 'Ahhh!' He began dialling. 'I hope he's not at lunch. Hello? Yes, this is Donal Cohan out in Erris for Mr O'Gorman.'

A faint female voice chattered into his ear.

'Oh my God!' said Cohan. 'When? Oh Jesus! And why was no one told?' He was shouting at this woman, who chattered on. 'The family? Arrah, what's the point now! Yes! Yes! Goodbye!' He put the handset slowly back.

'What is it?' asked Turlough.

'He's dead. Died in his sleep two nights ago. The funeral was this morning.'

Turlough covered his face with his hands.

'But sure you didn't know him at all Mr Walsh, did you?'

'No!' Turlough gasped, 'I never met him.'

They returned to the bar and Turlough sat silently for an hour drinking the tea until it was cold. Then he went outside and wandered up and down. Cohan had said O'Gorman was very old, likely to go at any time, but why now? What had he found out, or not? Or was anyone who meddled with that property in any way cursed? And to think he had almost involved Caitríona in this nightmare....

What about Cohan himself? Turlough walked back into Moran's Bar. 'Give me a pint!' he said, 'I have a few things to tell you about Uncle Bernie's acre,' and he began decribing in detail to Cohan, and Newspaper if he chose to listen, everything that had occurred since his granduncle's death.

The story seemed to go on and on, with occasional questions, and while he was recounting it the man with the waistcoat came in and took up his perch at the right hand end of the bar. Turlough was busy answering his questions when Morris Minor appeared, and he gave up and began again, the four listeners rapt as he went through it all, this time talking for over an hour without a single interruption.

'Extraordinary!' said Cohan when he finally finished with O'Gorman's death.

'Let me buy you a drink,' said Morris. 'I knew Bernard very well, you know.'

'There is a man,' said Waistcoat, 'lives the far side of the hill, who'd have known Bernard's parents.'

'My great-grandparents,' said Cohan, 'they're all buried in the same plot in Ballycastle. Now there's something! When did they stop using the small church, the one MacCurran is buried in?'

'This bit about Lorcan MacCurran being a graverobber is a bit hard to swallow,' said Newspaper. 'He was a bit of a local hero, you know. Our own Captain Midnight.'

'I didn't say graverobber,' said Turlough. 'He kidnapped the child while she was alive, killed her and ate her. He was a cannibal.'

'Merciful God! Mr Walsh, don't say such things ever happened!' said Morris.

'There are stories that were in the papers at the time about people being seen eating cadavers,' said Turlough, shrugging.

'Did you see him doing this?' asked Newspaper.

'No, but he told me he did. And I saw him eat a horse.'

'Ah well, still....'

'Anyway, forget him. Yes, Bernard's parents were Mary and Patrick Walsh. Bernard was seventy-four when he died, born in 1921, so my great-grandparents on my father's side must have been born around 1890, but that still leaves a gap of two generations or so before you get back to the time of the famine.'

'I suppose Bernard was baptized in Ballycastle,' said Cohan, 'and probably the pair of them too.'

'Brilliant!' shouted Turlough, jumping to his feet. 'Parish church records! Can somebody give me a lift down there?' Of course! He should have thought of it sooner.

'Oh, Father Luke wouldn't take too well to you showing up at this hour of the night with drink taken, Turlough,' said Cohan, head swinging pendulum-like from side to side.

'Tomorrow?'

'I'll drop by for you, about ten,' said Morris.

Father Luke's robes hung loosely from his tall gaunt frame. Turlough reckoned him not much older than himself, but there was something about those dark penetrating eyes that went back centuries. A memory of a time when the Latin rituals he practised would have set him, in the eyes of the people, closer to the world beyond the grave than theirs.

'Old baptismal records? I'm always very reticent about strangers poring over those,' he said, as the three of them stood outside the church's side entrance.

'Ah, well, I understand, but it might help me....'

'He's poor Bernie's grandnephew, Father,' said Morris.

'Who?' asked the priest.

'You remember mad Bernard Walsh, the funeral a few months back?'

'Oh yes! Unfortunate soul. Well, I suppose since you're one of our own, Turlough...Turlough? That's an unusual name. You won't find many of those in these books,' said Father Luke, leading them around to the sacristy.

'I'll come back for you about four,' said Morris. 'God bless, Father.' He screwed on his cloth cap and sloped away.

'I'd say that's a case of the kettle calling the pot black,' said the priest as they walked on.

'What?'

'Morris calling Bernard mad.'

'I'm sure you have quite a few characters in your flock, Father,' said Turlough.

'Oh don't talk to me! This whole parish is an open air asylum!'

They went in through the small arched doorway.

'How far back were you hoping to go, Turlough?' asked the priest.

'As far as the famine.'

'Ah, you won't get that far. This church was only built in the 1860s, and I don't think there are any records before that. Well, they're all on that shelf there.'

'Thanks.' Turlough put his notebook down on the small table in the centre of the room.

'I'll look in on you again when I've finished hearing confessions,' said Father Luke. 'Now you're sure you're not working for the Mormons?' Then he left, laughing, before Turlough could reply.

This task was much like searching through handwritten phone books with all the names in random order. He started by searching for Bernard's own baptismal record, which he found without much bother, since he knew the approximate date. But then the task became much harder. Neither of the parents' dates of birth were there, just their names, and there were four Patrick Walshs who might have been his great-grandfather. He would have to ask Father Luke for access to the marriage records to find out which of them had married a Mary O'Connor.

'What if she came from some other parish?' asked the priest when he returned. 'Then they would have been married there.'

'I know,' said Turlough, 'this could take a very long time, but I have to find out.' He looked at his watch. 'Could I come back and work on this during the week?'

'By all means.'

He reported his progress in Moran's Bar that evening.

'Just work your way back through the men,' said Cohan.

'The farms were never handed down through the women.'

'Aye,' said Waistcoat.

'Unless there were no sons,' added Morris.

'A widow would have to sell if she didn't have sons.'

'She might remarry,' said Newspaper.

'That never happened,' said Waistcoat. 'What man would be bothered with a woman that had been used before?'

Turlough shook his head, despairing at all the possibilities. 'I'll know every church in Mayo before I'm through,' he mused.

The bar filled up as the night wore on, mostly with older men. Some shook Turlough's hand and the general buzz of conversation was about the famine.

'I saw your ad in the paper,' said a stout ruddy-faced man in a tweed jacket, 'and if there was anything useful I could have said I'd have replied. I'm glad there's someone cares what became of his people.'

'Mr Walsh is in need of transport,' said Cohan, 'back and forth to Ballycastle.'

'For the dole is it?' asked the other man.

'That too,' said Turlough. 'I have no job and no car. My wife threw me out and she'll need all our money for the kids.'

'Be the hokey!'

'I deserved it.' Turlough raised his eyebrows, surprised by his own forthrightness with this stranger.

'Would an old bicycle be any use to you?' asked the man.

'That'd be perfect! How much?'

'Ah, don't mind that! Take a loan of it for now, and sure, you can pay me when you get back on your feet. I'll drop it off here with Donal tomorrow.'

CHAPTER SIXTEEN

More letters arrived every day the next week, none of any help, but quite a few wishing him well and asking him if he could let them know the outcome, because they thought they might have had relatives themselves who died in the famine.

He pinned up his maps against the bedroom wall, using them to plan his trips to Geesala, Bangor, Portacloy and a dozen other parishes. Ballycastle itself had yielded a long list of Walshs and these he had sorted into possible generations, all the way back to the earliest entry, a baptism in 1868.

He knew he would have had as many as thirty-two direct antecedents alive at the time of the famine, sixteen of them male, but he would follow up only the pure patriarchal line for now, the father of the father of the father, and see where that got him.

On Thursday evening he arrived home on his bicycle, whistling as he swung his leg off it, to find a small wooden table, paint peeling from its whittled legs, and a chair with a mostly intact rushwork seat by the side of the house. He felt a welling up of emotion inside himself at the idea that someone he had probably never met had donated this, exactly what he needed. People were talking about him, repeating his story. His back ached from sitting on his camp bed writing, and now he no longer had that problem.

That Saturday night Moran's was so crowded there were people standing in the street, but when Turlough wove his way to the bar Cohan, seeing him, tapped a man on the shoulder, saying: 'Here he is now! I told you that's Mr Walsh's seat,' and the man slipped away into the crowd.

'A pint, Turlough?'

'Absolutely, Donal. Where did all these people come from?'

'I thought you might be able to tell me that.'

'Mr Walsh?' Turlough felt a tapping on his shoulder.

'Yes?'

'Would you take a look at this?'

It was a woman, heavily clad, middle-aged, with a scarf tied tightly around her head. She handed him a photo, very old, brown, with the corners flaked away. In it was a family posing in front of a thatched stone hut, their features darkly shaded.

'It's, em, very old, very valuable,' said Turlough, handing it back.

'Well?' she asked.

Turlough was nonplussed.

'Would you say it's from the time of the famine?'

'Oh!' he said, 'I see! No, definitely not. I'm afraid there are no photos that go that far back. Let me see it again.'

He looked more closely at it.

'Do you know where it was taken?' he asked.

'I don't. I was hoping you might be able to tell me that too. And maybe who they are.'

'I'm sorry,' said Turlough. 'I wish I could. It's from the last century alright. All the children and the mother are barefoot. And see, the man has a clay pipe. But that's about all you could say.'

'Oh, then it is a hundred years old? An antique?' Her voice rose in excitement.

Others crowded around to see. Turlough passed it to the man next to him.

'It should be framed!' said someone.

'How much do you want for it?' asked Cohan.

'Oh, I couldn't sell it,' she said, 'but maybe you'd frame it and put it up on the wall, on loan?'

There were murmurs of assent to this idea and the photo was returned to Turlough, who handed it to Cohan. The woman disappeared only to have her place taken by another stranger, a man.

'Mr Walsh, when you're going back through the records do you ever come across any MacNamaras?' he asked.

'Yes, indeed, there seem to have been a lot of them around at one time.'

'I knew it!' said the man, pounding a fist into the other palm. 'They all went to America, you know.'

It went on all night, people coming up to him and asking him questions and then disappearing back into their own groups to discuss their own ancestors, or the famine in general.

The old picture was duly framed and hung on the wall inside the door to become a talking point itself. Two weeks later someone came in with a metal jug identical to one being held by the woman in the photo. Morris belted a six-inch nail into the wall and it was hung up also. Turlough reminded them that neither of these came from the time of the famine, but undeterred, people flocked to Moran's on Saturday nights as the summer wore on with questions, stories, more photos, tools, charts of their own family trees, a shawl, fragments of pottery, even some Confederate money sent from America.

On one such balmy night in July, Father Luke appeared in the bar.

'Ah, Turlough!' he said, ambling up to shake hands, as the people, like the Red Sea, parted for him. 'I'd heard about the great interest your research has aroused in the famine period, so I thought I'd come up and see for myself.'

'What will you have, Father?' asked Cohan, bowing over the counter.

'Oh, nothing at all, Donal.'

'Are you sure now? Maybe a drop of the good stuff? On me.'

'No, no! I really won't be staying, but tell me, where are you men headed with all this?'

Turlough and Cohan looked at each other.

'Oh, Father, I wasn't trying to make any money out of it if that's what you mean,' said Cohan.

'I know that, Donal,' said Father Luke, 'No one would accuse you of that, surely.'

'I'm so busy looking for my own answers I hadn't given that any thought,' said Turlough, 'but I think I've awoken old, old memories around here.'

'Couldn't have put it better myself,' said the priest. 'And it would be a shame if nothing were to come of it. This past couple of months the people seem more alive, more energetic, more giving....'

Turlough nodded at this. In the last two weeks he had been given a paraffin lamp, a cast-iron frying pan, a bicycle pump, and, most useful, a bookcase. He had only to mumble that he needed anything and someone in the community came up with it.

'Well, what can we do?' he asked.

'Now, don't laugh, Turlough,' said the priest, putting a hand on his shoulder. 'I know this may sound like doing hardly anything at all to a hard-nosed businessman like yourself, but what if we formed a committee, and went on from there....'

'Oh that's an excellent suggestion, Father,' said Cohan, 'and will you head it up yourself?'

'No,' said the priest. 'First of all, I know nothing about that period of history, and by all accounts Turlough has read everything there is on it. Secondly, this is not Church business, and thirdly, none of this would be going on if Turlough hadn't arrived in our midst, so it's up to him whether to do anything at all.'

'Well?' said Cohan, glaring at Turlough. 'Will you head it up then?'

Heart and mind raced. What had he set in motion here? How could they want him to help them, help them face the worst nightmare in their collective memory? What did he have to contribute? What did they expect of him?

'It would be a privilege,' he heard himself say. 'And I hope you'll join us Father, and of course you, Donal.'

The publican and priest both shook his hand.

'Let's agree to meet here, say, next Wednesday, seven pm?' asked Turlough.

'Very good,' said Father Luke, 'and if it's alright with you I'll make an announcement from the pulpit tomorrow at ten o'clock Mass.'

The three men adjourned to Turlough's cottage that Wednesday, and as the long summer evening lingered, the sky dimming imperceptibly slowly over the wild Erris hills west of them, he showed them his books, papers, maps and notebooks.

'Working along the patriarchal line,' he said, 'I'm back five generations. My great-great-grandfather was born in Glenamoy in 1866. This fellow here!' He pointed to a name on a diagram in which various other Walshs had been crossed out. 'I know that's him because no one else of that name was the right age to have married my great-grandmother.'

'You're almost there, then,' said Cohan.

'One generation away, but now I'm stuck. I just know that his parents' names were James and Eileen and that they were born in or around the end of the famine.'

'Still,' said Father Luke, 'you've narrowed it down very close. You know that your people have been here all the way back.'

'But I'm telling you,' said Turlough, slamming the book, 'this other family, the Kernens, were here right up to that time!'

'And have you found any reference to them?'

'Not one.'

'You're sure you have the spelling right?'

'Absolutely. I remember it perfectly.'

They made no reply to that, so he walked out the back with them, down to the end of the field to where the Kernens' cabin had once been and described it in detail to them.

'So you see, Father Luke, I'm haunted by these visions, experiences, whatever....'

'You're a very courageous man, Turlough, don't you see that?'

'No.'

Swifts flew by, zigzagging through the warm air, feeding on the midges that were hatching. A pair of rabbits bobbed nervously along by the far wall of the next field, stopping, starting, listening. A corncrake cried from some unseen refuge of disused meadow.

'We all have demons inside us,' said the priest, 'but few of us ever face them and...there is no better thing we can do than to make our suffering an example to others.'

'You don't think I'm just crazy?' asked Turlough, as they began walking back up the field again.

'Oh, God, no! If you were you'd be seeing moving statues of the Blessed Virgin or the like!'

That Saturday night Moran's Bar was abuzz with talk of the new committee. What were they going to do? Would volunteers be needed? What about a céilí to raise money? What was Mr Walsh planning to do with the money? Should they put up a memorial at the crossroads? Hadn't all the priests caught the fever and died too and wasn't that why the old church was abandoned?

Turlough was mulling over this last legend when a commotion began.

'I'm sorry now,' he heard Cohan saying, 'but you know I won't serve you. It only leads to trouble.'

An unwashed, wretched-looking man stood in the middle

of the bar, wringing a cloth cap in his hands. His dark hair was matted into clumps and his eyes darted from side to side with the extreme discomfort of being there at all.

'Go on then! Off with you!' said Cohan.

'I just wanted a word with the man himself,' said the unwelcome arrival, voice as rough and sullen as the rest of him.

'Bloody tinkers!' said someone.

'Thieving rogues, the lot of them!' said someone else.

'A word with who?' demanded Cohan.

'The potato famine man.'

'Yes?' asked Turlough, taking pity on the fellow. 'What can I do for you?'

'We heard about you down in Castlebar, sir,' he said. 'And we brought you something.'

Turlough held out a hand to examine whatever he had brought.

'Oh, it's outside,' said the tinker, so Turlough slid off his stool and followed him back out.

'I don't like the sound of this,' said Cohan, coming around from behind the bar to join them.

An old panel van stood in the street with the engine running. A tinker woman and two dishevelled looking children looked out the front passenger window. The back doors were open and as Turlough followed the tinker he heard a low metallic clanging and saw two other men lowering something heavy from the back of the van.

They rounded the near door and Turlough all but fainted at what they had brought. A huge dark bulbous cauldron, rusted through in places, stood in the road. The kind whalers of old had used to boil the blubber in. The kind they had left with South Sea cannibals. The kind from which the starving masses had been served stirabout!

'Will it stay in these parts if we let you have it?' he was asked by an older tinker.

'Where did you get it?' Turlough gripped the rim with both

hands and peered in. It was identical to the cauldron Pendleton had shown him in Westport, could well have been the very same one.

'Don't know,' said one of the men. 'Would you say it's the genuine article?'

'Yes!' Turlough declared. 'This was used for an outdoor soup kitchen during the famine. I'm sure of it.'

'Then you'll put it in this museum you're starting?'

He couldn't recall even answering that question before they were gone, slamming doors, and he was left standing there, alone in the street with a cauldron in which that greasy watery gruel had been boiled and served, in the twilight of their existence, to hundreds, no, thousands, of destitute people, maybe to the Kernens themselves. A museum! He smiled, then grinned broadly and clapped his hands together. Yes, a museum. They had given his committee its mission.

'Our topic this morning, listeners, is the great famine of 1845 and the years that followed, its aftermath and consequences...something we all learned about as schoolchildren, but which now appears to be the subject of renewed interest...and indeed interests with widely differing viewpoints.'

The veteran radio talk show host paused at this point in his script, slipping the sheet he had just read underneath the others.

'With me now to discuss this are our two guests, Bronagh O'Herlihy of UCD's history department, author of a forthcoming book, *Victorian Feminism in Ireland*, and the man they call Potato-famine Walsh, who is currently raising funds to establish a famine museum in the west of Mayo.'

Turlough watched as Bronagh smiled charmingly and nodded at the microphone, as if she could be seen over the radio.

'Let me start with you, Bronagh. First of all, congratulations on getting this important work published and I hope it does very well in the marketplace. Now, let me ask you, why do you see the famine as a turning point? Why is it so important in your mind?'

She focused on the microphone, joined her hands and leaned forward.

'There are two major reasons,' she began. 'First of all, the famine marks the final end of the old ways, to which so many of the peasant population had been clinging for, well, centuries. This was the moment of final realization of the folly of trying to eke out an existence from ever-shrinking little farms. That was the mainstream thinking of the populace before the famine, but it was completely shattered, and the new thinking, after the famine, was to seek out entirely new solutions. People married much later, so that there were fewer generations trying to use the land at the same time. They emigrated to Britain and America where they could participate in the industrial revolution, and of course they went about pulling themselves up by their bootstraps here at home, creating a new middle-class.'

'I see,' said the host.

'Could I comment on that?' asked Turlough.

'Please, let me finish!' said Bronagh. 'That's the first reason. The second is even more significant. The famine occurred, by coincidence, just after Queen Victoria came to power. Now, the two greatest rulers in Britain's history have both been women of course, Elizabeth I, and Victoria. Queen Victoria took the extraordinary step, in the face of all that was going on in Ireland, and against the advice of all the men around her, of making a royal visit here in 1849, which I think was a fantastic display of leadership, and which triggered the development of this middle-class, and of the new morality, and which gave us the high value we place on education to the present day, and this of course is what ultimately brought about the development of democracy and women's rights in this country.'

'Aaahhh!' said the host. 'Fascinating! Let's move on now to

hear the viewpoint of Potato-famine Walsh and then we'll take some calls from our listeners.'

'Yes,' said Turlough, 'I'd like to respond to Bronagh's remarks, with which I totally disagree....'

'Well, we'll give you a chance to do that, but first tell us about your own efforts.'

'Alright. As you said, I'm raising money to build a museum to the famine victims in Mayo.'

'I understand it was as bad there as anywhere,' said the host.

'Yes. Forty per cent of the population perished. An alomst incomprehensible human tragedy....'

'I don't know where you get those figures from,' said Bronagh.

'From a census before and after the famine. Your British friends were always counting their subjects.'

'But you say perished,' said Bronagh. 'There's no proof of that. They emigrated, as I said.'

'You and I have had this conversation before,' said Turlough.

'And your solution then was to dig up graves,' she said, 'Is that still what you propose to do?'

Turlough was taken aback. That remark could be misconstrued, could damage his cause, yet he could hardly deny it. 'So why doesn't everyone emigrate from Somalia and Ethiopia and all these other famine-stricken places today?' he asked.

'That's entirely different,' she replied, 'There's just no comparison.'

'Oh yes there is,' said Turlough. 'People who are reduced to living skeletons don't go anywhere. They can't! Your problem, Bronagh, is that you've got your head so far up Queen Victoria's arse you're blind to the truth!'

'I'm afraid we must stop here for a commercial break,' said the host. Some lights changed and he swung around to Turlough. 'Mr Walsh, if there's another outburst like that from you, I'll have you removed from the studio.'

'You ignoramus!' Bronagh hissed.

'She started it,' said Turlough. 'You heard her!' But the talk show host was tuned into another conversation with his producer through his headset, nodding away to the people beyond the glass walls until the broadcast light came back on.

'We go now,' he said, 'to a listener in Cork. Good morning madam.'

'Oh, hello,' said the caller. 'I just wanted to ask the lady who's writing the book what it is she thinks Queen Victoria did for Irish women?'

Bronagh cleared her throat. 'Well, obviously a tremendous amount. You see, we tend to look back on the Victorians as terribly stuffy, which by our standards they were, but the fact is that until that time you were either a peasant or an aristocrat, there was really nothing in between. Now, during her reign, when the middle-class came about, it could have developed in any number of ways. If we'd had a king instead of a queen, it's doubtful that there would have been any tolerance for women finding new roles for themselves.'

'Does that answer your question, madam?' asked the host.

'It does, yes.' There was hesitation in the caller's voice.

'Would you like to add anything, Mr Walsh?' asked the host.

A bone had been thrown to him. He thought frantically. 'I think Bronagh is talking garbage,' he said. 'The question is not whether we had a queen or a king, the question is where would we be if we hadn't had any help from this accursed empire!'

'Oh, wrap the green flag round me boys!' replied Bronagh. 'The Fenian movement didn't even get started until twenty years after the famine, and at no time in the nineteenth century did the people aspire to the kind of independence we have now.'

'Do you seriously believe that?' asked Turlough.

'Yes!' She banged a palm down on the tabletop, drawing

headshakes and signals from the production staff. 'Why else would everyone have voted for Parnell?'

'We have another caller. This one's for you Mr Walsh.'

A woman with a south County Dublin accent came on. 'What I'd like to ask Potato-famine Walsh,' she said, and Turlough noticed a look from Bronagh to the talk show host at the derisory name, 'is why don't we simply put all these artifacts into the National Museum in Dublin, where everyone can enjoy them?'

'First of all,' said Turlough, 'not everyone lives in Dublin. Secondly,' he paused, 'when was the last time you went to the museum?'

'Emmmm...I can't recall.'

'Yes, well then, who cares what you think?'

'Mr Walsh!' said the host. 'That was unwarranted. We apologize for that, caller.'

'Ah, I'm sure you do,' said Turlough, 'That's what you and Bronagh, and this caller here are best at, isn't it? Apologizing for everything. Sorry, sorry, sorry.'

'What is your point?' asked the host, nodding at something his producer was saying.

'My point,' said Turlough, 'is that you people insist on looking at everything to do with the past in whatever way makes you feel...feel most comfortable...and not the way it really was.'

'Aaaahh!' said the host. 'And how was it really, Mr Walsh? I understand you've actually been back there in some way!'

There were smiles all round. The trap was sprung. Turlough opened and closed his mouth a few times. Deny it, slough it off? He wouldn't do that. No more lies.

'Yes,' said Bronagh, 'I mean you have us at a disadvantage there.'

'It's not a...laughing matter,' said Turlough, fearful his voice was breaking up.

'Was this a vision you had, or did you actually participate in these events?' asked the host.

'It felt...very real.'

'The Victorians, you know,' said Bronagh, 'were great believers in paranormal events, seances, visitations....'

'I'm afraid we're running out of time folks,' said the host, evidently keen to finish on this sensational note, which would provide material for several more shows.

Turlough closed his eyes. They had made a fool of him, with half a million people listening. Cohan, Morris, all of them were gathered to hear this, his opportunity to appeal to the whole country. They should have sent Father Luke. Was he listening too? Nuala and all her friends listened to this show every weekday morning. At least now she would have no problem rounding up sympathizers. And the kids, what would they think?

He had let everyone down, had let his old conceit get in the way. He should have anticipated this, been ready with a few quick phrases. He could have done more. Then in his mind he flew back over Moran's Bar, and on up the road over Uncle Bernie's cottage, and the gorse on the hill flashed by below him, and he was at Nan's grave again.

He saw her, as he had seen her the first time, showing him the egg she had found, holding it up, trusting, a child that didn't know what betrayal was, and never would.

'I'd just like to say one more thing!' he said.

The producer nodded to the host.

'We just have a few seconds left Mr Walsh.'

'To me,' he said, voice steady, resonant, 'this whole society we have today is like a person who has been horribly abused as a child, betrayed in every possible way.'

No one moved in the studio. Neither Bronagh nor the host looked at him. He was not interrupted. He went on, slowly and calmly.

'This child, brutally beaten, grows up and unwittingly becomes just like the parent. Without knowing it, we ourselves have become as bad as our old oppressors. And I see no other possibility for healing our society than to look back and remember the past, all of it, honestly, no matter how painful, and that's all we're trying to do over there, in our own small way.'

The show's theme music came on and the three of them pulled off their headsets. Bronagh and the host shook hands. Turlough walked out without looking back at them, out of the building, past the security barrier at the main gate and on until a taxi came by. Bad use of his dole money, but he wanted to flee, and he might make an earlier train, wait somewhere far from here for the connection to Ballina. Far better to return there in disgrace, and hope that somehow, with distance, all these voices from this morning that were playing over and over again in his head would grow just a little fainter.

CHAPTER SEVENTEEN

All the way west he became more melancholy, staring out the train window as the land grew poorer, darker, and boggier, with less cattle and crops in the mean fields, more overgrown hedgerows, coarse rushes, rusted gates, and the red iron rooves of stone outhouses that had once been dwellings. The land distanced itself in every way from Dublin and all that it stood for, but Turlough couldn't even partially erase the sense of his own enormous failure.

He had not solved the puzzle of how and when that acre had come into his family. He did not know what had become of the Kernens and must assume they had perished. And though he had shown that it was possible, with painstaking effort, to discover your roots, even if you weren't descended from a tribal chieftain or the ascendancy, the task, at first liberating, had proved in the end as depressing as not knowing at all.

Ever since records began the story was one of emigration, of a continuous, uninterrupted exodus, an emptying of the land. Two, sometimes three times as many births as deaths in every parish. And still it went on, though now there were so few people living in those western counties it was just a final, meaningless trickle, draining the last of this human reservoir into the vast Irish diaspora.

The train lurched, brakes hissing, carriages clunking against the ones in front, as it slowed and finally stopped in Ballina. Morris Minor was there on the platform, waving his cap in a wide arc and jumping from foot to foot as if Turlough was returning victorious, against all odds, from The Great War, or the Crusades, or a hundred years of exile.

'You made it!' he said, falling into step beside Turlough. 'By God, you showed them, what?'

'Have you talked to the others?' He grabbed Morris Minor's arm. 'What do they think?'

'Oh, I couldn't say! I've been travelling all day. Heard it on the car radio down in Castlebar.'

They said nothing else all the way to Killala, Turlough reduced to brooding aimlessly now. Then, as they reached the traffic lights in the middle of town and he looked up to the windows where he had once seen the gold letters 'Thadeus O'Gorman, Solicitor', and saw they were no longer there, he pounded a fist onto the dashboard.

'Morris, you go on, I'm getting out!' he shouted.

'What?' asked Morris. The lights changed to green as Turlough opened the door.

'Go on! Leave me here! I'll be back tomorrow.'

He slammed the door and the car behind honked, so Morris continued on, leaving him to wander the streets of Killala.

Was this what it was like to be homeless, to have been evicted? He thought about that all the way to the small quay, with fishing boats huddled together at low tide, dark blue water in the bay beyond, where the French had arrived in 1798, the last allies that would attempt to foment rebellion by their very presence. But they had been no more than a pinch to the hide of the establishment in the east they sought to topple, and no ripple of their presence had affected the teeming communities to the west who would go on multiplying until the holocaust of fifty years later.

It was late, growing dark, the days dwindling with the end of summer. A sudden cold gust whipped at him and he turned back toward town to see the last leaves blowing from the trees and after a few paces he realized how dark it had gotten and that the road had changed, to a narrow, poorly cobbled lane.

Turlough peered ahead into the gloom and it seemed that the town of Killala itself was shape-shifting before his eyes, buildings melting away to be replaced by others, stone walls appearing alongside him where there had been none, and then the sky filled with bright winter stars. His breath came in grey puffs, short excited ones, and he quickened his pace, looking for someone, anyone, who could confirm for him what he felt sure must have happened.

But there was no one out on the streets; not even a candle flickered in any of the small windows. Should he bang on a door? Wake someone and ask them what year it was? He passed a long two storey building, and was sure he heard someone coughing, but he saw no signs of life in its dark windows, so he walked on, hoping he might see a proclamation of some kind with a date on it. He blew on his hands for warmth, then rubbed them together. It was freezing. His feet crunched on iced-over mud, snapped the silvery layers that covered the puddles and wanted to slither across the velvety white frost.

Then in the silence he heard a child crying, a painful chant that repeated itself over and over. It came from somewhere to his right, so he struck out down a side street, that gave onto a more important looking road, that led off into the distance out of town, in what direction he couldn't say. In front of him now stood an imposing building, of three or more storeys, surrounded by a high-walled courtyard.

It was from here that the crying came, stopping and starting. Two huge iron gates led into the courtyard, both of them open, leaving black arcs on the ground, as if they had been swung back just now, disturbing the frost. He walked toward them and other human sounds came across in the night from the windows of the building.

He heard coughing, moans, an occasional voice, but the words were too faint to make out. When he reached the gates he noticed tracks, sweeping away to the right and he followed them a few paces until he saw a wagon, the breath of its two horses steaming as they stood there. Three men in dark cloaks were loading objects from the ground into the the back of this rig, two of them handing them up to a third man who slid them up toward the front.

Turlough stopped, uncomprehending at first, and then a wave of nausea overcame him as he grasped what was happening. There were corpses laid out on the sparkling dirt, dark, stick-like, as if someone had spilled a box of giant matches, and the two men were prising them free, and handing them, frozen stiff, to the man in the wagon. This was Killala's poorhouse.

They could have accomplished their task entirely by starlight, but they had two oil-lamps. Turlough approached them purposefully and picked up one of the lamps.

'Don't mind me!' he announced, 'I'm looking for someone.'

The three men muttered to one another, not about to challenge someone who spoke such clear English. Turlough looked into the wagon first, but if any of these cadavers were the Kernens they were so horribly changed he did not recognize them. Then he roamed amongst the dead on the ground, emaciated, fever-wracked remains, some entirely naked, the rest partly clad in rags, all with hair that had been cut short in an attempt to fight the ever-present lice.

They all looked much alike, but he held the light over each face, hoping not to see one he knew, but not wanting to miss it if it was there. And when he did come to it, it was not the face, but something about the way her right hand lay that was familiar, the very way he had seen her asleep in the cabin after Maura had been taken.

Turlough hunkered down and held the lamp over the face of Sheila Kernen. 'Oh, merciful God, did she have to go like this?' he cried.

'Quiet there, you!' said one of the undertakers, 'or you'll have them all going.'

There were a few shouts from within the poorhouse, and when Turlough looked up he thought he saw faces pressed against the barred windows.

'Where are you taking these bodies?' he asked.

'To bury them, of course,' replied the same man.

'In the dead of night?'

'The only way these bodies will get taken out of here is frozen. You can see how they died, can't you?'

'Take this one!' said Turlough.

They looked over at him.

'We're full,' said the one on the wagon. 'We might get her tomorrow if there's a freeze.'

Turlough bent down and pried at Sheila Kernen's remains until they cracked free of the ground, then picked her up and carried her to the wagon. 'Well, leave someone else and take her!' he said angrily.

'Ah,' said the first man, 'alright then, throw her up on top.'

The wagon lumbered away out the gate to whatever paupers' grave they had prepared. Turlough was tempted to follow them, to find out where she would be buried, but instead he turned his attention to the poorhouse itself.

'Tomás!' he shouted, cupping his hands, 'Tomás Kernen!'

A babble of voices came back at him. 'Bríd! Are you in there?' he roared.

More voices responded and now the windows filled up with faces, too dark and too numerous to study. Then he heard heavy footsteps and a party of official looking men with long sticks rounded the end of the building.

'Off with you!' one of them shouted, while another threw a rock.

It missed, but the point was clear, so Turlough ran back toward the gate. They kept coming, two of them following him out onto the street, grunting the kind of wordless threats they might use on dogs, while the others manhandled the gates closed.

'Was he alone?' shouted one of the men at the gates.

'Looks like it,' said one of the pair in the street.

'Bloody animals!'

'No respect for the dead!'

'I was looking for someone,' said Turlough from a safe distance.

'Then come back in daylight!'

'Kernens! Do you know any Kernens in there?'

'Get away, man! There's two thousand dying in here, in a place meant for two hundred!'

'You've no name once you go through these gates!'

With this chilling advice, the two in the street slipped back in through the almost shut gates and helped the others to secure them. Their voices receded as they shuffled back across the yard together and the silence returned.

'Walsh? Is that you?'

Turlough swung around to see a band of men stepping out from hiding places on both sides of the road. The man who had spoken strutted out, hands on his hips, a sword at his side, a couple of pistols in his belt, wearing an outsized white shirt, an almost theatrical sight.

'Lorcan MacCurran?'

'I go mostly by the name of Captain Midnight these days,' replied MacCurran. Even his voice had taken on a new arrogance, far surpassing his previous mannerisms, but then time had passed for him too.

'Are they in there?' asked Turlough, gesturing wildly back to the poorhouse.

'Who?'

'The Kernens!'

'They might well be.'

'I'm sure that was his wife. You remember? You stole their child!'

MacCurran grasped the hilt of his sword. 'You hold your

tongue, Walsh, or I'll run you through! I was sure I'd left you
for dead back there in Glenamoy, but you're made of stronger
stuff than you pretend.'

'For God's sake, MacCurran, I just want to help these
people.'

'And what do you think we're all doing?' MacCurran took
on an exaggerated posture of indignation.

'Alright then, help me get them out of there!'

'That's impossible. And if you say the wife is dead, they
probably all are.'

'Well, can't I just look around?'

'That's not the way it works. If they were alive and you took
them out, then what would you do with them? They'd never
get back in. They'd have lost their places and they'd still be
destitute.'

'Couldn't they emigrate?'

MacCurran laughed. 'With what? Where would they go and
what would they do?' He pointed an accusing finger. 'And if I
recall, Walsh, didn't you send one of the Kernen sons to
America already, on a ship that everyone knows sank still
within sight of shore, and his poor sister praying ever since
that he'll send for her?'

'You mean Bríd?'

'Was that her name?'

The rest of the band gathered closer around, meaner
looking than the last time, down to a hard core now, perhaps
aware that their chances as marauding bandits were little
better than they had been before, and at the same time bitter at
living on while the whole world they knew was dying.
Whatever they had once been, their first words confirmed that
they were now a gang of very desperate men.

'Let's do him, Captain!' said one of them.

'There's meat on him alright,' said another.

'Ah, back off all of you!' shouted MacCurran, sliding his
sword back into its scabbard. 'We have much more important
business tonight.'

'Look,' said Turlough, 'I don't care about all your midnight antics, but is there any way, legal or not, to get my hands on the money to help them?'

'You don't have any?'

'No. A few pounds in my wallet, that's all.'

'And have you no land?'

'No.'

MacCurran stared at Turlough, sizing him up.

'I could use a fellow that's not half-starved to help out tonight, and with that accent of yours, wherever you got it, we might well put one over on his lordship's lackeys.'

'What are you up to?'

'Justice!' MacCurran cried. 'The kind we make ourselves!'

'The only kind,' said someone else.

'If I go with you,' asked Turlough, 'will you help me help the Kernens?'

'I will indeed,' MacCurran replied.

There seemed no other course but to go with Lorcan MacCurran, despicable and untrustworthy though he surely was, so he fell in beside the white-shirted Captain Midnight, who led his ragged bandits out along the main road into the dark countryside.

This was the winter of 1847-'48. That much was clear. Turlough mulled over the political situation in Ireland at that time as they walked. The revolt in France of 1848, William Smith O'Brien's subsequent farce in Ireland, and even the United Irishman newspaper were still in the future, but the movement called the 'Young Irelanders' was already afoot.

'Do you back Mitchel then?' asked Turlough.

'Whoever calls for us to rise up and stab these oppressors in the heart, that's who I'll follow!' said MacCurran. 'Land, Walsh, that's what this is about.'

'You're right there,' said Turlough dryly.

'Alright, we have to leave the road here,' said MacCurran quietly. 'Jimmy, you lads get on around the back and take care of the dogs.' The youngest looking group tumbled over the nearest wall, carrying a few pikes. 'Walsh, have you ever used one of these?' He pulled a pistol out of his belt.

'I know how,' said Turlough, taking the weapon. 'Give me some powder and shot.'

'There's none to spare,' he was told. 'What's in it is dry. It'll have to do you.'

They walked on some more.

'Who are we visiting?' asked Turlough, whispering.

'The home of Sir Clyde Montegrine.'

'Does he own the Kernens' land?'

'That, and miles more of the county.'

The left-hand side of the road now became a high wall and where it began it also led off back past grassy fields, so that they were gathered at the corner of a walled estate. The men began scaling the cut limestone and dropping to the far side. Turlough picked his way up, glad of the months of cycling and his own cooking, which had greatly reduced his intake of food.

He ran along the side wall with Captain Midnight at the head of his gang, through ornamental shrubs and cypress trees, and out onto the lawn, dotted with privet bushes shaped into Grecian vases and wedding cakes. Sir Montegrine's house came into view, not quite the pillared palace of other landlords in the east, but nonetheless an enormous Georgian mansion, far bigger than the poorhouse in Killala, with balustraded steps leading up to a panelled front door.

'Are you ready for this?' asked MacCurran.

Turlough held up the heavy pistol in reply.

The other men crouched down on the grass, or ran around the sides of the house, avoiding the squares of yellow light thrown out by the brightly lit downstairs rooms. MacCurran beckoned to Turlough and the two of them climbed the granite steps and pounded the door with its own cast-brass knocker.

There were footsteps inside, coming from further back.

'Who's there?' asked an unfriendly voice.

'I have a message for his lordship!' declared MacCurran.

There was a pause.

'Are you alone?'

'Just myself and my companion.'

'Where are your horses?'

MacCurran stared open-mouthed at the door, unable to think of a reply to that one.

'The gate was locked and there was no one there, so we had to climb your wall!' shouted Turlough. 'Nice hospitality after a three day ride from Dublin!'

They heard voices conferring quietly inside now and then the sounds of the door being unlocked. Turlough put his pistol behind his back, and MacCurran folded his arms as the door swung open to reveal two servants in uniforms and wigs.

'You have a message?' said one of them.

'This can only be told to Sir Montegrine himself,' said MacCurran.

'Then I'm afraid,' said the other servant, 'you've made a wasted journey. He's in London for the season.'

'The old bastard is never here is he?' asked Turlough.

'Seldom,' said the first servant, both of them taken by surprise as the two men pushed the door further back and walked in.

'So he won't be needing your services here, will he?' said MacCurran, drawing his sword. The two servants backed away and started shouting.

Now the whole situation became one of noisy confusion. Their yells brought forth the rest of Captain Midnight's gang, who hurled rocks through the windows from outside and streamed into the hall. This, in turn, alerted tougher looking guards from downstairs, who came up shouting and brandishing clubs, knives and a couple of blunderbusses.

The melee that followed spread into the rooms on both sides, the men bursting through the double doors, observed from above by the portraits of Sir Montegrine's forebears, simpering out from within enormous carved gilt frames, with their dogs looking balefully up at them, impatient for the artist to finish and the next hunt to begin.

Far above even these, Rococo birds of unknown species glared down their plaster beaks from where they were set into the ceiling alongside purple grapes, intertwined variegated vine leaves, and vivid, orchid-like blooms. A gun went off, its shot ricocheting loudly from the brass frame of the hanging candelabra, setting it into harmonic motion and with it all the shadows of the otherwise lifeless art.

Turlough backed into the room to his right, aiming his pistol here and there, but MacCurran's men had the upper hand from the start. Then he turned to see two men standing with their backs to the pedimented marble fireplace, above which hung a lavishly framed painting of a reclining nude woman, statuesque in a classical way, a piece of her discarded white robe covering her fleshy hips, blue ribbons trailing from thick locks of golden hair.

One of the men drew a sword, the other a pistol.

'Get out of here! We'll have none of your terror tactics!' shouted the man with the sword, but it was an empty threat and the hungry horde, some barefoot, enraged by their very surroundings, kept moving toward the stricken pair.

The swordsman slashed out across their path, as he made for the nearest of two sets of French doors that gave onto the back lawn. An engraved crystal decanter flew through the air, missing him and smashing both itself and some of the glass in the doors to shards. This was followed by Delft bowls, their basketwork sides causing them to make whirring noises, as they spun more accurately, so that he had to duck, and they too shattered noisily behind him.

'Come on Kincaid!' he yelled with an upper-class accent, reaching the doors.

Turlough whirled back to the man with the pistol. Yes, it was Kincaid. He advanced toward the little agent, his own weapon raised in front of him.

'You bastard!' Turlough shrieked. 'How many people have you been the death of this year?'

'Stay back you!' The landlord's agent aimed his pistol, hand shaking, 'Or I'll shoot!'

'Go on! But you better make it good, because it'll be the last thing you ever do!'

The rest of the mob had turned its attention to goading the swordsman, one of them taunting him now with a Chippendale chair, but he drew his blade down along the fellow's wrist, and while he recoiled, shrieking, seized the chair by a leg and struck out with it at a couple more of them, then pulled open the door and vanished into the darkness.

Turlough was about six feet from Kincaid, but either the agent's knowledge of anatomy was poor or the unrifled iron barrel of his pistol sent the bullet other than where he had intended, because when he pulled the trigger, Turlough felt only a slight pain in his left shoulder.

Kincaid staggered back with the recoil, falling over a tasselled footstool into the petit-point decorated upholstered armchair in which he must have been relaxing prior to this intrusion. Expecting no mercy, he scrambled for one of the fire-irons and lunged forward. Turlough pulled the trigger, but nothing happened.

'Cock it man!' shouted someone. He felt a blow to the side of his head from the poker, but there was little momentum behind it and, ignoring the pain, he pulled back the weapon's hammer, leaned forward and fired straight into Kincaid's skull. The little man's eyes looked up at him, then his head fell forward, and he tumbled out of the chair onto the ornately woven edging of the room's patterned rug.

There was a huge cheer at this sight, and a general ransacking began, men pulling the drawers out of the many cabinets looking for silver, flinging everything of glass and ceramic against the walls, hacking at the oil paintings with pikes, smashing the chairs to pieces and throwing these across Kincaid's body onto the fire.

Turlough walked back out into the hall, looking for MacCurran, who he found in the dining room on the far side, already wrecked and abandoned by more of his followers who were now working their way noisily through the floors above and below.

'Glass of his lordship's claret, Walsh?' asked MacCurran, sitting at the head of the table with wine bottles and stemmed glasses in front of him. Turlough sat down, weak now at the thought of what he had just done. MacCurran picked up one of the bottles, smashed the neck off against the edge of the table and poured two glasses of red wine.

'Was that Sir Montegrine who got away?' asked Turlough.

'Not at all, man! Didn't you hear what the servant said? He comes here once a year, if the weather's fine!'

'So why bother? He'll hire another agent.'

'And what's your solution, Walsh? To do nothing?'

Turlough reached for the wine, the growing blaze in the room behind reflected in the glass as he raised it.

'To all those who died this year!' he said and took a drink.

MacCurran looked at him for a few moments, frowning, as if troubled by these words, then raised his own glass.

'To all those who lived,' he replied quietly, and put the glass to his own lips.

Both men sat there for a long time then without talking, listening to the whoops of joy at this retribution, the crackling of the burning furniture, the sounds of horses galloping on the lawn outside, men shouting, their voices becoming fainter, as they ran off into the night with what loot they could carry.

CHAPTER EIGHTEEN

'Now,' said Turlough, 'you said you'd help....'

'You're fierce anxious to help these people you're not even related to, Walsh. Haven't you done enough for them? By God, you put a bullet into the agent that turned them out to die. You've avenged them, man, and many others.'

'What use is that?' asked Turlough.

'What use?' MacCurran poured himself some more wine. 'There's something very strange about you, if you can't answer that yourself!' He stood up. 'You see all this around you here?' He raised his arms, indicating the now smoking ceiling. 'All paid for with rent! I saw my own family turned out for the lack of it too. Left to die on the side of the road so that this house could be furnished the way it is, kept up by a staff of servants, and left empty!'

He threw his glass at the unused fireplace, the sound of its breaking muffled by the roar of the flames now rising through the far end of the house.

'Do you have family yourself, Lorcan?' asked Turlough, hoping to steer the conversation in a more compassionate direction.

'Not one. Sure, would I be risking life and limb leading these exploits around the countryside at night if I had? What would I do with a wife? And children?' He shook his head. 'But one day, Walsh, one day, these bastards will have to sell off their land. We'll see them all ruined. And when they do, I'll have the money to buy a plot for myself, and then I'll take a wife to keep me warm every night.'

'Then you have money?'

'Oh, I do! There's those that pay me tribute, and others we take it from!'

Turlough scoffed. 'The great revolutionary, patriotic saviour of his people, tells all.'

MacCurran rushed to the table and pounded both fists on it. 'You're a fool, Walsh! There isn't one man the length and breadth of this country that has any money that didn't make it by taking it from someone else.'

'Well, it doesn't have to be like that,' said Turlough calmly, ignoring the other's rage.

'What? How else can it be? There's only so much land to go around. Why should it all be in the hands of those that are descended from Cromwell's soldiers? It's our turn now! We'll have the upper hand again yet, you wait and see!'

His eyes would not stand still. It was as if his life depended on winning this argument. Was that it? Fear for his eternal life?

'Is that what you'll tell God when he judges you?' These were pre-Darwinian times, so surely he believed in an omnipotent deity, waiting near at hand to meet us all.

'God never laid eyes on this place!' retorted MacCurran. 'What kind of a God would have let this come to pass? I never want to meet the God that stood by while whole villages of his people were wiped out, the God that did nothing while all those that kept faith with him lost everything...this God of yours is on the side of the landlords. I hope I never lay eyes on that monster...I'll take my chances with the Devil. There might be more good in him.'

The timbers of the ceiling at the far end of the house crashed down on Kincaid's charred remains, sending up showers of red sparks. The staircase was now alight, fire spreading down from the upper two floors, and yellow flames licked their way across the varnished hall floor toward them. Turlough stood up and leaned over the table himself.

'You don't believe that!' he shouted.

'Don't I? Stay around for a while, Walsh, and I'll show you how much I don't believe it.'

'No matter what you've done, Lorcan, you can always go back. You can change. There is forgiveness....'

MacCurran recoiled at this phrase. 'Not for the things I've done!' he yelled.

'MacCurran, you're an evil person now, but you weren't always like that! Go back!'

Turlough watched him shake his head, rejecting this advice, out of hand, and it came to him that only one of them could be right. Either you were pulled along through life by unseen and mostly malevolent forces, and must reconcile yourself to what you became on the way, or you weren't, and were free to leave the path trampled ahead of you by family, society and the events of your time, and beat a new one yourself to some new destination. MacCurran believed he had been driven by the inhumanity of the famine to abandon all laws and morality and seek vengeance wherever he could, whatever the consequences, while he, Turlough, had freely given up his place in his own society and went on making ever more difficult choices in the hope of undoing what he himself had become. He had met his opposite.

'Do you smell him?' asked MacCurran.

Turlough fixed his gaze on the two fire-filled eyes across the table and now it was as if they, and not the flames behind him were the source of all this heat. He felt again an unnatural dread that rooted him to where he was, as if some truth he never wanted to face was here with him, swirling around, unseen, hidden in the thick smoke now billowing in over them. 'Smell who?' he asked.

'Kincaid!' shouted MacCurran, laughing at him. 'His flesh is roasting. You don't know the taste of human meat, do you?'

'Look,' said Turlough, reaching out to grab the other man's arms, 'whatever you've done, if you help me now, give me the money to send the Kernens on their way, it'll be proof to God almighty that you mean well!'

MacCurran jerked himself free of Turlough's grasp and struck out at him, an unexpected blow to the side of his head that sent him staggering back toward the flaming doorway.

'Just three fares to America!' Turlough screamed. 'That's all! What do I have to do to get you to part with that?'

MacCurran's nostrils flared and he tilted back his head, inhaling the hot acrid air, savouring a last whiff of what had once been the landlord's agent. 'Once you've done that, there's no going back, Walsh! Ask the others who've eaten with me!'

'Alright then,' said Turlough, voice like gravel from the smoke, grasping at last the extent and the nature of the other man's madness, 'me!' He jabbed at his chest with both hands. 'You give me the money and you can eat me!'

MacCurran's eyes met his again, wild, with bright orange pupils, his whole face drawn back, as if he too were now starving, but animal-like in his hunger.

'Done!' he proclaimed, in a voice Turlough hardly recognized. 'There's a well.' He laughed up at the ceiling, a river of flame pouring along it over him. 'A holy well, further out along this road, about a mile. Be there by dark tomorrow, and we'll have you!'

Then, in a last frenzied act he bounded onto the table, ran along its length and hurled himself through the back window. Instantly, the inrush of oxygen ignited the overheated material in the room, and Turlough backed into the flaming hall, burning both hands as he pulled open the front door and dashed down the steps onto the lawn.

The conflagration reached its height as Turlough walked toward the road, heating his back while his face froze, and he knew by a great crashing sound that the roof had fallen in. They had chosen the night well, with no chance of rain to douse the flames. He climbed the wall, dropped onto the dark road and began walking back toward Killala. People began to pass him running in the other direction, then soldiers on horses, the first in the hope of plunder, the second to prevent them.

No one accosted him, seeing that he was empty-handed. Was that all they thought about? Was that how everything was measured and judged, even back then? The law, the police, the whole structure of society just one cruel hoax to preserve the wealth in the hands of those who then possessed it?

Reminded that he was in the past, Turlough began to brood on the complicated metaphysical issue of allowing himself to be killed and devoured here. Would he also be dead in the twentieth century? On both of his previous trips, his physical condition when he awoke had mirrored what he had experienced here.

Still, there was every possibility that he would not find any of the other Kernens, and therefore would not be obliged to keep his rendezvous with the detestable, barbarous MacCurran. What drove a man so far, beyond all moral boundaries? He smiled at his own question, as if he had any right to ask it. After all, how far would he have gone to preserve himself in the same circumstances?

He thought of Tomás Kernen refusing a day's work because they still had some food. Where did courage like that come from? How did some people find the strength to avoid doing wrong, while others pursued every temptation? Why had he chosen all his life to do whatever was to his own advantage?

But then he had never met anyone like Tomás Kernen. The thought struck him with the force of MacCurran's punch. Was that the answer? Had all morality perished here in the time of the famine? Were all the good people long dead and gone, as they say? Were they literally the dead and the gone? All emigrated or perished?

Then what did that say about him? His own last few sentences on the radio interview came back to him. He had got that right, but no one would listen to the metaphor of a crackpot from Mayo, just one more character in Father Luke's outdoor asylum, a place to visit in summertime, but not one whose people should be taken too seriously. No, best to forget about him, leave him cycling harmlessly around the desolate countryside, not changing anything.

'It doesn't have to be like this!' he roared up at the stars.

The streets of Killala remained almost deserted long after the sun brightened the east side of its round tower, just a few women in black shawls and cloaks moving slowly about, and here and there a half-starved dog sniffing through the dung. Fever had taken a heavy toll here, discouraging those that remained from contact with others.

Turlough could find no one who might be able to inform him as to the workings of the poorhouse. It had been locked when he passed it again, and he had returned six more times with no change. The yard remained empty, but for the bodies that had not been taken on the wagon the night before. Would freezing actually kill the typhus germs?

Two soldiers came by on horseback, but they spurred on to avoid him, ignoring his questions. He returned once again to the iron gates. Now he was not alone. A crowd of people had gathered there, as wretched as any he had yet seen.

'Are you trying to get in?' he asked, but they were all too far gone to answer, in acute pain, some begging from him with gangrenous hands. They were joined by others, and, while the gate remained closed, the crowd grew to a hundred or more. Turlough, exasperated, pushed through to stand at the bars, and wait.

Finally, with the sun halfway across the southern sky, an official looking person came shuffling across the yard, followed by rougher looking men, carrying sticks, an unnecessary precaution in the face of these waifs. Arriving at the gates, the man inside shook his head, then made a gesture as if shooing the crowd away.

'The outdoor relief is finished!' he said. 'And there's no room in here! Go on someplace else!'

If any of the hungry heard and understood this, they ignored it, surging forward around Turlough to push their hands in through the bars and howl.

'There's nothing here for you!' shouted the man. 'There wasn't yesterday, there isn't today, and there won't be tomorrow!' He turned and began walking away.

'Sir!' shouted Turlough, 'I'm looking for some people that are in there!'

The man turned back, peering out from under his three-cornered hat to see who had said this.

'I was here last night!'

'Aye, that's him!' said one of the guards, pointing with his stick. 'Making an awful commotion so he was!'

'What is it you want?' asked the official.

'I'm looking for a man and his two children, by the name of Kernen.'

'Well, my good fellow, I'd look them up in our record books, but we're so overcrowded the chances are they're not listed.'

'Couldn't you let me in to find them?'

'That's not allowed.'

'Why not?'

'Because if it was we'd lose what little control we have. Every scrounger and riff-raff in Mayo would be in here! Every union's as bad as this one. Just look around you!' He began walking away again. Turlough's mind raced. Half the day, a short winter day, was gone.

'I'm a works inspector, working for Colonel Jones!'

The official was arrested by this remark and came right back up to the gate. 'That's all been closed down this long time,' he said. 'Will the Relief Committee be starting any new works?'

His question caught everyone's attention. The starving crowd hushed themselves, and the guards sauntered forward to hear Turlough's response. He could say anything he wanted here, whatever would get them to open the gates, but he could not bring himself to inflict one more lie on them all.

'I'm afraid not,' he said. 'England has turned its back on us.' He could have told them more, that there would be blight again next year, that Trevelyan and his 'leave everything to natural causes' had the upper hand now, and would soon be knighted anyway for all he had done, and would grind away at all attempts to increase aid. He could tell them that there would be a foolish rebellion that would harden attitudes still further against Ireland. He could tell them that before it was over, half the population of Mayo, at least, would be dead. Instead he left it at that one short, bitter, true remark.

'Then what brings you here sir?'

'Just to help these people. They're old friends.'

The official pondered this for a moment, then signalled to his men, who came forward and unlocked the gate, opening it just wide enough and long enough for Turlough himself to slip through. 'I'm afraid,' he said, leading the way toward the main building, 'you'll just have to go through the place and look for them. I hope you have the stomach for it.'

He had hoped it would be dreamlike, not fully real, like so much of his life up to now. If he could withhold real emotional contact from those closest to him, then surely he could view these spectres as though they were no more than scenes in a documentary, pass them by, unaffected, and forget them.

But it was not like that. Every dying face in every overcrowded room he walked through reached out to him, penetrating the very space where memory and feeling met, chiselling themselves into his consciousness forever, and only the urgency of his search made his legs pull him along past more and more of them.

The stench too clung to him, inescapable, a mind-dulling mixture of excrement and putrefaction, proof beyond words and images that he was in the very midst of the immolation of a whole people, experiencing an atrocity that would shape the destiny of all who survived it, leaving them scarred, to the point of psychic paralysis, by the immeasurable shame of what they had seen and done, and not seen and not done, in these times.

The low sun beamed heartlessly in the windows, providing no warmth, just unwelcome, painful light, against which most were powerless to squint or raise a shading hand, only sitting or lying there, enduring this bright picture of suffering all around them.

And these, Turlough reminded himself, were the lucky ones, given food and shelter. But to look at them was almost to agree with Trevelyan, for this legislated charity would not save them, would only prolong their sentence on this earth. Those few who might emerge with some semblance of their health in the spring would suffer the same nightmare again. They would go and plant potatoes and again their crop would be totally blighted.

Even if he could have held it all at arm's length, it was apocalyptic, beyond all rationalization. Not even the coldest application of logic could ever explain it. He was glad of the tears that streamed down, glad because they blurred his view, the only respite available to him. He stumbled through yet another room of the half-dead, wiped his eyes, focused one more time, and saw him!

'Tomás! Is that you?' He rushed over to the man, sitting on the edge of a bed on which another skeletal form huddled behind him, and the once keen eyes of what was left of Tomás Kernen turned slowly up to him.

Turlough knelt down in front of him. 'It's me, Walsh!' he cried, 'I've come for all of you! I have a way to get you out of here!'

There was a glimmer of recognition and Turlough felt a bony hand seize his wrist. 'Did they bury her yet?' asked Tomás Kernen.

'Sheila?'

Tomás nodded.

'Yes! Last night. I was there.'

'I thought...I heard you.' There was no strength in his voice, a feeble monotone. He would never be able for the journey to America. He couldn't walk and Turlough would not be there to carry him. He was probably too far gone to ever recover now.

'Where's Bríd? And Séamus?'

'Will you look for them? Take them away!' Tomás's grip tightened, and his eyes fixed themselves on Turlough.

The other two were not in the room, not there in the mosaic of ravenous faces.

'Where are they?' asked Turlough again.

'They took them,' said Tomás. 'The other place.'

Turlough began to panic. Where would they be? After all this he had found only the father, too weak to be helped. The day was passing. MacCurran was an outlaw who would not risk waiting around if they didn't show, and so unstable it would be impossible to make another deal with him, if the encounter did not prove fatal anyway. s'What other place?'

Tomás Kernen's eyes looked out from behind a mask of exhaustion and despair. 'Did they bury her right?' he asked again.

'Yes! Oh, yes, Tomás!' Turlough sobbed through the words, then embraced the man, as tightly as he dared without hurting him. 'I'll find them,' he said, standing up. 'They'll make it!' There was the faintest nod by way of reply. 'I have to go, now, Tomás...'

He left, ignoring everything around him now, and returned to the ground floor, then out into a small courtyard where he found the same official again.

'What other place have they taken the children to?' he asked.

'Oh! Ah, yes...Under the new laws we're only supposed to take in able-bodied men here...'

Turlough shook his head at this statement after what he had seen.

'...and what with the crowding, we've got an auxiliary workhouse down toward the harbour. A two storey building on the right. You can't miss it.'

Turlough nodded, remembering that he had passed the place the previous night. He fled, running through the town, the day already turning to dusk, and arrived breathless. This place was more disorganized, with people hanging around everywhere, but still there were guards at the door of the building itself.

He ignored everyone, cupped his hands and shouted up to the windows: 'Bríd! Bríd Kernen! Are you there? Bríd! It's me, Walsh!'

Strong arms seized him, but he went on shouting. 'Séamus! Séamus Kernen!'

The windows filled up with curious faces, the same haggard, dull-skinned, lice-ridden ones as before, but with far more women and children. And then he saw her! She smiled and waved a thin white hand.

'Bríd! Get Séamus and come down! Hurry!'

'If they leave they won't get back in,' said one of those holding Turlough.

'They won't have to,' he said, 'I'm taking them away from here.'

They loosened their hold on him and he stood there, for what seemed like forever, and then Bríd appeared, with Séamus by the hand. Though thin, they were in far better shape than their father, and he knew that both parents had sacrificed everything to keep them going.

Bríd wore the same dress he had first seen her in, now a shapeless grey ragged smock, and she still had her shawl. She had on a pair of worn out boots, of which she was surely not the first owner. Séamus was barefoot and entirely in rags, but he did not look sick. Turlough hugged the two of them and held Bríd there, crying into his chest, heedless of her lank, infested hair, arms around her, warming her bony frame as it shook with joy at this unexpected salvation.

'We have to go,' he said, turning to pick the boy up in his arms and leading Bríd out into the darkening street.

They knew their mother was gone.

'Is Dad going to die?' asked Bríd as they walked past the poorhouse.

'I'm afraid so. But he wants you to go, now, away from here, to America! He told me.'

He put Séamus down and the three of them stood outside the gates for a few moments, while he took off his socks so that the boy could use them as footcloths, then they hurried on along the cold road, Turlough making Bríd recite as they went the names of all the towns he could think of between there and Dublin.

He told them he had arranged for enough money and more to get them to America.

'Use some of it to buy shoes for both of you as soon as you can, but keep the rest of it hidden. When you get to Dublin make for Kingstown right away and buy tickets on the ship to Liverpool. Don't tell anyone where you're headed. Don't buy tickets on any other ship out of an Irish port.'

'How will we find Mick-Óg?' she asked.

They had reached the charred ruin of Sir Montegrine's house, smoke still streaming up from within the gutted building. Black, misshapen funeral pyre to a landlord's agent. In a way MacCurran was right. Those who owned the country would never let go until it was taken from them. Greed was truly the most persistent of all human traits.

What should he tell her? Did she need to believe that Mick-Óg was over there, ready to wave to her from the pier? Would the promise of seeing her older brother again be the only thing that would keep her going on the long trek across the desolate midlands? Did he have to tell one more lie?

'You may never find him,' he replied instead. 'His ship might have sunk on the way, or, if he did get there, he could be anywhere. The country is huge, Bríd. Imagine if you could fit the whole of Ireland into just one parish, that's how big it is by comparison.'

Séamus looked up at his sister. 'You won't let me get lost, will you?' he asked.

'No, no!' she said, bending down to him. 'I'll look after you the whole way. I'd never leave you alone. That would be worse than anything....'

They both looked back along the road toward Killala, realizing they had left their father there to die alone, but he must have implored them before they were split up to try to get away, because they said nothing and walked on again, hand in hand.

'And get a ship to the United States, not Canada, not British North America. The Saint Lawrence is frozen now anyway.' He did not want them to go through all that was ahead of them just to become statistics of the fever on Grosse Isle, or in Montreal itself. What else could he tell her? 'If you can, work your way right across the country to San Francisco, but at least get away from the port towns.' In the west she would find it easier to climb the social ladder, and Séamus would be less likely to be slaughtered in the Civil War.

They came to a place where the brambles had been adorned with scraps of clothing, pieces of hair tied to stems with ribbon, Saint Brigid's crosses piled on the ground, the greenness of the rushes telling which were new, and up close they saw amongst these offerings that in a cleft between two granite boulders an underground stream gurgled by.

'This must be it.' Turlough looked all around into the gloom but saw no one. He scrambled up over the rocks, the start of a low hill of similar granite debris, coated in wet turf and bog grasses. s'Wait here!' he told them, then climbed further up. 'MacCurran!' There was no reply. The silence of the winter dusk unnerved him. Was he too late or had he been deceived? Had Captain Midnight been arrested?

'Up here!'

Turlough heard the voice from above and pushed himself hurriedly up with deep knee-bending strides. MacCurran, white shirt making him look all the darker himself, stood with his back to a dolmen on the hilltop, stars in the patch of sky that showed through the three upright rocks that supported its huge portal slab.

'Have you the money?'

'Have you the Kernens?'

'Yes.'

'All three of them?'

'No. Just the two children. The father is dying.'

'Are you sure about that?'

'I am.'

'Will he hang on much longer?'

'Don't make light of this, MacCurran!'

'Oh, I'm not. Alright then, here, here's two fares to America. More than enough.' He held up a small bag of coins.

'Three! We agreed three fares!'

'There's only the two of them.' He walked forward to Turlough and leered at him, calm now, but no doubt capable of going berserk and ruining anything if he were provoked. He shook his head slowly and his face lost even that mockery of humour.

'I tell you what, Walsh,' he said in a low voice, 'I won't ever have it said of me that I treated any of my own worse than a landlord!' He reached into his shirt and produced a handful of gold sovereigns. 'Give them this then! And mind you tell them to hide it well!'

Turlough took the little bag and the pile of heavy coins and began back down the hill.

'Tell them,' shouted MacCurran, 'that I paid for everything! Not Captain Midnight, mind, but Lorcan MacCurran!' A strange laugh came down the hill. 'And then be back to pay your own share of the price!'

A pagan burial mound atop a hill that gave forth holy water, he thought as he bounded down the slope. And a river springing from the underworld, flowing with who knows what magic. A good place to die.

'Here!' he said, excited himself at the newly improved prospects of the two waifs. 'Let no one see the gold until you get to a ticket office in Liverpool! Then buy provisions for the trip. There might be fever on the ship and the healthier you are the better your chances.'

Bríd gasped at the sight of so much money, secreting the sovereigns in the torn lining of Séamus's jacket, and tying the little sack into the knot that held both ends of her shawl together.

'Won't you come with us a part of the way, Mister Walsh?' she asked.

'I can't. But get started, walk as far as you can tonight. No one will harm you. Captain Midnight's men are all around. It was from him I got the money.' He did not mention MacCurran's name. It was beyond him to leave them with the impression that they had been saved by that abomination. And they must never know the real cost....

'Thank you!' she said, throwing her arms around him one last time. 'May God look after you always!' She was in tears again.

'Remember everything I told you!' he said, crouching down to Séamus. 'And you look after her in America, do you hear?' The boy nodded, took his sister's arm and both of them left. In the gloom he was sure he saw some gaiety return to her walk, some semblance of the way she had bounced along beside him that first day.

'Mister Walsh?' It was Bríd's voice, though she was already out of sight.

'Yes?'

'Do you remember the first day we met?'

'Of course,' he called back, glad of the dark, tears starting down his cheeks now.

'Remember you asked me did I believe in magic?'

'Yes!' His voice cracked and failed and he was sure the night had swallowed up his last word to her. Then, after a long pause, and yet perfectly clear though she must now be well down the road, he heard her say calmly, 'I do now.'

MacCurran was no longer alone by the dolmen. The hill was dotted with shadowy figures, silent, unmoving, perhaps incredulous that anyone would do this, perhaps, like MacCurran, hungry for human flesh. Yes, that was it. They had all crossed over with him, beyond the pale, the Rubicon, the edge of the solar system, to where there was no light, deep into the instinctive primal void, from which they could never return. Deprived of everything, they had conquered the last taboo. Like some tribe of speechless aborigines, they had tasted long pig and found it to their liking.

It was a good place and a good time to die. He too had nothing left, and might well, if he lived on, become like them, and so, sooner this one moment while his spirit soared beyond all imagining than that he flinch and plummet now to endure a lifetime of doubt. He had done that. He knew all those possibilities. Whatever else, whatever happened, he could never return to the life he had known up to now.

'Give me your pistol!' he said to MacCurran.

He took the weapon and cocked it. From the dark hill he could see Killala Bay shimmering to the north, knew that Tomás Kernen would die now in some peace, eager to join his family, loneliness a worse fate than death itself for him. To the west lay the dying civilization of Erris, tumbled, ruined, plagued and blighted, where people went on crawling into ditches to die with their mouths full of grass.

Bríd and Séamus he knew were walking slowly south, toward Ballina, where they would turn east for the long trek across Ireland and out of this accursed land. And there, in the east, lay his own past, a distant regret, a wasted existence, but in the end he had done this one good thing. It had been given to him to do this and he had.

Turlough raised the weapon, pointed it straight into the right-hand side of his skull and pulled the trigger.

CHAPTER NINETEEN

The bullet travelled through the dark like a slow cannonball, then struck from above an ocean of still water, starting a series of circular ripples that went on growing long after it had sunk to the black depths, slowing, trailing silver bubbles and, as the waves on the surface grew, light flashed from above, a dappled brightening of the primordial fluid and its unknown contents.

Illuminated on the inert blue-green bottom was the wreck of a ship, shell-encrusted wooden hull, weed-waving spars and undissolved shreds of rigging, and below its forgotten deck were the unhungry bones of Mick-Óg, current-swept into a great uncounted pile of others, their last whale-like moan returning to them from around the planet, its power echoing away into silence like all the others, sídhe-mounds of oak that dotted the wind-trail to the New World, linked by a chain of fevered remains, slid overboard one by one, a memory of the dead that would never leave.

He was pulled by a force that opposed the current, seeking out the mouth of a river to push him up against its flow, then sending him leaping, salmon-like, upriver and pushing him through its foaming upper reaches, to glide, his eyes just above the surface, across a freezing cirque. In front of him a woman rose slowly, back to him, but turning. Long wet black hair, he knew it must be Bríd, until the familiar curves of her cool flesh brought back other wished-for would-be memories and the fingers of the hands beckoned to him and he saw it was not her, but Caitríona, and he swam into her and found she was an illusion.

Dark Rosaleen, the nurturing land, the island soil that would give and give, dark, rich, fecund, renewing, over and over, wanting him there, in her loins, unmoved by all the centuries of carnage, but bitter beyond all telling at this new desertion. Do not fear. The French are on the ocean deep. Deep in her. On her. On Caitríona in Paris. But he had recoiled from her and now they were both drowning in that sterile water at the source of the river, her river, her spring.

Above, the keel of a wooden ship passed by and he spun down and away from it and he was sorry, and the all forgiving God that was man that was God blew away the ocean and he stood on the bridge over the duckpond in Stephen's Green and Nuala sat on a bench and beckoned to him, but he couldn't move. She smiled and lay back as she liked to do on the side of their bed and he wanted to tell her but she wouldn't let him. There was no Goddess of forgiveness.

Forgive and take. Worse than the cannibals. Beneath the brackish duckpond when he looked over the parapet were more bones, laid out long ago for a burial that had never been, submerged now beneath the rising waters of time, lost far below the paths we tread today, but there was human marrow in every bog and stream and it would all have to be forgiven because there was no God of forgetfulness.

Spires rose above the green plain, the pinnacles of great edifices, that would have been a century in the making in the medieval times of their design, but now they sprang into being all at once as a repentant populace gave a thousand donations to each of a thousand Father O'Connells, who blessed them and sanctified their sorrow and built them mighty churches. The French are on the sea. They come to make us priests.

Nuala. Gaia. Anu. Dana. An island womb, spawning people

beyond count, all slipping downriver, they would not flow inland, only out to sea, faster than she could make more of them, and though the Gobán Saor filled the land with cathedrals so that they could be with their Christ-God, still they left. Even Uladh, to whom the first people had come to taste the fish of her middle lake, and the last new people to farm her immortal soil, was forsaken now, and all of the forgotten Gods shrank into their sídhes, fleeing this confusion, this denial, this lingering horror. Yes, this island tomb!

The steeples rose higher and sharper above the flat earth, crying out to the one God above, trying to rend the sky that hid the Christian heaven. Below now, the fires of eternal suffering blocked all other paths, swirling through the ruined mansion. A tongue of flame struck out into the dark, from the pistol, following the bullet, into Kincaid, over and over, and he fell, but he was MacCarthy and he lay there, screaming his high-pitched abuse. Diabolical curses from the occult. Words not known, but guessed at, from some other ancient time of hideous carnage.

A great beating of wings arose, like the sudden filling of a mainsail, over and over, and Turlough looked up to see birds flying by in long diagonal lines. The Wild Geese, off to France, to die in foreign wars. Caitríona beckoned again, both hands cupped, water flowing from her black hair over her white skin, but he was rooted where he was, could not go to her, could not escape whatever was pounding toward him across the dark sky, unseen, behind.

He was afraid to turn, to look, and his feet were in snake-filled water, and they would be drawn by his heat. He was erect, naked, ashamed, all his lust in the open as the mist shredded away and a blue sky lit the stony mountain. He should go, give in, fall over backward and let the river carry him back down, away from here, out of this empty hinterland, through the city-state, and beyond its granite walls.

East into the heart of the empire where Flaherty, Mulholland, O'Toole and all the other knights sat at the huge round table, waiting for the king. Not him. There was no seat for him, but Larry Kent's was empty. And this was the only castle. The rest were in ruins, just tumbled ivy gardens. Nuala would have to make them let him in.

He looked down at the water, to see his own face, to know that it was him, but he had to lean forward to make sense of the dark reflection, and he was afraid of falling over. Still, his face came close to the water and he was surprised to see he was wearing a white shirt and then when he turned his face to the light that it was Lorcan MacCurran looking back at him, a madman, irredeemable, all gone to the other side, peering through the thorny thicket of a wilderness of cruelty from which he would never again emerge.

The children wanted to know. Were they planned or accidental? Lust or love? Wanted or not? They blamed her. She blamed him. Gearóid threw the rugby ball, but once again Turlough felt himself rooted, couldn't move, and it went past and the boy wouldn't look him in the eye. Emily's smile faded. No matter what he said it would not come back. They did not want to be saved. They did not want the gold coins to go to America. They wanted to stay where they were.

Above, the keel of a wooden ship passed by, leaving a foaming wake, and the howls of Sheila Kernen rent the air, following the wind that drove the brig away. Dark Rosaleen losing one of her own but he hadn't known. He had wanted to help. He was neutral, wasn't that it, taking no part in any war. No pawns for the knights of the lords of the monarchs of an alien power. No help for any of them. Yanks or Nazis. Let the Catholics and Protestants hurl insults and burn each other until the end of time.

The queen came riding by, the spokes of the wheels of her shining carriage going the wrong way as she waved a wizened claw and bobbed a wooden head at the ogling, awestruck throng. The human hoarding raised their festive hats and she never saw beyond them, pulled by laughing horses to her steamboat in Dun Laoghaire, to ply the friendly sea and return in righteous glory to the palace of her choice.

He ran after her, all the way out to the end of the harbour's granite arm, but the smoking funnels raced past and when he threw himself into the green swell it was too late and too cold and when he rose to the surface the mists had closed in and he was back in the still mountain source where Caitríona saw him and turned away again, thigh deep in the lake, making him see her in a way he never had. A woman. The woman. Not for lust. More than that. Did the salmon spawn up here? Had he come too far?

'I didn't mean to leave you! I didn't know!'

White vapour hid the cliffs that made his words echo. She looked to where the echo came from. The door of her flat closed. Again and again and again. Nuala shook her head. He had not left her. She had thrown him out. The bench in the park was empty. He was too small to see over the parapet of the bridge.

His mother bent down to point out the different skaters but his parents would not let him walk out on the ice. It was thin at the edges. It was broken there so that the water lapped at the concrete. They never let him do anything but his mother talked to her friends about the things he tried to do. He would have to work much harder to get the points to go to university. Half the students failed their first year exams. Him or the fellow next to him.

Dog eat dog. Man eat man. That was the way it was, with or without the dancing and shouting round the fire. The eternal hunger. You could do it quietly. You learned not to let them know. How to keep everything secret. Say no but mean yes. Like a woman's clumsy protest. But she could trust you...to withdraw and come all over her. Are you sure? Yes. There are millions of them in the stuff. Let him get it in first without coming. All over now.

'And how are we this morning, Mr Walsh?'

She asked the same question every day. There were

forty-three planks to the floor and one hundred and seventeen rows on the candlewick bedspread, but he did not know how many times she had said that.

'Oh, isn't that a grand day?' She whisked back the curtains to allow the daylight in at the room's four occupants and then he knew for sure she wasn't the one that came to wake him up to give him his sleeping pills and that he could stop dreaming now and let it all fade away until tonight again. Turlough usually sat up before the other three, but they were all older than him. One was sixty-four, the priest was fifty-five, and the other was seventy-two. Maybe. If you added up their ages and divided by five you would get his own age.

It was a sunny day. Windy but sunny, the wind blowing the last of the leaves from the branches he could see from his bed. The nurse bustled around checking to see that the other three were still alive, which they always were, blinking and grunting at the unwelcome new day.

'Now, gentlemen, go on down for your breakfast!'

She always said that with her back to them as she was leaving to wake up the next room.

'Are we ready for our treatment this morning, Mr Walsh?'

This nurse had a stethoscope around her neck. She led him by the arm down the long corridors that led to the room where they did this. He was always afraid going in there. They told him everyone was, but that it was good for him. They didn't know how bad it was for him.

'Just take a few deep breaths, Mr Walsh,' said the anaesthesiologist, putting the mask to his face.

He felt them slipping on the headset, adjusting the electrodes, connecting him to the machine. Sometimes they did it right away, sometimes they made him wait for a while. While he waited he remembered all the other times. It was the same, the very same, as when he had pulled the trigger himself, the bullet going into the water, and his whole life rushing past. This was his regular punishment for it all.

The jolt came quickly this time but to his own surprise he did not have the same dream. Out in the middle of the cold cirque a perch jumped, a silvery red flash that left an innocent ripple. He smiled. They were all gone, at last. There were no voices this time, just the still, clear water of the lake. There was nothing to fear in there any more.

'And how are we this morning, Mr Walsh?'

The curtains pulled back revealed a grey winter sky. There were no leaves on the branches now, but if he concentrated hard he thought he saw buds that would become new ones.

'I'm fine! Never felt better!' he replied. 'Ravenous for the institution's fine cuisine! And you're looking positively radiant yourself, Sister!' He got out of the bed and walked to the window, waiting for her to leave before dressing himself. There were patches of snow on the lawn and in the fields beyond, old snow that hadn't gotten around to melting yet. The end of winter, no better time to be leaving this place.

'You've made a remarkable recovery, Turlough,' said the doctor, sitting behind his desk in his book-lined office. 'Clearly now we can tell you were traumatized by some sort of blow, but there was no evidence on any scan.... And knowing the history of mental illness in your family....'

He picked up a manila folder, thick with documents.

'Your granduncle's file. Bernard showed the very same symptoms. Obsessional. A paranoia about characters from the past. Manic depression. But nothing we did worked on him.'

Turlough clasped his hands in front of himself. He wanted to tell the doctor that it wasn't their medical science which had cured him, but that might cause him to be held back yet again for more observation. Better to say nothing, get out of here and write him a letter in a few months' time.

'Well, thank you for everything,' he said, standing up and shaking the doctor's hand. 'I'd better go, I don't want to keep my friends waiting.'

The office door reverberated when he closed it. He took one last look down the polished corridor that led to the institution's interior and made off the other way, for the entrance, a small overnight bag of his belongings in his left hand.

Turlough's face broke into a broad grin when he saw Donal Cohan and Father Luke standing there waiting for him, murmuring away in hushed tones until he came up to them.

'You needn't both have come,' he said, shaking their hands. 'I was just expecting Morris!'

'Ah, sure, didn't he lose you the last time!' said Cohan.

'It was the very least we could do for you, Turlough,' said Father Luke, putting an arm around him and leading him out to the car.

The cottage looked the same when they pulled in beside it, but as soon as they began walking round to the back door he noticed changes. The grass had been scythed back, the privet bushes sawed down to stumps. The nearer of the two steel drums had been removed, the other straightened up on bricks.

'Morris has been keeping an eye on the place for you,' said Cohan.

'So I see.' Turlough fished out his door key and swung back the upper and lower halves of the back door. 'Come on in! If there's any gas I'll make you a cup of tea.'

They followed him in and watched as he looked round. It had all been repainted, white. The floorboards had been stained and varnished, dark brown. There was turf stacked up on both sides of the fireplace. His camp bed was gone and in its place a sofa took up the middle of the room.

'That folds out into a bed,' said Cohan.

They had put his maps back up on the wall after painting it, his desk and chair below them.

'I'm afraid we did nothing with the bedroom, other than put your bike into it, but look at this!' Cohan reached over to a switch on the wall by the door. 'Let there be light!'

Turlough looked back up at the ceiling and noticed that two bulbs dangled on wires from it, flashing on and off as Cohan demonstrated the newly connected electricity.

'Now,' he said, 'all you need is to sink a well and throw a pump down into it and you'll have running water.'

'I don't know what to say.' Turlough shrugged.

'They'd have done more, but they didn't like to meddle too much,' said Father Luke.

'But why?' He watched as it dawned on the two men that he really had no idea why the community was so appreciative.

'You remember your radio interview?' asked Father Luke. 'Well, you started a huge controversy, one that's still going on. I'm not sure I agree with your analogy to a child growing up, it almost seems to let us off the hook too easily, but thousands got the point.'

'It's just as well you're an accountant,' said Cohan, 'because we've been sent so much money we're not sure what to do with it.'

'And the government has promised us a grant.' Father Luke shook his head in wonder at his own words.

'For what?' asked Turlough.

'Our museum. And a staff to handle enquiries about the famine.'

'We've been on TV since.'

'I've been opening your mail,' said Father Luke. 'I hope you don't mind, but we just didn't know when....'

'No, no, that's just as well. I'm glad you did that,' said Turlough.

'A publisher wants to talk to you,' said the priest.

'Well, eh, great! Tell me...was there anything from someone by the name of Caitríona?'

Father Luke and Donal Cohan looked at one another, then shook their heads.

'No. No definitely not.'

CHAPTER TWENTY

In the days that followed Turlough was so glad at what they had done for him he often found himself choked up, so it was as well that they left him mostly alone or his emotional state might have caused them to form new doubts about his recovery. They wanted him to stay there and had done everything in their power to persuade him, despite his having shown them no proof whatever that his insight into the famine was genuine. He stood at the half-door one morning reflecting on all this and decided that if he were to go on living here it would be sacrilege to leave the land idle like that.

He bought a spade and fork and began restoring the potato beds. It was too early to plant yet. Working his way down each row he pulled or dug out every weed, loosened and turned the soil, and raked away the stones. It took him a month, not because he didn't work hard, but because he was thorough, careful that it should look like all those other fields long ago. When he was finished he took to sitting out the back on the evenings when the weather was fair, surveying the neat brown ridges and the landscape beyond, by no means fully at peace with himself, but nonetheless capable of reviewing events in his life with a certain newfound sagacity.

Gearóid and Emily came to visit around then and he took them fishing in a rowing boat on Lough Conn. They had lots of news.

'Mam has moved in with Larry Kent,' said Emily.

'Oh? Why? Didn't she get a good price for the house?'

Gearóid, less able for such discussions than his sister, kept his eyes on the end of his rod.

'They're sleeping with each other,' said his daughter, voice even, demanding a reasonable reaction.

'Where's Philomena?' he asked.

'Gone off to live on some Greek island with her hairdresser,' replied Gearóid.

The three of them sat silently in the creaking boat for a while, one waiting for a fish, one for a word of approval from her father, and the father himself for the right words to come.

'I wrote to your mother when I got out of hospital, you know,' he said.

'Yes.'

'We read it.'

'Then you know that I'm not in love with her, I probably never was, indeed I doubt that I was ever capable of such feelings.'

'You mean until now?' asked Emily.

'Yes. Yes, I think you could say that.'

'Why?' It was of the utmost importance to her to know the answer to that question, and whatever he said or didn't say would be chiselled into her young mind for all time, so he would have to give it his best attempt.

'Because I was brought up in a very strange society, one in which you were just not free to express your feelings, and didn't know how, since you never saw anyone else do it either, and yet one where you were free to think the worst of everyone else, because they thought the worst they could of you. They were out to discover your weaknesses and use them against you. The world was a place of palpable malice and its citizens were constrained only by one thing, the fear that they would be found out, otherwise they would engage in all manner of wrongdoing.

'In a way that's true. There are no laws or commandments against what we don't want to do and, yes, we live in a society where lying, cheating and stealing is a way of life, so invasive that everyone sooner or later compromises themselves. And when you become like that you just lose your capacity for giving, and people who are not generous cannot love. It is beyond them.'

'Wow!' said Emily.

'Makes sense,' said Gearóid.

'But, listen carefully, nothing is predetermined! We all have free will, we all have the wherewithal to change ourselves, and our lives. No matter how you feel in years to come about how we brought you up, don't let it get in the way of your own spirit!'

They caught two small trout, hardly worth keeping, but he fried them one each anyway back at the cottage and listened to them for hours talking about school, their friends, asking advice about which subjects they should or shouldn't take the next year. They told him too that it had been in the papers that his old boss, MacCarthy, had been forced to retire and been replaced by a new fellow called Finucane and that Dara Mooney had been all set to win the 470-class World Championships but he had lost his mast and now he might not even be going to the Olympics because he was doing so badly in the frostbite series.

He was sorry when they got on the train at Ballina, but deeply, profoundly relieved that they were no longer angry at him for the way things had worked out and that they were talking of coming back again at Easter and bringing their mountain bikes.

It was a night so dark and so wet, with rain pouring steadily down and water streaming everywhere, that it was easy to imagine the cottage was the Ark, about to float free of its foundations in an otherwise submerged world. Turlough sat by his small turf fire, reading Ellmann's biography of James Joyce, searching, as always, for clues. And that was the way he led his life now, finding a few paragraphs, or maybe just phrases, in one book, that led him to read two more, and so what had once been a collection of history texts had now grown into an unruly and eclectic pile of Irish literature and philosophy, their words the building blocks of a new inner castle that would replace the outer ringfort of deception, with its chevaux-de-frise of ancient witticisms and blasphemy, that he had now toppled.

The half-door was open so that he could listen to the rain, a percussion symphony, a sizzling curtain, beyond which even a rare passing car was inaudible, only the sweep of its lights across the wall betraying its presence. Did the Irish mind have a conscience or not, he asked himself, and what were the arguments for and against?

If the entire Catholic nation consisted of the descendants of dispossessed individuals, did they view themselves collectively as a dispossessed nation? Was the prevailing moral ambiguity today inevitable, a consequence of these events, a manifestation of these latest layers of the Irish collective unconscious? Or was that, however logical an explanation, an anthropological impossibility?

He rubbed his eyes, resigned that he would get no further with these cogitations that night, looked up at the black square beyond the half-door and, for the first time since he had moved into this house, believed he was seeing an apparition.

Caitríona was standing there. He stood up, convinced that he had slipped once more into the realm of the surreal and that she would surely vanish at any moment. She had no hat on and her wet hair clung to the sides of her face as it had in that unending dream.

'Can I come in?' she asked.

He hurried over and unbolted the lower half of the door,

swung it open and saw that it really was her, standing there
clutching the same travelbag he remembered from Paris.

'You're soaked!'

She shrugged, smiling up at him, then dropped the bag as
he embraced her.

'Oh God! I was sure I'd never see you again!' he said,
pulling her against him. 'I wrote. I called. I had friends go
round to your flat, but you were just gone, quit your job and
vanished.'

He felt her quiver, but he was not sure if it was emotion or
cold.

'Oh, Turlough! You know I went to Ballina, to see you in
that awful place?'

He shook his head. No one had told him that.

'But they said you might never recover, and they just let me
look at you through a glass window, and you were really out
of it....'

He laughed. 'Well, I'm back! But I'm a different person now.
The old use-and-abuse Turlough is gone!'

'You look very well,' she said quietly, drawing back, 'and
younger, somehow.'

'Must be the light! Let me get you a towel. Are your clothes
wet?'

'No. Just my jacket.'

He stoked the fire and made her a mug of tea, watching, as
she took in his surroundings.

'You were right,' he said, bringing her eyes back to meet his,
'coming here was the solution.'

They sat down together on the sofa and he recounted his
experiences since leaving her the last time. It took him hours to
go back over it all, and toward the end she stopped
questioning him, exhausted, eyelids closing together.

'This is the bed,' he said, springing up. 'Well, let's say, this
is your bed, for as long as you want it.'

If it was awkward for her she hid it well. He unfolded the
seat, the sheets and blankets already there, made up, then set

up his old camp bed while she undressed and pulled on a long flannel nightdress, catching a reflected glimpse in one of the windowpanes of those perfect groin-tingling lumbar curves, a flashover into his own inner underworld of which she was now so much an enduring part.

He turned off the light and closed the door and, standing there, with only the glow of the fire between the two of them and utter darkness he wanted to say something...significant. He wanted to tell her that he really desired her, wanted her not to feel in any way imperfect, to know that he wanted her, but was not sure he was up to it.

Yet he couldn't say that because he wasn't sure it was true. Was he avoiding her because he was afraid Bríd and Séamus would appear in the room again? Was he just terrified the whole cycle would start all over again if he went near her?

He sat down on his camp bed and shook his head. He had been philosophizing here on his own for too long. Here he was, speculating on reasons why he might decline an invitation he hadn't been given. She hadn't in any way even hinted that he might join her. She too must be troubled, deeply enough to leave her own job, and the city she had always lived in, and come here to seek out a madman who lived in a haunted house. He would listen to her story, and help her in any way he could, and then see what came of it.

'Show me where you buried the little girl,' she said next morning. The rain had stopped and a wind was drying the topsoil as they trudged up through the gorse to where you could see both the cottage and the old church.

'Here!' he said. 'Right here.'

He pointed to the exact place.

'If you disinterred her you'd prove to everyone that you're not inventing all this,' she told him.

The wind was whipping her hair about and she had to hold it free of her face to look down along his arm when he pointed out the church.

'No. They wouldn't want her buried far from here and that unspeakable savage MacCurran lies in the only piece of consecrated ground in the valley. I won't disturb her bones just for some theatrics.'

'You're still not free of them, are you?' she asked, echoing his thoughts of the night before.

'No. I don't know what became of Bríd and Séamus and I don't know how we got the land.'

They walked back down in silence and for the next few days talked about their feelings toward themselves, their families, and their society. Turlough was astonished at how similar Caitríona's were to his own. She enlightened him though on one point. She told him that she believed now that even the first time they had met, at some club function, he had struck her, though she hadn't understood it at the time, as being in conflict with the goings-on around him, and they laughed at how impossible it would have been to put that into words that wouldn't have sounded like an adolescent come-on before now.

Was it, he wondered, that anyone provoked into going on this journey was destined to eventually come to the same place? His spirit soared, so much so that when the letter that came answering the first of his two remaining questions, it was almost as if he had been expecting it. It was postmarked Santa Cruz, California, USA.

Dear Mr Walsh,

Thank you very much for your letter last month which was fascinating and prompted me to research my own past, a somewhat easier task than I had expected.

I married Thomas Kernen in 1938. He was a lawyer in San Francisco, a good catch for a girl like me. His family were well off and I have never wanted for anything, although we weren't married for very long. He died when his ship was sunk in the Pacific during World War Two, leaving me alone with two daughters, both long since married and divorced and remarried now with children of their own.

Now, here's what I think you wanted to know. My father-in-law, John Kernen, was very proud of the fact that he was the grandson of an officer who fought on the side of the Union in the Civil War. And his name was Séamus Kernen.

The paper shook in Turlough's hand. It had to be them. They had taken his advice and gone to San Francisco!

I had to take a trip up to San Francisco to find out the rest of it, and with my eyes the way they are I seldom do that any more since I can't drive. But it was well worth it. With the help of some friends I found a newspaper article about Séamus Kernen dating to 1867 and I think if you read that it explains everything.

I would love to go back and see the land they came from but at seventy-six years old my health is not up to it. It is good to know that we are not all forgotten. If you are ever over here please come and visit me and I hope I'll hear from you again.

Yours faithfully,

Gloria Kernen.

Turlough sat down on the sofa and unfolded the photocopied newspaper article.

WAR HERO MARRIES HEIRESS

Dashing cavalry officer Major Séamus Kernen, twice decorated for bravery, today married Miss Annabelle Phelan, daughter of the well-known banking tycoon. This is surely a marriage of the purest love, Major Kernen being the brother of the widow of Patrick Hayes, the famous hotelier, and in no need of marrying further wealth. He is to be all the more admired for his achievements when one thinks back to the orphan's beginnings, crossing both Atlantic and continent hand in hand with his sister, then the youthful Bríd Kernen....

He handed the letter to Caitríona and cried, shaking with joy that they had survived, and more, had gone on to lead such extraordinarily successful lives. And he had almost given up, was on the last list of names sent to him by the Irish Network. Now, not to have ever known was too painful to contemplate.

'Oh my God! Oh my God!' shrieked Caitríona over and over.

They laughed and hugged one another, then he took her

down to Moran's Bar on the crossbar of his bike and they spent all afternoon showing the letter and newspaper article around. By evening word had spread and everyone he knew was there to see this evidence. Whatever their views of him before, Turlough saw he was now revered, a kind of holy man. He had found out, by incomprehensible means, what had become of victims of the famine, people who had been swallowed without trace a century and a half earlier.

He and Caitríona walked home late that evening, he pushing the bike along, she clinging to his arm.

'I take it as a sign,' he said.

'Absolutely. No doubt about it.'

'If they're over there they can't be here.'

'Nope. Just the two of us.'

He stopped and embraced her, they kissed, languorously, every nerve and neuron alive, her face, her lips, every morsel of her irresistible, tantalizingly close, soft, fine, wanting to be gentle, to give, to be held like this, to do more.

'Caitríona!' he whispered. He had never spoken her name in those other times, long ago, when they had been together. She would have laughed, and been right to, at the gesture. They walked on, into the little cottage and helped undress one another in the light of the hot, slowly-flaming peat fire.

He didn't know where to begin, but she pulled him down onto her, onto her bed, still unmade from the night before and he kissed her all over, as she deserved, until she had to have him inside her, and he pressed down into her and rubbed his cheek eagerly against hers, and then she hesitated.

'Turlough,' she whispered in his nearby ear, 'I want you to know, it's right in the middle of the month for me, and I'm not using anything. Are you sure this is what you want?'

'Yes!'

'Me too!'

He fell on her, and they writhed together in a long ecstasy of copulation, a tangle of limbs and searching scratching fingers, and in the demented moments of his orgasm he felt the last webs of confusion blow away. He knew the sperm would reach her source, that it was meant to, that they would have a child here, that, erupting in the darkness inside her, he would start a ripple that would become a wave that would eventually turn back the tide of death here.

There was no one in the room with them, whatever had lingered here down all those years was gone now too, and if Bríd and Séamus, and even little Nan were outside the uncurtained window, they went away again, far, far away this time, beyond time and space, forever.

Two days later Turlough, whistling, surveyed the little cottage with a new eye and decided there was a lot more that could be done to improve it. It was time to plant the seed potatoes, which would nourish mother and child all through her pregnancy, but why not make the outside more aesthetically pleasing, plant lots of flowers for the coming summer?

He fell to it, scrounging cuttings of whatever seemed to do well in the area. Fuchsia, of course, and clematis for the front wall of the house. Morris promised to bring a trailerload of gravel, and in preparation for that Turlough began laying out the would-be paths. He was on his knees digging around for the bricks that had once outlined Uncle Bernie's flowerbeds on both sides of the gable end's brick chimney when Donal Cohan pulled up and sauntered around holding a salmon by one of its gills.

'A present for the two of ye!' the publican announced as Turlough straightened up, rubbing his hands together to rid them of clay.

'Oh Donal, that's fantastic, but we'll never eat the whole thing....'

'Ah, sure, between the pair of you, you will!'

Caitríona walked around to meet them, clapping her hands in delight at the sight of the fish.

'Now!' she exclaimed, wagging a finger at Turlough, 'I take that as a sign!'

'Of what?'

'Hey, they were your dreams!' she replied.

'And?'

'I'm definitely pregnant!'

He laughed. It had not occurred to him because he already believed, without any evidence, without waiting for even the first menstrual absence, that she was indeed with child.

'She's becoming more superstitious than the locals themselves!' said Turlough, taking the fish.

Cohan looked from one to the other, grimacing. 'Well, at least this puts paid to the scandalous talk that this was a platonic relationship between the pair of you,' he declared, and all three of them laughed.

'Will you come in?' asked Caitríona.

He shook his head. 'No, no, I just wanted to drop that up while it was fresh.' He began walking back to the car and Turlough joined him.

'Donal, something I've never understood....'

'What's that?'

'Well, you wanted to buy this place. Now, it's obvious the only way I'm going to leave is in a wooden box, which I hope won't be any time soon, and yet you don't have any grudge against me....'

'Oh, Christ, no! We all want you to stay!'

'And the land?'

Cohan opened the car door.

'Ah, it wasn't for me we were trying to buy the place at all, Turlough.'

'What?'

'Ah, no. I thought you knew that.' He sat into the car.

'Then for who?'

'That tinker fellow. You remember him: he was the one came into the bar when they brought the old cauldron. Father Luke is always on at us to watch out for run-down old places that might be going cheap, for young tinker couples....'

He slammed the door, started the engine, waved a beefy

hand and left. Turlough returned to his gardening, irritated at his seemingly endless capacity for misjudgment. Still, he was improving all the time. He even thought well of people now regardless of what he suspected, or even knew, they themselves were up to.

On his knees again, the trowel scraped along the side of one of the bricks. They were deeper down than he thought. Not surprising really, it was nearly thirty years since he had seen a flowerbed here. Yellow and purple pansies. Yes, he remembered those. And pink and blue snapdragons. Flowers from Victorian times. Plant them for old time's sake. He went on clearing away the muck from the first brick, then struck another. Maybe if you kept digging you would find other things too. He paused, considering that. Maybe things you wouldn't want to find?

An old dread crept up on him but he tried to ignore it. The flowerbed had been hopelessly overgrown, layer after layer of humus laid down over the years. If he hadn't known it was there he would never have found it.... He leaned back on his haunches, stunned by this new thought. Wasn't that the very essence of this whole quest?

Everything he had discovered had come from some outside intervention, or had it? Now it was apparently over he was incapable of placing the one remaining piece of the puzzle. He leaned forward and stabbed away at the earth again. Or was he? Just who were the parents of James and Eileen Walsh?

There were no more records of Walshs. He ripped out the trailing roots of more scutchgrass, feeling it snapping away from under the bricks. And her last name could be anything....

He stood up and leaned weakly against the wall, which appeared to be slipping, over and over, to one side as he fought to balance himself. If you kept digging.... He threw down the trowel and walked down the hilly field between two of his well-dug potato beds. He heard Caitríona calling after him but he ignored her. Things you wouldn't want to find.... He climbed out into the lane, and followed it past the point where Bríd had left him and on to the old church.

Was it that simple? All the blood drained from his face, all the strength from his limbs. He looked over the wall and saw Lorcan MacCurran's tombstone. He was back at the dolmen under the stars taking the readily offered gold. 'Tell them that I paid for everything.' Turlough scrambled over the wall, and walked, shaking, across the overgrown graves.

He read the inscription again. Lorcan MacCurran, 1814-1850. May God have mercy on his soul and forgive us all. Not just him, but all of them. Why? And how did the living know in advance they would have to be forgiven for something? He was back in the landlord's burning house. MacCurran's words rang out clearly.

'...will have to sell off the land...I'll have the money....'

Turlough knelt down and began ripping away the weeds and grass that had grown up around the tilted, perhaps sunken, tombstone. Things you wouldn't want to find. There were more words, lower down, embedded in the soil after all this time. He clawed frantically, not daring to read the individual letters until he had uncovered it all.

Then he stopped, screwed his eyes shut, opened them again, and let out a primal scream that went on and on, frightening the birds in the ruined church into flight, at what he saw there. It read:

Erected By His Only Daughter,
Eileen.

The Irish Famine
An Illustrated History

Helen Litton

This is an account of one of the most significant – and tragic – events in Irish history. The author, Helen Litton, deals with the emotive subject of the Great Famine clearly and succinctly, documenting the causes and their effects. With quotes from first-hand accounts, and relying on the most up-to-date studies, she describes the mixture of ignorance, confusion, inexperience and vested interests that lay behind the 'good v evil' image of popular perception.

This is a story of individuals and of a society in crisis. It should be read by anyone who seeks a fuller understanding of the Irish past.

ISBN 0-86327-427-7 Paperback

Famine Diary
Journey to a New World

Gerald Keegan

1847... Gerald Keegan, a schoolteacher, and his young bride left County Sligo to travel aboard the now infamous coffin ships to Canada. This book is based on the diary he kept.

ISBN 0-86327-300-9 Paperback

Famine
A Novel

Liam O'Flaherty

'I gladly accept one of the claims on the dustjacket of this novel: **"A major achievement – a masterpeiece,"**....it is the kind of truth only a major writer of fiction is capable of portraying.' *Anthony Burgess, Irish Press*

'O'Flaherty is the most heroic of Irish novelists, the one who has always tackled big themes, and in one case, in this great novel, succeeded in writing something imperishable...Mary Kilmartin (the heroine) has been singled out by two generations of critics as one to the great creations of modern literature. And so she is.' *John Broderick, The Irish Times*

'The author's skill as a storyteller is at times breathtaking. This is a most rewarding novel.' *Publishers Weekly*

Famine is the story of three generations of the Kilmartin family set in the period of the Great Famine of the 1840s. It is a masterly historical novel, rich in language, character and plot, a panoramic story of passion, tragedy and resilience.

Liam O'Flaherty was born on the Aran Island in 1896. His work includes the novels *Skerrett, The Black Soul, The Assassin*, a novella called *The Ecstasy of Angus*, and several acclaimed short story collections.

ISBN 0-86327-043-3 Paperback

All published by Wolfhound Press. For a copy of the catalogue, please write to Wolfhound Press, 68 Mountjoy Square, Dublin 1.